NEVER TRUST A PARTNER
The Con Games of Robert Edward Eckels

Introduction by BRIAN SKUPIN

NEVER TRUST A PARTNER
The Con Games of Robert Edward Eckels

Introduction by BRIAN SKUPIN

CRIPPEN & LANDRU PUBLISHERS
Cincinnati, Ohio
2021

Copyright 1969, 1970, 1971, 1972, 1974, 1977, 1978, 1982, 1986

All other materials copyright © 2021 by Robert Edward Eckels. All characters in this publication are fictitious and any resemblance to real persons, living or dead, is purely coincidental.

All rights reserved.

No part of this publication may be reproduced, stored in a retrieval system, or transmitted, in any form or by any means, without the prior permission in writing of the publisher, nor be otherwise circulated in any form of binding or cover other than that in which it is published and without a similar condition including this condition being imposed on the subsequent purchaser.

For information contact:
Crippen & Landru, Publishers
P. O. Box 532057
Cincinnati, OH 45253 USA

Web: www.crippenlandru.com
E-mail: info@crippenlandru.com

Jeffrey Marks: Publisher
Douglas Greene: Senior Editor

ISBN (softcover): 978-1-936363-54-4
ISBN (clothbound): 978-1-936363-55-1

First Edition: June 2021

Contents

Introduction: Confounding Expectations	7
Sources	13
The Blue Lady	15
A Question of Honor	22
Only Bet on a Sure Thing	30
The Waldemeer Triptych	41
Never Trust a Partner	52
The Kidnaped Painting	60
Hobson's Choice	68
The Switcheroo	77
Lang and Lovell Go Legit	83
Quit When You're Ahead	92
The Canadian Caper	99
The Bellman Portrait	112
Bread Upon the Waters	129
Nobody Can Win 'Em All	141
The Long Arm of the Law	153
Sufficient Unto the Day	164
Never Play Another Man's Game	174
Bibliography	188

Introduction: Confounding Expectations

By Brian Skupin

From the end of the 1960's to the late 1980's, *Ellery Queen's Mystery Magazine* (*EQMM*) and other magazines published a remarkable run of stories written by Robert Edward Eckels. They included a wide range of subjects: bank robbery, domestic suspicion leading to murder, ordinary men caught up in extraordinary circumstances; smuggling, kidnapping gone wrong, and large-scale manhunts.

But the majority of them of them showed Eckels excelling at two related types: stories of confidence men, and the world of spies crossing and double-crossing each other. The structure inherent in each marks both a strength—the appeal to detective story fans who enjoy plot twists or reversals—and a weakness—the very nature of the form foreshadows the surprise, lessening its impact.

Yet for 20 years Eckels was able to surprise again and again, repeatedly designing dazzling new variations on the swindle. Most of his stories were standalones, but he wrote two popular series, both of which are collected here in their entirety: The Lang & Lovell art forgery stories and the tales of Major Henry T. McDonlevy, the "world's greatest adjutant."

Eckels' second published story, "The Blue Lady" in the October 1969 issue of *EQMM* was the beginning of a series of tales about Lang & Lovell. Lovell is the inside man, the forger who can reproduce any painting by any artist living or dead, but who is so nervous that he "jumps around like a bean on a string." Harry Lang is the breezy, confident outside man who knows how to find wealthy buyers and how to push their buttons to make a profit.

Here it would seem that the even-more-constrained formula would make it too difficult to tell repeated stories, let alone a series of twelve is even more constrained than one would think the format is too constrained to be repeated. In each story we know that Lovell will forge or already has forged a painting, and that somehow Lang will perpetrate a scam for money. But Eckels time and again found a new trick and was able to surprise readers with the solution.

All the Lang & Lovell stories are briskly told, largely in dialogue, and are compulsively readable. The reader gets a little bit of inside information about the art business or forgery techniques, and roots for Harry to make his score while wondering how he can pull it off. There are some delightful grace notes in the writing that set them apart from the average magazine stories of the time: note the byplay Harry Lang engages in with receptionists—he is forever trying to get past receptionists—a moment in "The Blue Lady when "cupidity and caution battled to a standstill" behind a mark's eyes, or the reason for Lovell's indignation at the end of "Only Bet on a Sure Thing."

The stories do not need to be read in sequence, although there is a character in "The Waldemeer Triptych who reappears in both "The Kidnaped Painting" and "The Canadian Caper." Perhaps the best L&L stories are "The Kidnaped Painting" which packs an immense amount of plot into six pages, and "Quit When You're Ahead," with its cat-and-mouse game and interesting sidelights on art auctions. "Never Trust a Partner" was included in the *Best Mysteries of the Year—1973*, edited by Allen J. Hubin and published by Dutton.

The five Major Henry T. McDonlevy stories included here are something else again. The Major is an old school rogue, amiable and intelligent, always interested in a proposition bet or a night of poker. He refers to himself as the "world's greatest adjutant," an Army adjutant being an officer performing executive duties as needed for the commanding officer. Eckels explains this was an inside reference from his own service: "I once overheard the officer I worked for—and whose physical description I used for the Major—jokingly use this phrase about himself in a conversation with a fellow officer. The Major, however, isn't joking."

McDonlevy's partner and the first-person narrator of the stories is Tom James, who we meet in jail for disorderly conduct at the beginning of the first story, "Bread Upon the Waters," when the Major frees him by paying his fine. But Tom's role is different from Harry Lang's. He's the equivalent of a three-card monte man's shill, lending substance and believability to the Major's game. The cons are more substantial, and the stories reflect that in length and complexity.

The Major McDonlevy stories are all outstanding but "Bread on the Waters" is clearly the best. It's also Eckels' favorite of his stories, and he reports that according to Eleanor Sullivan, editor of *EQMM* at the time, "Fred Dannay said it was the best story he'd read in years." The ending seems to come out of nowhere, and yet the groundwork has all been laid in advance. Eckels says: "If you parse it, you see that it follows the classic strong magazine plot line to a tee."

Robert Edward Eckels was born December 7, 1930 in Christian Welfare Hospital in East St. Louis, Illinois, a descendant of Scots who immigrated to Ireland in the 1600's and then later in the 1700's to America. His father, Wilbur Rivers Eckels had been born in Kentucky but at a young age his father, a railroad worker, moved the family to East St. Louis, Illinois. Wilbur also worked for the railroad his entire career. In 1929, he married Dorothy Robert Beardsmore, a typist in a business office.

Wilbur had hoped his son Robert Eckels would attend the United States Naval Academy in Annapolis, Maryland, but by an early age Eckels' poor eyesight ruled that out. Eckels decided that since he liked to read, he would be a writer.

In Grade 7, Eckels borrowed the *Complete Sherlock Holmes* by Arthur Conan Doyle from the library, and over time checked it out to read repeatedly. Eventually his mother allowed him to spend $2.49 on his own copy, which he still has today. Other favorite writers included Agatha Christie, Erle Stanley Gardner, John Dickson Carr, Ellery Queen, and, notably, O. Henry, in particular the "Gentle Grafter" con man stories featuring the Old West swindlers Jeff Peters and Andy Tucker.

Later, in high school, Eckels borrowed a copy of *EQMM* from a teacher. Inspired, he wrote a mystery and submitted it. It came back rejected and Eckels was upset because "they sent back a subscription offer with the rejection, which said to me that they really didn't consider me a serious author."

Eckels persisted. In college he wrote a short story for a class assignment and submitted that for publication: "They rejected it and, this time, they didn't send me a subscription offer so I figured I had stepped up. "

After graduating from the University of Illinois, Eckels volunteered for the Army and attended Basic Training at Fort Leonard Wood Missouri. Eckels trained to be an engineer but found he was inconveniently sized: "Big enough to be placed in the 1st platoon which did all the heavy work, but small enough to be one of the smallest men in the platoon."

After Basic, Eckels was posted to Germany where it was discovered he could type, and he became a headquarters trooper. Eckels had taken typing, along with algebra, as an elective in school: "I've long forgotten most of the algebra, but typing has remained one of the most useful things I learned in 17 years of education."

Eckels left active military service in 1955, and left Reserve duty as a Sergeant First Class in 1961. The U.S. Social Security Administration (SSA) was hiring. It was doing work he believed in: "Its intent from the beginning has been to insure that old age or disability did not entail dependency on others or a descent into poverty, and that young widows with children would be able to keep their families together. Who couldn't believe in a program like that?"

Eckels passed the Civil Service examination and became a claims representative. For a young man ready to relocate as needed, the SSA offered tremendous opportunity for promotion, and Eckels took full advantage, moving several times and advancing his career.

The moves had another benefit. During a stint in Baltimore, Maryland, Eckels noticed the name Margaret Heindel on an office list, and remembered having met her during an earlier posting in Battle Creek, Michigan. He contacted her and they married less than a year later. They would have two sons: Thomas Robert and James Edward.

Eckels made another rediscovery in Baltimore, where he saw *EQMM* again on the newsstands and finally subscribed.

At around the same time, while sorting through belongings after his father Wilbur died in 1966, Eckels found some of the short stories he'd written, and started thinking about writing again. "I was reading a mystery which had a pretty tired plot. I came up with a variation that I thought would be better." Eckels submitted it to an agent along with a $5 fee. "I got it back with a really long letter from one of his staff that said 'I'm sorry, this story really has no merit.'"

But Margaret didn't agree, saying it was "as good as anything I've read in a magazine." So with his wife's encouragement Eckels submitted it to *EQMM*. "The Man in the Revolving Door" was published as the 329th First Story in the October 1969 *EQMM*, and Fredric Dannay, writing in the headnotes as Ellery Queen, called it "an extremely smooth and unusually entertaining story for a 'first'."

Now the stories came tumbling out of Eckels' typewriter. The first Lang & Lovell story was published in 1970, and by the end of 1972 22 of his stories had appeared in the magazine, three of them under a pseudonym—"E.E. Roberts"—at Dannay's suggestion. When asked how he produced so quickly Eckels replies, "Damned if I know. Plots just seemed to be there just waiting to be picked up."

"Bread Upon the Waters" appeared in 1973, and although the pace inevitably slowed Eckels wrote and sold a total of 55 stories through

1986, 45 of them to *EQMM*. Margaret proofread the stories before submission—except one. "He wrote one about a little boy who was kidnapped ("A Little Ride in the Car"). And I refused to proofread that story because I thought of our boys."

Eckels notes that Dannay was very hands on with *EQMM*. After two acceptances, Eckels' third story was rejected, with a handwritten note. "The last line read 'If you have any questions, call me,' with Fred's phone number. I called and he spent a long time explaining why this particular story didn't work out. I think the purpose was to tell me not to let this rejection stop me from writing. And it didn't."

Eckels participated enthusiastically in the mystery community. He joined the Mystery Writers of America (MWA), was President of the Chicago chapter, joined the Chicago Sherlockian society Hugo's Companions, and attended conventions. He recalls being impressed by Mickey Spillane at the 1981 Bouchercon: "I did pick up a lot of respect for Mickey... He showed himself to be a thorough professional who knew exactly what he was doing: putting comic book plots into adult novels."

Several of Eckels' stories have been reprinted in anthologies over the years, but there has been no collection as such. In 1989 Castle Books published *Tales of Espionage,* edited by Chris Dorbandt and *EQMM's* Eleanor Sullivan, which featured the stories of Eckels, Edward D. Hoch, and Brian Garfield. It includes eight of Eckels' CIA stories, fashioned into a "series" by grouping the unnamed agent protagonists as "Anonymous Men of the CIA." Eckels found out about the collection "when they sent me a copy of the book." (Note that because *EQMM* at the time purchased first anthology rights they would have already owned the rights to publish the stories in a collection.)

Since the September, 1986 publication of "The Bellman Portrait," the last Lang & Lovell story, there have been no new stories by Eckels. He explains why:

"I ran out of plots. When you come right down to it, all con games are essentially the same; so the number of variations you can use is limited. I talked to Ed Hoch about this and he agreed, having a con game series of his own. I didn't want to mechanically write the same story over and over with only the characters and setting changed; so I stopped."

As a present for his 90th birthday in 2020, his son Jim Eckels decided it make sure that Eckels' grandchildren understood his literary achievement, and arranged for Evan Eckels to build a website listing and commemorating his work, and for Alyssa Eckels to conduct an interview which was posted there.

At the same time, this collection was being discussed and prepared, and as part of the enterprise Eckels wrote a new Major McDonlevy story*.

Against the odds Eckels has now started writing again. "Once I started I found it hard to stop. I have finished a second McDonlevy story. And I'm currently working on a non-series story."

And so, after 35 years Eckels has once again found a way to surprise readers.

We hope you enjoy the stories.

---

* "Major McDonlevy Does the Math" was published in 2021 as a pamphlet included with the clothbound edition of this collection.

Sources

Emails exchanged between Robert Edward Eckels and Brian Skupin, January–February 2021

The website www.roberteckels.com by Evan Eckels

Interview with Robert Edward Eckels conducted by Alyssa Eckels and published at www.roberteckels.com

Tales of Espionage, Edited by Eleanor Sullivan and Chris Dorbandt, Castle Books, 1989

The Blue Lady

Lovell was waiting for me in the park across from Carter's mansion. As I walked up the path I could see him fidgeting on the bench. If he'd been a less sedentary man he would have been pacing back and forth. If he'd been less of a health nut he'd have been on his second pack of cigarettes. That's how nervous he was.

"You're late," he said accusingly as I came up to him.

"Only fourteen minutes," I said. "That counts almost as being on time."

"That's easy to say, but now you'll be late seeing Carter."

I sat down on the bench beside him. "How can I be late when he doesn't know I'm coming?" Nodding toward the package he clutched in his lap I said, "Is that the painting? Let me have it and I'll beard Mr. Carter in his lair."

Lovell let go of the painting with one hand and clamped onto my arm. "Maybe we shouldn't go through with this, Harry."

"Don't be silly," I said. I pried his fingers loose and flicked my own across my sleeve to smooth out the creases. "Of course we're going to go through with it. If that painting is half as good as you say it is, Carter might as well start counting out the money right now."

I took the painting from him and hefted it in my hands. It was surprisingly light; most of the bulk came from the wrapping. The picture itself was perhaps a foot and a half high by a foot wide. "Van Diemen's *The Blue Woman*," I said, "and our key to fortune."

"*The Blue LADY*," Lovell corrected. "And it's good all right." The quality of his work was the one thing you couldn't shake Lovell on. "Van Diemen himself couldn't tell this one from the one he painted two hundred years ago."

"Then there's nothing to worry about," I said and left him still fretting on the bench.

I walked up the curving white gravel driveway to Carter's front door. Arriving by car would have been classier, but cars have license plates and can be traced. Not particularly wanting to be traced, I walked.

There was a fancy bell-pull arrangement beside the door. I ignored it and rapped with my knuckles. A few minutes and several raps later, the door swung open and a girl in a black and white maid's uniform gazed at me out of dark, liquid eyes.

"Yes?" she said.

"My name is Lang," I said. "I've come to see Mr. Carter."

"I don't know," the girl said doubtfully. "Mr. Carter is very busy—" Her voice trailed off indecisively. She spoke with a heavy accent—German, I supposed. And from the way she acted she hadn't been in this country very long—at least, not long enough to lose her awe of Americans or to acquire the arrogant attitude that most rich men's servants display to their masters' supposed social inferiors.

Nevertheless, she wasn't going to let me in. But I'd expected that.

"Tell him it's about *The Blue Lady*," I said. When she still hesitated I made a shooing motion with my fingers. "Go ahead," I said, "tell him. He'll understand what I mean."

"Wait," she said and closed the door gently in my face.

I turned away from the house and rocking back on my heels casually inspected Carter's front lawn. It was a beauty. A lot of time and money had been spent on that landscaping. Carter's money, I surmised, but somebody else's time. Nothing in my research on Carter had led me to believe that he was the type to find the slightest pleasure in puttering with petunias. His sole passion was collecting. He'd started with money. And when, after his 20th or 30th million, that had palled, he had turned to art—particularly Van Diemens. Hence, Lovell's carefully recreated masterpiece. Carter had tried to buy the original six months before but had been outbid by a consortium on behalf of the Whitfield Museum.

There was a slight noise behind me and I turned around. The maid was back, holding the door open for me. I smiled at her encouragingly.

"Come with me, please," she said.

She led me to a small office off the entrance hall where a man with a round unlined face and a shock of startling white hair sat behind a desk.

"Mr. Carter?" I said although I knew he wasn't.

"No," he said. The frost in his voice contrasted with his southern accent. "I'm Mr. Ward, Mr. Carter's secretary." A good part of his duties must have been performed around the swimming pool, because his face and hands were deeply tanned. It set off the white hair well and vice versa. And I'm sure Ward was well aware of it. "Now what's all this about?" he asked.

"I have," I said, "a painting here that I'm sure Mr. Carter will be interested in seeing." I started to take off the wrapping. It was an awkward job because I had to hold the package steady with one hand and use the other to rip off the bits of sealing tape that Lovell had stuck on every conceivable crease and opening. Finally I smiled apologetically at Ward, set the package down on his desk, and went to work with both hands. It wasn't class, but it was efficient. I had the picture out in a matter of seconds.

In the meantime Ward had risen and was now staring distastefully at the jumble of brown paper and sealing tape on his desk. His attitude changed quickly enough, though, when he saw the painting. He took it from me and examined it front and back. He pursed his lips and clucked his tongue and went through all the other little mannerisms that people use when they're called on to inspect something they really don't understand.

"Yes," he said finally, "I believe Mr. Carter *would* be interested in seeing this. Wait here." Almost as an afterthought he waved a hand airily in the general direction of some modernistic assemblages of improbable curves and angles. "You may use one of those chairs," he said.

And with that he bustled out of the room. I picked out the chair that looked least uncomfortable, sat down, crossed my legs, and lit a cigarette. And waited.

In exactly 17 minute the cops were there.

There were three of them, two blue caps and one plainclothes detective named Ryker, from the Fraud-Bunco squad. Ryker left me in the custody of the two blue caps and went upstairs to confer with Ward and presumably with Carter himself. I did my best to look properly ruffled and indignant but gave it up when I saw it wasn't impressing the blue caps.

I was on my fourth cigarette when Ryker and Ward came back. Ryker was holding Lovell's copy of *The Blue Lady* negligently in one hand. He shook his head sadly at me.

"Of all the dumb crooks," he said, "that I've met in my life you sure take the cake. Not only do you pick the one guy in the country sure to spot a phony Van Diemen a mile off to sell your fake to but the picture you copy is one even an idiot would know is now hanging on the East Wall of the Whitfield Museum."

I was tempted to ask Ryker when he'd learned that last interesting bit of information, but I didn't. Instead I merely said, "I'm afraid there's been some mistake."

"Sure has," Ryker said, "and you made it." His free hand made an upward lifting motion. "On your feet. We're going downtown."

I remained seated. "No," I said. "What I meant is, I never claimed that painting is an original Van Diemen. Nor did I indicate in any way that I intended to try to sell it to Mr. Carter. As I recall, all I said was that I believed Mr. Carter would be interested in *seeing* the painting."

Ryker's eyes narrowed. He swung to face Ward. "Is that right?" he demanded.

Utter dismay swept across the secretary's face. "I—uh—well—" He wet his lips. "Well, I—uh—really don't remember his exact words, but—"

But it was only too clear—to Ryker as well as to me—that Ward was remembering only too well.

Ryker turned back to me. "Smart guy, aren't you?" he said. "Well, we'll keep an eye on you. So you watch your step."

I stood up and smiled at him. "May I have my painting back, please?"

Ryker handed me the picture roughly. "Okay," he said, nodding toward the door, "you can go now."

I kept the smile on my face and shook my head politely. "No," I said. "I still think Mr. Carter would like to see this painting."

Ryker glanced at Ward, got no response, shrugged, and left the room followed by the two blue caps.

"All right," I said to Ward, "the fun and games are over. You can take me to your boss now."

Ward turned his back on me, picked up the phone on his desk, and spoke softly into it. Then he listened for a few moments, put the phone down, and beckoned me to follow him. He didn't look as if he enjoyed it.

Carter was seated at his desk at the far end of his office when Ward and I entered. He didn't look up but kept his head bowed so that his face was partially hidden and only the bald top of his head showed clearly. I was willing to bet that what he was scribbling away so furiously at was something like "The quick brown fox" or "Now is the time for all good men."

He let us stand in front of his desk for several minutes before he threw down his pen violently and scowled up at me.

"All right," he said, "how much?"

"How much?" I said. "How much for what?"

"Don't be coy with me," Carter said. "You baited your trap and I let this"—he glared at his secretary and Ward paled beneath his tan—"stampede me into falling for it. I mean, how much to assuage your wounded feelings and maligned reputation." He paused to pick up his pen again. "You might as well settle now," he went on. "Lawyers' fees will eat up anything more you'd get by going to court. I guarantee my lawyers will see to that."

"I think it would be best if you and I spoke in private, Mr. Carter," I said.

"Not a chance," Carter said. "Any time I talk to someone as tricky as you I want a witness."

"As you wish," I said. Without waiting for an invitation I sank down into one of the armchairs facing Carter's desk. His frown deepened and Ward looked as if I'd defiled a cathedral. I ignored them both and went on blandly, "I'm afraid you've misjudged me, Mr. Carter. I'm not a swindler. I'm a thief."

Carter's eyes dropped from my face to the painting lying on my lap, then flicked to his secretary. "You," he said. "Get out!"

As the door closed behind Ward, Carter's gaze swiveled back to me. "You mean to say," he said, "that that—" His voice failed him.

"Really is *The Blue Lady*—the genuine one?" I smiled and shook my head. "No, it's a copy. But a very special copy made by an artist associate of mine using the same techniques used by that Dutchman who passed off so many fake Old Masters on the Germans during the second World War. You may recall that the fraud was only discovered when he confessed to save himself from being charged as a collaborator."

I passed the painting over to Carter. "Frankly, Mr. Carter," I continued, "nothing short of a detailed spectrographic analysis will distinguish this painting from Van Diemen's original. No, let me take that back. There is only one other way. If you'll look closely on the back you'll notice there is a small x in indelible ink in the lower left corner—put there to preclude any possibility of confusion among those few of us who are—ah—shall we say, in the know."

Obediently, Carter reversed the canvas, nodded when he found the x, then resumed his study of the painting itself.

Finally he set it down on his desk and sighed somewhat regretfully. "Very interesting," he said. "But I wouldn't be interested in a copy—not even one as good as this."

I nodded. "I didn't expect you would be, Mr. Carter. For a true collector like yourself it's the real thing or nothing. But," I added seriously, "isn't it true that the fact of possession is what's important? That what others think doesn't matter as long as you possess the original and you know it?"

Carter's eyes were now narrow-slitted with interest. "Yes," he said slowly, "I suppose that is true. What's your point?"

"Very simply this, Mr. Carter," I said. "As I told you I'm a thief." I hitched my shoulders, then let them drop. "I propose to steal *The Blue Lady* from the Whitfield and leave this copy in its place, then sell the original painting to an interested collector—yourself for example—for $100,000, payable on delivery in, say, five weeks."

After a long moment he shook his head. "You'd never get away with it. Somebody would be bound to notice."

"Would they?" I said with a hint of amusement in my voice. Then, more seriously: "Tell me truthfully, Mr. Carter, wasn't your initial decision that this painting was a fraud based largely on the assumption that the original was hanging in the Whitfield Museum?"

"That did play some part in my thinking," Carter admitted gruffly.

That was as much of an admission as I'd get from him, but it was enough. "In the same way," I said, "art experts and critics the world over look at paintings in museums and galleries and assume that because the paintings are where they are they must be what they purport to be, the originals."

I shook my head slowly, "I'd hate to tell you, Mr. Carter, how many beloved masterpieces are actually fakes. It would be years, if ever, before the Whitfield submitted *The Blue Lady*—this copy—to the kind of testing necessary to expose it. And you could display *The Blue Lady* in your possession confident that everyone who saw it would assume it to be a copy." I permitted myself a small laugh. "You could, in effect, have your cake and eat it too."

I watched cupidity and caution battle to a standoff behind Carter's eyes. Finally he said, "No, it's still impossible. The Whitfield is the most security minded museum in America."

"More security minded than the Prado or the British National Gallery?"

That was the clincher. Carter's mouth dropped. "You mean," he said, "that you've substituted paintings in the Prado and the British National Gallery?"

I just smiled.

It took Carter a moment to recover his composure. "You understand," he said at last, "that I couldn't afford to be implicated in this in any way."

"You wouldn't be. I have a reputation to maintain, so protecting you is as much to my interest as to your own."

Carter nodded. "All right then," he said. "It's a deal. $100,000 for *The Blue Lady*." He looked up at me from under his eyebrows. "I suppose you'll want the payment to be in cash."

Now it was my turn to nod. "Yes," I said. "Checks have such an embarrassing habit of turning up where you least expect them to."

Carter stood up and I rose to meet him as he came around the desk to hand me back the painting.

"Good luck," he said.

I tucked the picture under my arm. "Luck," I said, "plays no part in my operations."

He started to ring for his secretary, but I told him I could find my own way out.

Lovell caught up with me when I was two blocks away from the house. He was breathing hard, as if he'd been running.

"Man," he said between gasps, "I thought I'd die when the police showed up. I mean, it really got me."

"It shouldn't have," I said. "We expected him to call the police. It was part of the plan."

"I know, but still—" Lovell shook his head. "I'm not cut out for this sort of thing. And the worst is yet to come—robbing the Whitfield Museum!"

"Lovell," I said patiently, "you are an excellent artist. You may even be a genius in your own twisted little way. But you have one very bad fault. You don't listen. How many times do I have to tell you? We're not going to rob the Whitfield Museum. We are going to take this painting back to your studio, remove the supposedly indelible mark from its back, and then in five weeks sell it to Carter for $100,000.

"After all, we're swindlers, not thieves."

A Question of Honor

The girl behind the secretary's desk looked up and appraised me coolly. If she was impressed she did a good job of concealing it. "Yes?" she said.

"My name is Lang," I said. "Please tell Mr. Frelling that I'm here to see him," I smiled.

The girl drew a short line with her pencil through something typed on a sheet of paper in front of her and placed the paper in a metal tray at one side of her desk. "Do you have an appointment?" she said.

She was, I decided, very like her desk—sleek and modern and functional. Only her eyes kept her from being beautiful. They were hard and brittle around the edges.

"No," I said, "I don't, but—"

The girl turned her attention back to the papers before her. "Mr. Frelling sees no one without an appointment," she said.

I sat down in the visitor's chair beside her desk, folded my hands across my stomach, leaned back and crossed my legs. "Oh," I said, pretending I didn't notice her frowning stare, "I imagine he'll see me. Just tell him the man who sold him the Westmacott painting six months ago is back."

The girl's eyes turned thoughtful. I could appreciate her dilemma. On the one hand there was the rule—no appointment, no admittance. On the other was the fact that Frelling was almost as passionate about collecting art as he was about collecting money. She tapped the eraser end of her pencil against the desk while she tried to make up her mind.

I winked at her. "Go ahead," I said. "Live dangerously and call him."

She shrugged, swiveled around, and picked up her phone. She spoke softly and quickly into it, listened for a few moments, then swiveled back to face me. Her eyes had grown appraising again.

"Through there," she said, nodding slightly to point the way.

"There" seemed to be a solid oak wall. But the girl didn't look like the type that went in for fun and games, so I stood up and stepped out briskly. My faith was justified. As I was about to bang into the wall it slid apart silently from the middle and I went into Frelling's office.

Actually, it was more like a throne room than an office. Frelling sat in a high-backed armchair at the far end of the room, where light from the windows cast him and the man who was standing slightly to his left rear in sharp relief. Instead of a desk, a large, low coffee table stood before him. Only the intercom on one corner indicated that the table served any purpose other than decoration.

"Well," Frelling said jovially as I approached, "Mr. Lang. This is a surprise." He was a stocky man with a leonine head set low and forward on his shoulders so that he seemed almost neckless. Surprisingly for a man of his bulk, he spoke in a hoarse tenor voice.

Now he turned to the man beside him. "You remember Mr. Lang, don't you, Charles? Mr. Lang sold me a painting by Abner Westmacott some six months or so ago. A very fine painting—and a bargain too."

"Yeah," Charles said, "I remember him."

I remembered Charles too. He was Frelling's bodyguard and all-purpose goon. A giant ape of a man whose carefully tailored suit couldn't disguise the fact that he'd have been more at home in the prize ring—or swinging from a tree.

"I suppose," Frelling went on to me, "that you have another bargain for me."

"No, sir," I said, sitting down uninvited in one of the smaller and, of course, lower-backed chairs across from him. "As a matter of fact, I've come to buy back the Westmacott."

The smile disappeared from Frelling's face. "Buy it back?" he said sharply. "Why?"

"Well," I said, "this is rather embarrassing to admit. But I'm afraid we've both been victimized. I've just found that the painting I sold you is a forgery. Naturally—" I smiled earnestly—"I want to make good."

Frelling's eyes had narrowed to two unreadable slits. "I see," he said. He laced his fingers together and rested his chin on them. "How did you learn about it being a forgery?"

"How I did," I said, smiling more earnestly than ever, "isn't important. What is important, though, is that I have here—" I patted my breast pocket—"a certified check for the amount you paid for the painting, $25,000, which I'm prepared to refund for the painting."

"Mm-mm," Frelling said. "Let me ask you again: why?"

"Why?" I said, bewildered. "Why, what else can I do?"

"You could," Frelling said, "do nothing. From what my lawyers have told me, a person can't be held liable in cases like this unless it can be proved that he wasn't acting in good faith—or had knowingly misrepresented the object."

"Well," I said, "I suppose from a strictly legal point of view I'm not liable. But I look on this as a question of honor."

"Now that," Frelling said, "is very interesting. Especially since when you sold me the Westmacott I was given the distinct impression that it had been stolen. And that was why I was getting it at half price."

I stopped smiling. "Now," I said, "I'm certain that I said nothing—"

"No," Frelling interrupted, "you didn't. But you worked very hard to give that impression without saying it." He waved a hand impatiently. "In any case, it's immaterial now. I couldn't return the Westmacott even if I wanted to. I sold it over a month ago to the Municipal Museum of Art. For, I might add, $60,000. I'm surprised you haven't heard of it; it was in all the papers."

"You sold it!" I cried. "You don't know what you've done. You—" I caught myself and bit the words off. I stood up, the smile back on my face. "Well, in that case," I said, "I won't take up any more of your time. I'll—"

"Not so fast," Frelling said. "There's something going on here that I don't understand. And you're not leaving here until I get to the bottom of it." He spoke over his shoulder. "Charles, help Mr. Lang back into his seat."

Charles covered the distance between us in three brisk strides. "Sit down," he said. He put a huge hand on my chest and shoved.

I sat down.

"Now," Frelling said, "I want the truth. And so that you won't waste time telling more lies, let's get a few things straight. You," he went on, pointing a blunt finger at me, "are nothing but a cheap con man. I spotted you for that when you first walked in here with that phony Westmacott."

"Then why—" I began.

"Why did I buy it?" Frelling finished for me. "Because it was an unusually fine copy, and I saw a chance to make a profit on it. With my reputation behind it no one would think of questioning authenticity." He smiled dreamily. "So all I had to do was wait a few months and then sell it for more than twice what I paid you for it."

I laughed bitterly. "I hope you're happy with your profit."

Frelling studied me thoughtfully. "Maybe you'd better explain that remark," he said at last.

I glanced up at Charles glowering down at me, then I shrugged. "The game's over," I said. "So why not? The truth of the matter is that

I work partners with a character named Lovell." I smiled wryly. Lovell's a nut about the food he eats and he's as nervous as your Aunt Nelly in a hailstorm. But he has some compensating characteristics.

"For one thing, he's an artist with a large if somewhat specialized talent. He can forge a painting by any artist living or dead and do it so well that the original artist himself would be hard put to tell the difference. Although to be on the safe side we generally stick to the dead ones." I grinned up at Frelling. He didn't grin back.

"Go on," he said.

"Well, anyway, Lovell mixes his own paints—using only the materials and methods the original artist would have used. And he has his own special ways of 'aging' the painting."

"The big problem is getting the right kind of canvas. They literally don't make canvas like they used to. What we do is buy a cheaper painting of about the same age as the one Lovell is going to forge and then he paints over it. It's easier than scraping the canvas clean. And the practice wasn't uncommon among the Old Masters themselves. They weren't ones to waste a canvas if they could help it."

"All this is very interesting," Frelling said, "but I fail to see the point."

"You will," I said. "We bought the canvas the Westmacott was painted on at an estate auction. There were two paintings by the same unknown artist for sale. And as luck would have it, one other character besides Lovell and myself was interested in them. Rather than bid each other up, we made a deal and split the two paintings between us."

I paused and shot a sour glance up at Frelling. "The other painting has been identified as an early work by Pieter De Jong. It sold for a quarter of a million last month. Now I think you can see why I wanted to get the Westmacott back."

Frelling leaned forward. "A De Jong," he said, almost reverently. Then more harshly, "And I let it get out of my hands."

"Yeah," I said, "but you didn't know what you really had." I furrowed my brow in thought. "But then," I went on slowly, half to myself, "neither does anybody else—including the museum." I turned my attention back to Frelling. "Maybe the game isn't over yet. I wouldn't stand a snowball's chance of getting the painting away from the museum. But you just might."

Frelling looked at me speculatively. "And how might I do that?"

"By simply telling the truth," I said. "Or rather that part of the truth we want the museum to know—that you've found out the Westmacott is a forgery and want to buy it back from the museum. It's a natural and if we can work it right I'm sure we can pull it off."

"We?" I said. "I'm the guy who can prove the painting's a forgery. You can't do it without me." I smiled. "And, of course, I'd expect you to be properly grateful when it's all over."

Frelling smiled back, a wintry twist of the lips that didn't quite reach his eyes. "Of course," he said. He settled back in his chair. "Well, Charles," he said to his bodyguard, "what do you think?"

"I don't like it," Charles said gruffly. "I wouldn't trust this guy a dime's worth. He's the kind that can go in a revolving door after you and come out first."

Frelling nodded slowly. "All in all," he said thoughtfully, "I'm inclined to agree with you, Charles, about Mr. Lang's character. But in this particular case self-interest seems to have bound us together. And," he went on, his eyes fastened on my face, "I think Mr. Lang is smart enough to realize I'm not the kind he can safely play any tricks on. So, on balance, I think we'll go along with his little scheme."

He pressed down one of the buttons on his intercom. "Miss Ryan," he said, "what's the name of the managing director at the Municipal Museum?"

The girl's voice came back, clear but slightly tinny: "Murchison, Mr. Frelling."

"Yes," Frelling said, "that's the one. Well, call him and tell him I want to see him right away in my office. Tell him it's a matter of the utmost importance."

He released the button without waiting for a reply and gave me another of his bleak smiles. "It won't be long," he said. "Now tell me, just how did you plan to handle Mr. Murchison?"

"Oh, dear," Murchison said. "Oh, dear, this is terrible." He was a slight, balding man with a sharp nose in a thin face and a jawline that merged almost imperceptibly with his throat. His eyes flicked around the room like a nervous bird's. "I don't suppose," he went on, "that there's any possibility that it isn't true."

"None whatsoever," Frelling assured him. "The forger himself confessed to Mr. Lang here, who of course immediately got in touch with me." For obvious reasons we weren't letting Murchison in on my part in the original swindle. "I investigated thoroughly," Frelling added. "Most thoroughly. And there can be no doubt. The Westmacott is a forgery."

"Oh, dear," Murchison repeated. "I wish I knew what to do. There's going to be the most awful scandal when this gets out."

"Why should it get out, Mr. Murchison?" I said smoothly. "Surely the three of us can agree to handle the whole thing discreetly."

"You don't understand," Murchison wailed. "I've got to report this to the trustees. And I'm sure they'll demand a full investigation." He looked down mournfully at his hands clasped in his lap, "and no matter what happens I'm going to be made to look like the most awful fool for recommending the purchase in the first place."

Frelling shot a quick, anxious glance at me. The last thing he wanted was a thorough examination of the painting.

"Oh," I went on to Murchison, "I think we can avoid that. What would happen if you presented the trustees with a *fait accompli*? Suppose, for example, you were to tell them that on further investigation *you* had discovered that the Westmacott was a forgery, that *you* approached Mr. Frelling, and that he insisted on taking the picture back and refunding the purchase price."

"Yes," Murchison said slowly, "that might work…No." He shook his head emphatically. "It's too risky. If I went over the heads of the trustees that way they would fire me."

"Now listen—" Frelling began, his face flushed with anger. I cut him off by standing up and motioning with my head for him to follow me. I walked over to the window, and after a moment he grudgingly got up and came after me.

"What is it?" he demanded.

I glanced back at Murchison. He seemed too preoccupied with his own problems to pay any attention to us. Still, I kept my voice low and confidential. "Look," I said, "Murchison's afraid to jump because the way he sees it he's going to lose either way. So what you've got to do is make it profitable for him to jump your way."

"You mean a bribe?" Frelling shook his head. "I doubt if that would be wise. He'd be bound to suspect something then."

"If the money's enough," I said, "it won't matter what he suspects. Offer him $25,000. That's twice what he makes in a year. And you're still getting the De Jong cheap."

Frelling thought it over for a long minute, then turned abruptly on his heel and went back to his chair. "You know, Mr. Murchison," he said as he sat down, "I feel somewhat responsible for the predicament you find yourself in. And I think it would be only fair that I compensate you for the possible damage to your reputation…"

In a quarter of an hour Murchison was on his way back to the museum with Frelling's refund check for $60,000 in his pocket. Charles was to follow later to pick up the painting and give Murchison his "compensation"—$25,000 in cash.

"Well," Frelling said after Murchison had gone, "that wraps everything up very neatly."

"Except for one thing," I said, smiling.

"Except—oh, yes," Frelling said, "you expect me to be properly grateful. Well, rest assured Mr. Lang, I am. Thank you very much."

Charles was grinning from ear to ear, and for the first time that day Frelling's smile had reached his eyes. I opened my mouth to say something, but Frelling held up a hand to forestall me.

"Don't press your luck, Mr. Lang. You can't have everything. Just be thankful that nothing worse happens to you."

There was, of course, no answer to that, so I turned and left.

Their laughter followed me until the oak doors closing behind me cut it off.

I found Murchison later that evening sitting in the rear booth of a small bar halfway across town from the Municipal Museum.

"Hi," I said, sliding in opposite him. "Charles pick up the painting all right?"

"Yes," he said. He shoved a thick white envelope across the table to me. "Here—take this. It's yours."

Out of force of habit I riffled through the bills in the envelope. "Hey," I said, looking up surprised. "This is the whole $25,000. Our deal only called for me to get half."

"Take it all," Murchison said fervently. "I'm going to have enough trouble explaining this to the trustees without having to account for an extra $12,500." He rubbed his hands across his eyes and shook his head. "I don't know why I let you talk me into this anyway. When you first came to me and I checked your story out and determined that the painting really was a forgery, I should have gone right to the trustees and let them handle it. Legally."

"Sure," I said, "and then Frelling would have sat back and claimed that he'd acted in good faith and couldn't be held liable for the museum's bad luck. And the museum would have been stuck with a phony painting because you never could have proven otherwise. Lovell and I didn't think the museum deserved that. So we came up with a plan where everybody ends up with what he deserves. The museum has its money back. And—" I patted my jacket pocket where the envelope now resided—"Lovell and I have our just reward."

"And Frelling?"

I grinned at Murchison. "Oh," I said, "more than anybody Mr. Frelling gets just what he deserves. I do regret that I can't be there when he scrapes the paint off that canvas and finds absolutely nothing beneath it.

"But then," I finished up philosophically, "you can't have everything."

Only Bet on a Sure Thing

Grierson leaned back in his chair and placed his fingertips carefully together. "Let me see if I understand this, Mr. Lang," he said. He was a short fat man with a round baby-smooth face out of which jutted an incongruous sharp-pointed chin. His deep booming voice clashed sharply with this innocuous appearance. So did his quick mind. In fact, his mind was so quick that I was beginning to suspect that I'd made a mistake in approaching him. But nothing ventured nothing gained, and I had a deep faith in his basic dishonesty.

"Let me see if I understand this," he repeated. "You propose to substitute this copy of Mazzaratti's Adoration of Narcissus for the original in the Snowden Galleries and then turn the original over to me for $50,000."

"That's right," I said. We were in Grierson's study, a pleasantly bright room paneled with three kinds of blond wood and furnished to match. The copy in question lay between us on Grierson's highly polished desk. I leaned forward and moved the painting closer to him.

"As you can see," I said, "the copy is an unusually fine one, made by an artist friend of mine using Mazzaratti's exact technique and only the materials available at the time the original was painted. For all practical purposes it's an exact duplicate of the original." I smiled to show my sincerity. "In fact," I went on, "short of spectroscopic or electroluminescent examination there's no way to tell the two apart."

Grierson pursed his lips and nodded slowly. It was a thoughtful gesture. And I didn't like that at all. I preferred my—ah—clients to be openly consumed by greed, by the true collector's passion for a new thing—not calmly thinking things over and analyzing my proposition from every angle. Grierson was a collector all right. Proof of that hung on the walls surrounding us, but most of his collection had been an inheritance from his grandfather. And maybe that's what makes the difference.

"Oh," he said, "I'll grant you that it is an excellent copy. I'll even grant you that it would take a most thorough examination to distinguish between it and the original. What concerns me, though, is how you plan to switch the paintings."

I smiled and shook my head. "Professional secret, Mr. Grierson," I said.

Grierson shook his own head in return and more emphatically than I had. "I'm afraid that answer won't do," he said. "If I'm going to risk my money and my reputation I have to be sure the plan has a very good chance of succeeding. Especially since museums are becoming more and more security-minded."

Since he put it that way I had no choice but to explain. And that called for some quick thinking on my part. Since, of course, I had no intention of switching any paintings. Instead, I intended to return in six weeks and sell him the copy that lay before him now. It was a simple scheme but one that had worked very well—or had until now.

Figuring the best defense was a good offense I said, "Are you familiar with the security system at Snowden, Mr. Grierson?"

Grierson waved a hand negligently. "Not in every detail," he said in an offhand voice.

Which meant of course that he had no idea of what security precautions the Snowden had taken. I kept the relief out of my voice and face and went on smoothly. "Well, like most places with valuable things to guard, the museum has set up its security system to keep people from breaking in and taking things out. Accordingly, it's not really able to cope with someone who's already inside." I spread my hands. "And that, quite simply put, is the essence of my plan. I go into the museum through the front door just like any other visitor. But then just before closing time I'll duck into a small storage closet on the third floor near the Managing Director's office. When it's dark enough, I'll sneak out, switch the paintings and sneak back again. The next morning, as soon as there's enough of a crowd to make me inconspicuous, I'll simply walk out the front door."

"And," Grierson said sarcastically, "of course no one will notice the painting tucked under your arm."

I beamed at him. "Of course they won't," I said, "because it'll be hidden in a hollowed-out artist's pad. And there are always enough would-be artists floating about the museum sketching so that one more won't arouse any comment."

Grierson nodded thoughtfully. "Just audacious enough so that it might work." He sighed. "It's almost a pity that I have to turn you down."

"Turn me down!" I said, and the surprise in my voice was not at all pretended. "In heaven's name, why?"

"Because," Grierson said flatly, "I only bet on a sure thing. And in this case I could never be sure I had the original or not—" he nodded toward the painting on his desk "—this or another excellent copy just like it." He shook his head. "I'm afraid the odds just don't appeal to me."

I stood up. "Well," I said huffily, reaching for the painting, "If you don't trust me—"

Grierson didn't move. "Oh, come now, Mr. Lang," he said, "just because we don't trust one another is no reason we can't do business together. Except that we'll do it on my terms, not yours."

I sat down. "What did you have in mind?" I said. "And call me Harry."

Grierson smiled, a wintry twist of the lips that left the rest of his face unmoved. "All right, Harry," he said. He leaned forward, elbows on the desk, and pointed the eraser end of a pencil at me. "This artist friend of yours, is he still available?" His voice had suddenly become crisp and businesslike.

"Lovell?" I said. "Sure. We're partners. He does the painting and I do the selling. Why?"

Grierson swiveled in his chair to fact the wall behind him. There were several paintings hung there but your eyes were inevitably drawn to one. It was a seascape with dark, almost black rocks in the foreground and in the distance the sun setting through a cloud formation. The water between the rocks flowed liquid gold in the reflected sunlight. It was a wonderfully warm and beautiful painting and I sensed that the entire room had been designed to complement it.

Grierson didn't speak for a few moments, then he said, "Can he duplicate that?"

"Very likely," I said. "But why should he?"

Grierson swiveled back. "Because," he said, "I'll pay $10,000 for the copy. That should be reason enough, shouldn't it?"

I shook my head. "Now it's my turn to say the answer isn't good enough," I said. "It's not that we wouldn't like the money. But I would have to be sure that you're not planning to lure my partner and me into a police trap."

Grierson regarded me closely for a long minute. "Fair enough," he said at last. He turned back toward the painting. "Do you recognize it?" he said.

"It's Glover's *Sunset with Clouds and Rocks*," Grierson said. "My grandfather bought it in 1939 for $250." He studied the picture thoughtfully for a moment, then went on. "At today's prices, it's worth a quarter of a million."

"Now that," I said, "is what I'd call a smart investment."

"Yes," Grierson said absentmindedly. "The ironic thing is that grandfather didn't intend it as an investment. He just wanted to help out a struggling artist. It was the kind of thing he was always doing," Grierson added distastefully. "This one just happened to pay off."

I thought idly that Lovell, who before teaming up with me had spent a number of years as a struggling artist himself, was going to really love this guy.

"Of all the paintings I inherited from grandfather," Grierson went on, "this is the prize." He sighed and turned back to me once again. "Are you aware of the terms of my grandfather's will?"

I shook my head. "No," I said, wondering why he thought I might be.

"Briefly," Grierson said, "it provides that I must give the local art museum its choice of any one of the paintings in his collection. If I don't within a year, his executor is directed to sell all the paintings and give the money to charity."

Suddenly I began to understand. "And the museum wants the Sunset," I said.

"Precisely," Grierson said. "But I can't bear to part with it. If I don't, though, I stand to lose everything."

"Tough," I said. "On the other hand, you could go to court and try to break the will."

Grierson nodded. "I could," he said. "And my lawyers admit that it's not impossible that I might win. But they indicate that image-wise it wouldn't do me any good." He smiled wryly. "And in these days of nosey Internal Revenue agents and anti-trust suits, none of us can afford to neglect our public image."

His smile lightened. "But now I have the ideal solution to my dilemma. Your artist friend duplicates the Sunset. I give the copy to the museum and everybody's happy. So how about it? Do we do business?"

I nodded slowly. "We do," I said. "Only the price is $20,000—half in advance."

I'd told Lovell to wait for me outside a small restaurant several blocks from Grierson's home. And there he was, fidgeting on a bench which according to the sign on its back was furnished through the courtesy of the McBee Funeral Home. He bounced up as soon as he saw me coming.

"Oh, lord, Harry," he said, "am I glad to see you." He peered nervously around my shoulder. "Everything went all right, didn't it?"

"Almost," I said. I motioned with the fake Mazzaratti under my arm. "He was too smart to buy this, but we've got another deal cooking. Smaller profit but less risk. Come inside and have a cup of coffee while I tell you all about it."

"Coffee is a diuretic," Lovell said earnestly. "And the caffeine—" He shuddered with distaste but followed me into the restaurant anyway.

Besides being nervous as a cow, Lovell is a health food nut. I've never seen him eat a steak—too many steroids, he says—but he'll guzzle down the oddest concoctions of wheat germ, fermented mare's milk, or what-have-you without turning a hair. He has other qualities, though, which more than offset these peculiarities. I hadn't lied to Grierson when I said that Lovell could duplicate the Sunset. He's a master at copying other artists' styles. He can with equal ease duplicate any existing painting or create an "original" in the style of any painter you care to name. It's a rather limited talent, I admit—but a profitable one.

We sat down at a corner table where we couldn't be overheard. And after the waitress had taken our orders—coffee for me, yogurt for Lovell—I explained Grierson's proposition to him. He didn't say a word throughout, but his face gradually took on a sulky, stubborn cast. I gave him until the waitress had brought our orders and left again. Then I said, "All right. Let's have it. What's bothering you?"

He shook his head stubbornly and let his spoon drift through his yogurt. Finally, still without looking at me, he said, "Does your conscience ever bother you, Harry? Because of the things we do?"

"No," I said. I took a sip of coffee. "Does yours?"

Lovell frowned and chewed his lip as he thought that one over. "No," he said at last, "but sometimes I think maybe it should."

I put down my cup and said patiently, because we'd been over this ground before, "Well, the next time you get to feeling that way just remember these three things." I began to count off on my fingers. "One, the people we take can easily afford the loss. They wouldn't be art collectors if they weren't rich to begin with. Two, they always believe they're getting the clean end of the stick. And three, they're only getting what they deserve because we couldn't take them if they weren't dishonest at heart."

"I know," Lovell said. "But—" his voice broke indignantly "—this time we'd be helping a rich crook swindle a museum."

"Not," I said, "if we switch paintings and let Grierson keep the copy."

A smile brightened Lovell's face. "Harry," he said, "that's brilliant." Then as I knew it would, the reaction set in almost immediately. The smile faded and he looked at me anxiously. "Do you think we can get away with it?"

"Of course we can," I said. "You just eat your yogurt and leave everything to Old Harry."

I didn't know it then, but I'd just underestimated Grierson for the second time.

Since Lovell had to work from the original and since Grierson obviously wouldn't let us take it away with us, we had no choice but to work at his home. I helped Lovell pack his equipment—it filled a large-sized suitcase—and we taxied over to Grierson's house.

Grierson himself met us at the door. He frowned at the departing cab. "Was that wise?" he said. "That driver might remember having brought you here?"

"What if he does?" I said. "He doesn't know who we are or why we're here. There isn't a chance in the world that he'll connect us even remotely with your turning the Sunset over to the museum—assuming he bothers to keep up with donations to museums."

Grierson half turned and I saw for the first time that he wasn't alone. A stocky man with a cynical, horseplayer's face stood in the hallway behind him. "What do you think?" Grierson said to him.

The stocky man shrugged his heavy shoulders. "He's right," he said as if he were talking about someone 500 miles away in another state. "If they'd played it cute and tried to sneak in, they'd have only made themselves more conspicuous."

Grierson turned back to Lovell and me. "This is Murphy," he said by way of introduction. "Murphy does odd jobs for me."

Looking at Murphy, I could guess what sort of odd jobs. And I didn't like the implications of what I was thinking.

"You know," Grierson said as he escorted us back to the rooms he'd set aside for our use, "I really don't know which is giving me more pleasure—keeping the original Sunset or putting one over on those prigs at the museum." He laughed shortly. "Have you ever met Watson, the Managing Director?"

I assumed the question was directed to me alone since Grierson and I were leading, with Murphy and Lovell following. Murphy, of course, was letting Lovell carry his own suitcase.

"No," I said.

"The man's a fool," Grierson said contemptuously. "Always prattling about how art should be enjoyed by all and not hoarded like a miser's trove." He snorted. "As if everybody were capable—" He broke off. "Ah, here we are," he said. He flung open a door leading off the corridor. "I think you'll find this suitable for your needs."

It was a large airy room, bright with the afternoon sun streaming down from a skylight. The chairs and other furnishings had been moved back along the walls to make room for the two large easels set up in the middle of the floor. On the right-hand easel rested the Sunset minus its frame, and on the other an empty canvas the same size and shape. As far as I could see it was everything you could want for an artist's studio.

The only incongruous note was an electric oven installed along one wall.

Lovell set his suitcase down and walked over to the easels. He studied the setup for a long minute, then adjusted the painting slightly and stepped back to study it some more. "This will do fine," he said at last. He went back to his suitcase, heaved it up onto a table, and began to unpack. Murphy lounged in the doorway and watched him idly.

Grierson beamed. "Good," he said. He rubbed his hands together. "How long will it take, do you think?"

Lovell paused in his unpacking and shrugged. "A couple of days," he said. "Three or four at the most."

"So soon?" Grierson said, surprised. "Remember, this has to be a perfect copy."

"It will be," Lovell said haughtily. The quality of his work was the one thing he was really touchy about. And the only thing you couldn't shake him on.

I said smoothly, "The actual painting itself doesn't take very long at all, Mr. Grierson. Usually, it's mixing the paints so they match perfectly that gives the most trouble. But since the Sunset is a fairly recent painting, that shouldn't be too much of a problem."

"I see," Grierson said. His eyes shifted toward the oven. "You asked for that, so I got it for you. But what's it for?"

"It's used for the aging process," I said. When Grierson looked at me curiously, I went on, "As paint gets older and drier it tends to contract and a network of tiny cracks forms across the surface of the painting." I smiled at him. "You get the same effect," I said, "if you bake a new painting."

"Very interesting," Grierson said, obviously impressed. "And that, I suppose you use for mixing paints." He nodded to indicate the blender that Lovell had just unpacked.

I laughed. "No," I said, "Lovell uses that to mix his food."

"It's a high protein milk shake," Lovell said with the sincerity of a true believer. "You start out with a base of honey, add malt and milk powder, eggs, ice cream, soybean oil—"

Grierson held up a hand, palm out. "Spare me the details," he said. He turned back to me.

"That's about it," I said. "Unless you have some more questions, you can leave us to our own resources."

Grierson regarded me thoughtfully. "I don't think so," he said slowly. "You see, it occurred to me that if your copies are as good as you claim, you could easily make two instead of one, smuggle the original painting out, and leave the museum *and* me holding the bag."

He looked at me expectantly, but I didn't say anything. There were at least a couple of holes in the scheme he'd just outlined, but pointing them out would only confirm his suspicions. So would a denial.

"So," he continued, "the only way I can have peace of mind to make sure you don't have even the slightest chance of doing that. I thought at first of marking the original in some way. But marks can be found and then erased or duplicated. So I decided that the simplest and best way was to leave Murphy here with you all the time you're doing the painting. I don't think you'd be foolish enough to try anything with him around."

Murphy grinned at me from the doorway, almost as if he wished I would try.

"Suit yourself," I said. I made my voice as offhand and casual as I could.

"I intend to," Grierson said drily. He moved over to the door and paused. "One other thing before I go," he said. "Your sleeping quarters are in the next room. As an added precaution, though, Murphy will sleep here. And I should warn you, he's a very light sleeper."

And with that cheery thought Grierson left us. Murphy closed the door after him and settled down on a straight wooden chair beside it.

Lovell cast an anxious glance at me.

"You know what we came here to do," I said. "So begin. One more in the audience won't make any difference." That, I hoped, should get the message across to Lovell and yet be natural enough not to alert Murphy.

But from the mocking glint in Murphy's eyes I couldn't be sure.

Lovell looked dubiously from me to Murphy, then turned to the empty canvas, struck his horizon line and began to paint. Within two minutes he was completely absorbed in his work.

That left Murphy and me to amuse ourselves.

"How about a little gin rummy to pass the time?" I said. "Penny a point."

Murphy grunted something I took to mean no.

"Well," I said cheerfully, "if you don't care for gin, how about—"

Murphy grunted again.

It was, I decided, going to be a long three or four days.

And it was. We left the room only to sleep. Our meals were brought in—or rather Murphy's and my meals were brought in. Lovell kept a supply of his high-protein malt mixture standing ready in the blender to be shaken together whenever the need for nourishment moved him. For the rest of the time he labored diligently and silently on the copy.

Murphy's most characteristic pose was sitting next to the door with his chair back propped against the wall and his feet dangling beside the bottom rungs. His eyes were half hooded and seemingly somnolent. And yet I'd have been willing to swear that a gnat couldn't have blinked in that room without Murphy spotting it.

As for me, I wandered aimlessly about the room, fiddling with this or that as the mood struck me.

I had just begun to conclude that Lovell would never finish when he put down his brushes, lifted the copy off its easel, and went to stick the painting in the oven.

Murphy let his chair legs come down with a thud. "Time to call Grierson," he said. "He'll want to see this."

"Not yet," I said. "Something still could go wrong. Better wait until it's through cooking and Lovell's had a chance to check it over."

Murphy settled back in his chair, apparently as stolidly as before. But when I started to move about the room he shouted at me to settle down.

I settled down.

Finally Lovell shut off the heat and, after giving the oven time to cool thoroughly, took the painting out. He had moved the original over to the far right-hand side of the easel and now he placed the copy immediately to the left of it and began to go over every square inch of both paintings with a magnifying glass. He took an inordinately long time about it, and Murphy began to fidget more and more. It was comforting to know that he was human enough to have run out of patience as soon as he saw the end in sight.

At last when he could stand it no longer, he burst out irritably, "Aren't you done yet?"

He started to get up, but I forestalled him by crossing casually in front of him and going over to stand beside Lovell. As I stood there peering over his shoulder I let my hand brush lightly against the copy. It was cool to the touch, the last trace of the oven's heat gone. I nodded to Lovell almost imperceptibly.

Lovell straightened up. "All done," he said. He turned from the easel and walked over to his blender. "Go take a look if you like," he said to Murphy over his shoulder as he punched the button to start the machine.

It was an act Lovell had done at least a dozen times since we'd come to Grierson's. But this time the blender top was loose; it flew off and the high protein malt spewed out all over the room. One glob caught Murphy on the side of the face as he stood up.

Fortunately the paintings were at a sharp angle to the machine or they too would have taken the full blast.

Murphy stomped angrily over to the blender and yanked the cord out of its wall socket, sending the machine crashing over. "You jerk," he said, turning on Lovell and drawing back his fist.

Lovell, however, seemed too upset to be frightened. "I don't know how it happened," he complained. "I was sure I put it on tight."

Murphy swung around to face me. "You!" he cried, pointing with his stubby forefinger. "You were fooling around this thing earlier—" His eyes narrowed as a sudden thought took hold of his mind. He pushed past Lovell and covered the distance to the paintings in three quick strides. He stood before them frowning.

"Look, Murphy," I said, "I—"

"Shut up," Murphy said harshly. He continued to study the paintings. Finally a slow grin began to twist his face. He reached up to touch the right edge of the painting to the left. He brought his hand away a second later, rubbing his thumb against the tips of his fingers. The grin broadened.

"All right, wise guy," he said to me, nodding to indicate the wall intercom, "call Grierson."

His eyes gloated over me as I buzzed Grierson in his study and told him the copy was done.

Grierson turned back to the paintings. "The ironic thing is," he said, "that Murphy wasn't really necessary. Oh," he went on, flicking a hand at the Sunset on the right, "this is a good enough copy and I'm sure the museum will accept it without question. But—" he picked up the other Sunset "—when you see the two of them together, you can't help but notice the small signs that distinguish the work of a true creative genius from that of a competent hack. If you have the eye for it, that is," he added after a second.

Blood suffused Lovell's face and he began to swell with indignation. I recognized the signs and grabbed him and got out of there fast before he said something that might have made Grierson change his mind about turning Murphy loose on us.

As it was we were barely out of the house when Lovell exploded. "Did you hear that man, Harry?" he said. "Did you hear him?" His voice deepened to mimic Grierson's. "'The small signs that distinguish the work of a true creative genius…If you have the eye for it…'" He clamped his hand on my arm, pulling me to a sudden stop. "Harry, I swear he was talking through his hat. There isn't one cent's worth of difference between those paintings and I've a good mind to go back and prove it to him."

I eased his fingers loose from my sleeve with my free hand. "I wouldn't do that if I were you, Lovell," I said. "You see, I didn't switch those paintings. All I did was smear some of your malt mixture along the one edge where Murphy was sure to see it and *think* I had pulled a switch.

"That was your painting Grierson was praising."

The Waldemeer Triptych

As I came through the door a clerk materialized from somewhere beyond the paintings that lined the walls and started forward to greet me. But then he took in my straight-off-the-rack suit and the flat newspaper-wrapped package under my arm and decided that anyone who so obviously couldn't afford the kind of prices the Browder Galleries commanded wasn't worth his attention. When I refused to dry up and blow away, he raised his eyebrows and turned his gaze on me as if he were just discovering I was there.

"Yes," he said with that polite insolence that only clerks in exclusive shops ever really master.

"My name's Lang," I said in the half-apologetic tone he'd expect. "I have an appointment with Mr. Browder."

The clerk's eyes were frankly skeptical, but after a moment he sighed and nodded his head to the left. "In his office," he said.

I thanked him, clutched the package tighter under my arm, and set off in the direction he had indicated. The clerk sniffed and went back to whatever he'd been doing before I came in.

There was a small door inconspicuously marked *Office* set in the far wall. I went through it without knocking, gave my name to the harried-looking middle-aged woman at the secretary's desk just inside, and waited while she buzzed Browder. When the box on her desk squawked back his permission for me to enter, she smiled tentatively and got up to open the inner door for me.

I was tempted to wink at her as I went by just to see the reaction I'd get. But that would have been out of the character I was trying to project, so I let it pass and went on into Browder's private office.

He looked up from behind his desk and measured me carefully as the clerk had done. And reached pretty much the same conclusion. But since he wasn't on salary plus commission and had more to lose if he were wrong, his reaction was less obvious.

"Yes, Mr. Lang?" he said. "What can I do for you?" He was a slight elderly man with a pinched face and bright restless eyes. What was left of his thinning gray hair had been let grow long on one side and combed carefully over the bald spot that stretched from his forehead to the nape of his neck. It was about as convincing as the friendliness he tried to put in his voice.

I cleared my throat. "Well," I said, "as I told you on the phone, my aunt died recently and I found this painting among her things." I put the package down on his desk and began to undo the wrappings. As usual Lovell, my partner, had used up at least half a roll of tape, sealing it. I smiled apologetically at the mess I was making. "I don't know much about these things," I said. "But she'd had it for a long time and I thought it just might be valuable."

"Hmm," Browder said, not committing himself one way or the other. He waited until I had the wrappings completely off, then took the painting from me. It was a fairly conventional still life—assorted fruit and jugs—and was really notable only for the pattern of light and shade and the bold brilliant colors.

"Hmm," Browder said again, still not committing himself. He studied the painting closely, then flipped it over to inspect the back of the canvas. I'd been working with Lovell long enough now to recognize that Browder was checking the edges of the canvas and the condition of the wooden stretcher holding it taut. As he looked he made a clicking sound with his tongue that could have meant anything. But since the wooden stretcher had been carefully aged in potassium permanganate, the clicking sound probably meant nothing.

After a moment or two he flipped the painting over and without taking his eyes from it opened his desk drawer and took out a large magnifying glass. This he moved back and forth across the face of the picture, pausing now and then as a particular detail caught his eye

I moved around behind him and peered over his shoulder. "What's that little squiggle down there in the corner?" I said, pointing.

Browder looked up at me obliquely. "That little 'squiggle,' " he said drily, "is the colophon used by Jan de Beck as a signature."

"Jan de Beck," I said breathlessly. "Then this thing must be worth a *lot* of money."

"It would be," Browder said, his voice drier than before, "if it was genuine. But this is a forgery." He moved the magnifying glass to cover a brightly decorated jug a little left of center. "You see that faience jug?" he said. "That's the giveaway. Back in the Seventeenth Century those jugs were as common as television sets today, and they show up in at least half of de Beck's paintings."

Browder put the magnifying glass down and looked at me disgustedly. "The shape of this jug is all wrong. It's too round and the handle's at an impossible angle for use. De Beck would no more have made that kind of mistake than a contemporary artist would paint a perfectly square TV screen."

I'd wondered how soon Browder was going to notice it. Now that he had I wet my lips and said quickly, "Now remember, I never said it was a de Beck. You're the one who brought it up, not me."

Browder smiled nastily. "That's right, my friend," he said. "But your protestation of innocence was just a shade too quick for an innocent man. You knew this was a fraud when you brought it in."

I let my eyes drop from his and said sullenly, "You'll never be able to prove that in court."

Browder's mouth twisted again. "Prove it?" he said. "Why should I want to prove it?" He transferred his gaze back to the painting. "Except for that one flaw—which only a handful of experts would spot—this is an excellent forgery." He pursed his lips and let his eyes wander over the painting. "I'll give you $500 for it."

"And sell it for ten times that," I said bitterly.

"No," Browder said, "I'll be lucky to get two or three thousand for it, because to cover myself in case anyone does notice the jug later, I'll have to describe it as a studio picture—or 'attributed to de Beck.'" He took out a check book and poised his pen over it. "So," he said, "do you want the $500 or don't you?"

"I want it," I said. "But I'd prefer cash."

"I'm sure you would," Browder said, "but this check is my evidence that I bought this painting from you openly and in good faith." He gestured slightly with the pen. "Now how do I make this out?"

I shrugged and told him. He rapidly filled out the check, ripped it off the pad, and handed it to me. Then in an obvious gesture of dismissal he picked up the magnifying glass and began to inspect the painting once more.

When I didn't take the hint after a couple of minutes, Browder looked up again. "Was there something else?" he said coldly.

I shifted my weight from one foot to the other. "Well, yes," I said. I wet my lips. "I can get you other paintings like that."

Browder set the magnifying glass down to one side and regarded me thoughtfully. "Can you now?" he said slowly.

"Yes," I said, letting a little more assurance creep back into my voice. "I work partners with an artist named Lovell." I smiled and shrugged, half embarrassed. "Lovell's kind of a nut about some things," I said, "particularly the food he eats. But he does have a large if somewhat specialized talent. He can forge a painting by any artist living or dead and do it so well that most of the time the original artist himself would argue that it was genuine."

Lovell, if he ever got to hear about it, would never forgive me for that "most of the time." The quality of his work was the one thing you couldn't shake him on. But there was that small matter of the wrong-shaped jug to explain.

"Of course," I went on, smiling now even more confidently, "just to be on the safe side we generally stick to artists who are dead. Like Jan de Beck."

Browder nodded soberly. "I see," he said.

I'd thought he would; I'd researched Mr. Browder pretty carefully before approaching him in the first place. "Anyway," I went on, "Lovell mixes his own paints, using only the materials that would have been available to the original artist. And he has his own special method of 'aging' paintings, improved after the methods used by that Dutchman who passed off so many fake Old Masters on the Nazis."

"Very interesting," Browder said. Frowning, he bent back over the forged de Beck. I waited, but after a while when he still hadn't said anything more, I began to edge slowly toward the door. Browder let me almost get there. Then without looking up, he said, "Don't run off. I haven't finished with you yet."

Obediently I moved back to his desk.

Browder continued to study the painting thoughtfully. After another minute, he murmured half to himself, "My old mother always did say that when you had a job to do, the Lord would put the tools in your hand." He chuckled sardonically. "Although in this case maybe I should credit the devil." He put the painting aside and looked up. "Sit down, Mr. Lang," he said briskly. "I think I do have a job for your artist friend."

I pulled a chair around, sat down, and leaned forward eagerly. "Call me Harry," I said. "And what kind of a job?"

"All right, Harry," Browder said. He put his forearms on his desk and leaned forward himself, his hands clasped before him. "Do you know what a triptych is?" he said.

"Sure," I said. "It's a painting in three parts."

"More precisely," Browder said, "a set of paintings on three hinged panels."

I shrugged. "Have it your way," I said. "In any case, as I understand it, you want Lovell to paint a triptych."

Browder smiled bleakly. "More precisely," he repeated, "two panels of a particular triptych." He swiveled suddenly on his chair, pulled a book off the shelves lining the wall behind his desk, and began to leaf through it. Finding what he wanted, he swiveled back and laid the book before me. "That one, to be exact," he said, stabbing his bony forefinger at a full-page color plate.

I picked up the book and examined it more closely. The legend at the bottom of the plate identified the painting as Waldemeer's The Trials and Triumph of Job. All in all, it was pretty much what you'd expect, given that title and theme. So after a cursory glance or two I devoted my attention to the accompanying text.

"According to this," I said when I'd finished reading, "these paintings were part of the loot that the Nazis gathered out of occupied Europe during the second World War and were destroyed along with most of the rest of Berlin when the city fell to the Russians in 1945."

Browder regarded me with sly amusement. "That's what everyone has assumed," he said. "But one of the panels turned up recently."

"After all these years?" I said. I shook my head skeptically.

Browder shrugged. "Why not?" he said. "No one really knows all that happened in those last days of the war. And as recently as 1963 two paintings by Antonio Pallaiuolo, which were thought to have been in Berlin in 1945, turned up in California. I'm sure there would be more if it weren't for the fact that the original owners would immediately put in a claim for them.

"In any case it really doesn't matter whether the Waldemeer is genuine or not. The present owner believes it is and is convinced that the other two panels also exist—probably behind the Iron Curtain. And has commissioned me to get them."

"Why you?" I said bluntly.

Browder coughed delicately. "Because," he said, "I have in the past performed similar services for other collectors and have certain—er—contacts in Eastern Europe."

"I see," I said. "But you figure there's more profit in passing off a forgery."

"Precisely," Browder said. "Particularly since my contacts deny any knowledge of the Waldemeer triptych at all." He fixed his eyes on mine. "So do we have a deal?"

I nodded. "We have a deal," I said, "but it's going to cost you more than $500 a painting."

Browder showed his teeth in a shark's smile and we got down to the really important business. I asked for a 50-50 split, but of course Browder balked at that. And in the end we settled on 25% of the gross sales price as my share and Lovell's. Which was what I'd have asked for in the first place except I'd known he'd argue down from any figure I first named.

On my way out I did wink at Browder's secretary. She winked back. And that just goes to show that you never can tell about people.

"It's impossible," Lovell said flatly.

It was the afternoon following my visit to Browder's and the three of us—Browder, Lovell, and myself—were in a small cafe that Browder had decided would be a safe meeting place.

"It's impossible," Lovell repeated. "I just can't work from a photograph. There are too many things that don't show up—whether the surface is *impasto* or smooth, the exact type of paint used, the condition . . ." His voice trailed off under Browder's steady gaze.

Browder drummed with his fingertips on the table and let the moment drag out. Finally he said, "I agree. In fact, I was rather surprised when your friend didn't bring it up yesterday."

Lovell gulped and blinked nervously. Browder turned his solemn stare on me. I shrugged.

"Lovell's the artist," I said, "not me. I have to leave that kind of thing to him."

Browder nodded slowly and turned back to Lovell. "The only problem is—how do we get the existing panel for you to work from?"

"Now there," I said, "is something 1 am an expert on. Just leave it to old Harry to take care of that little detail."

Browder hesitated, and I could guess what was going through his mind. He didn't want to introduce us to his client because then we might be tempted to make a deal on our own, freezing him out. On the other hand we had to have the one original panel to work from. He said at last, "We'll do it together."

"Suits me fine," I said. And we traded smiles of equal insincerity.

The apartment house was set off in a little park of its own with a clear view of the river on one side and the city skyline on the other. There was nothing sleek or modern or flashy about it—just that quiet elegance that spoke of generations of inherited wealth.

The interior matched the exterior, and I looked around with frank curiosity as Browder and I crossed the entrance lobby.

"Your client lives well," I said.

"What would you expect of someone who can afford to collect art on a large scale?" Browder said drily.

I nodded to show I conceded the point and followed him into the elevator.

The girl who opened the apartment door was young—no more than 25—with long blonde hair that looked as if it might be natural and an open, almost ingenuous expression. She looked blankly at us for a second, then smiled shyly in recognition. "Why, Mr. Browder," she said.

"Forgive me for dropping in on you unannounced like this, Miss Horgan," Browder said smoothly. "But I couldn't wait to tell you my news."

Miss Horgan's face lighted up like a beacon. "The other panels!" she exclaimed. "You've found them!"

Browder beamed back. "It appears we have," he said. Then his face sobered again. "Unfortunately, their condition has suffered somewhat as a result of the treatment they were given in 1945 and immediately thereafter."

"Oh, no!" Miss Horgan sounded so heartbroken that I was almost ready to cry with her.

"Now, now," Browder said soothingly. "It's nothing that can't be remedied and fortunately the face of the paintings hasn't been affected at all. But under the circumstances I felt we had better examine the panel you have to determine if it suffers from the same defect." He half turned to indicate me. "That's why I brought Mr. Lang along. Mr. Lang is an expert art restorer."

Miss Horgan looked at me anxiously.

Browder took her hand in his. "It's quite all right, my dear," he said. "We can trust Mr. Lang's discretion."

If there hadn't been a large amount of money involved, I would have been sick right to his face. As it was, though, I smiled reassuringly, and after a moment Miss Horgan smiled tentatively back.

She led us through a sumptuously furnished apartment to a sun-bright studio on the river side of the building. It was a casual room and the right-hand panel of The Trials and Triumph of Job looked curiously out of place on one wall.

"As soon as I have the other panels," Miss Horgan said, "I'm going to redecorate this room around them."

"Of course," Browder said, not really paying any attention to her. He nodded to me. "All right, Mr. Lang," he said.

I lifted the painting down from the wall carefully and pretended to poke at its back with the blade of a small penknife. Fortunately, like most paintings of its age and type, it had been painted on a wooden panel instead of on canvas. And after a moment or two I looked up and said with convincing authority, "I'm afraid the rot has set in on this one, too."

"Oh, no!" Miss Horgan wailed for the second time.

I turned to her and gave her another reassuring smile. "It's not that serious," I said. "The rot hasn't penetrated too deeply. So all we have to do is plane off the affected parts, seal it, and your painting's as good as new. Better, in fact. So, with your permission, I'll take it to my shop and have it back to you repaired before you even have time to miss it."

Miss Horgan's eyebrows drew together in a frown. "I just hate the thought of parting with it," she said. "Couldn't you do the work here?"

I took a deep breath, then blew it out again, as if I were considering her request. "I could," I said slowly. "But," I added, "I couldn't guarantee results—or that the painting itself wouldn't be damaged."

"In that case," Miss Horgan said hastily, "take it."

"That's right, my dear," Browder said unctuously. "Better safe than sorry."

We packed the painting in one of Miss Horgan's spare suitcases and Browder and I carried it downstairs in the elevator. Outside, he said, "That was easier than I expected."

I looked at him obliquely, then shrugged. "Most things are," I said, "once you make up your mind to do them."

"Perhaps," Browder said. He laid a bony hand on my arm. "There is one thing I want you to remember, though, my friend, in case you're thinking it would be easy to cheat me. I still have that forged de Beck you sold me *and* the canceled check. If you try anything funny, they both go to the police with a formal complaint." He chuckled complacently. "I'm sure you're an old hand at dodging the police, Harry. But an arrest warrant would at the least seriously cramp your style."

And with that happy thought between us we drove back to town.

Browder dropped by twice while Lovell was working on the paintings. The first time Lovell had just started to plane down the back of the original panel. There was no rot of course, but having told Miss Horgan that was what we were going to do, we had to carry through.

"Careful you don't damage that," Browder said.

"If I do," Lovell replied haughtily, "I'll paint you another just like it."

Browder snorted and left.

The second time the paintings themselves were finished and Lovell was in the process of testing to see if the first coat of varnish had dried sufficiently hard. But when Browder came in, he stopped and set the paintings up for Browder to inspect.

Browder looked them over critically, then shook his head. "They don't look right," he said.

"Of course not," Lovell said. "They're still too clean." He took the paintings down off their easels, laid them flat, and before Browder's astonished gaze poured a bottle of black ink over them.

Lovell gave the ink a minute or so to seep down into the networks of cracks that he had carefully nurtured across the face of the paintings in imitation of the genuine aging process. Then he set to work to mop up the excess ink with a towel. When he was finished, the result was very like the accumulation of dirt that builds up over the years in a genuine work of art.

"How's that?" Lovell said proudly, sure of his answer.

It was grudging, but finally Browder nodded his approval. "How much longer before they're ready?" he said.

"A couple of days," Lovell said. "They need another coat of varnish and we have to give it time to harden thoroughly."

Browder nodded again and left. I closed the door after him, then turned to lean against it and give Lovell an "O" sign with my thumb and forefinger. But he had already gone back to getting the paintings ready for revarnishing.

Right on time three days later I delivered the paintings to Browder. It was after hours, so none of his regular employees would be around to witness the transfer. But Miss Horgan was there.

She was beaming like an excited child on its birthday. "I've been pestering Mr. Browder about the paintings ever since I knew they were available. And I was just lucky enough to be here when you, called to say you had finished your repairs and were bringing them over."

"That was lucky," I said.

Browder smiled insincerely and helped me remove the protective packing and set the paintings up for Miss Horgan to admire.

"Oh," she said, clapping her hands together, "aren't they lovely?"

"Yes," Browder said, "indeed they are. But we mustn't I detain Mr. Lang any longer. It's getting late and—"

"That's all right," I said cheerfully, realizing what Browder was driving at. He wanted me out of there before the price was mentioned so that he could cut the price in half before arriving at our 25%. "I don't mind at all."

Before Browder could say anything more, I made quite a show of turning the pictures over and explaining the "repairs" to Miss Horgan. She kept nodding politely as I spoke, but her heart obviously wasn't in it. And as soon as I paused she turned eagerly to Browder.

"We might as well get everything settled now," she said. "$200,000 was the price agreed on, wasn't it?"

Browder winced, but recovered smoothly and even managed to drag up a smile from somewhere. "That's right," he said.

Miss Horgan sat down in the chair beside Browder's desk and took an alligator-bound check book from her purse. "I'll give you a check now to close the deal," she said. She wrote swiftly, tore the completed check from the pad, and held it out to Browder. "I'm afraid I'll have to ask you to wait a day or so before cashing this, though," she said, smiling apologetically. "Just until I have time to transfer sufficient funds into my checking account."

"Quite all right," Browser said, smiling in return. He took the check from her and held it clutched in his hand, waist high. "I'll have the paintings repacked and delivered."

"Fine," Miss Horgan said. She stood up. "Well," she said, "I guess that takes care of everything, doesn't it?"

Unconsciously, Browder's fingers caressed the check lightly. "It does indeed," he said.

Miss Horgan shook hands with each of us, then left.

As soon as the door was shut behind her, I turned to Browder and rubbed my thumb rapidly over the first two fingers of my left hand. "$50,000," I said. "And this time I'll take it in cash."

Browder nodded soberly. "Under the circumstances," he said, "I agree." He went to the wall, swung out a picture to reveal a safe behind it, and after a quick glance back to make sure I wasn't watching, he spun the dial rapidly through the combination and pulled the door open.

He took out several thick packets of bills, glanced at them briefly, then handed them to me. I didn't think he'd risk a short count but just to make sure I riffled through them quickly before sticking them in my pocket. The $50,000 was all there.

"Satisfied?" Browder said drily.

"I would be," I said, "if I had that canceled check from the previous sale, too."

Browder hesitated for a second. Then he shrugged and turned to the safe again. A moment later he came back and handed me the canceled check. I stuck it in my pocket with the packets of bills.

"Keep in touch," Browder said. "You never know when something like this will turn up again."

I promised I would and left. We didn't shake hands.

The car was parked two blocks away. I walked around it and got in on the right-hand side. Miss Horgan, behind the wheel, smiled at me sardonically. "What kept you so long?" she said.

"A few minor details," I said. "Like getting the money."

Her smile broadened. "Speaking of money," she said and held out her hand.

I counted out $15,000 and handed it to her. "One third of the profits," I said, "after deducting the expenses of painting the panel you used to bait Browder and the other two he sold you. Not to mention a month's sublease on that gilded cage you called an apartment."

Miss Horgan put the money in her purse and sighed. "I'm going to miss that apartment," she said. "But under the circumstances I imagine it would be best for all of us if we were long gone when Browder tries to cash that check."

I smiled, remembering how Browder had used the same phrase. "Under the circumstances," I said, "I agree."

Never Trust a Partner

The girl at the typist's desk looked at me dubiously. "I don't know," she said. "Mr. Kelmartin doesn't like to be disturbed unless it's somebody with an appointment." She was a stocky girl in her late teens or early twenties with a pleasantly unintelligent face.

I smiled and scribbled on the back of a business card: *There are 10,000 reasons why you should see me.*

"Give Mr. Kelmartin this," I said, "and see what he says then."

The girl looked even more dubious than before, but she took the card and went through the door marked "Private" behind her. A couple of moments later she was back.

"He'll see you," she said. She sounded surprised and vaguely let down.

I winked at her and went past her through the door, letting her close it after me.

For one of the city's more successful art dealers, Kelmartin certainly was Spartan in his tastes. Although paintings lined the walls of his showroom outside, his own office was bare of decoration and scarcely large enough to accommodate the old-fashioned rolltop desk set square against one wall and two armless wooden chairs. In some ways, though, it was the kind of office you'd expect to find a man like Kelmartin in. He was tall and spare, with the thin sharp-featured face of an old-time Yankee trader and frosty eyes behind small, octagonal, rimless glasses.

He removed his glasses as I came in and began to polish them carefully with a handkerchief he drew from his breast pocket. "Just what is it I can do for you, Mr. Lang?" he said. "Or better still"—he glanced down at my card on his desk—"what did you have in mind to do for me?" His voice was so precise as to be almost biting.

I smiled affably. "I understand you're cataloguing the art collection of the late Bernice Magruder," I said.

Kelmartin resettled his glasses on his nose, folded the handkerchief and stuffed it back in his pocket. "That's hardly a secret," he said. "It was in all the papers."

"Yes," I said. "It was also in the papers that Miss Magruder was as eccentric as they come and bought pretty much as the fancy moved her. And kept what she bought stored away in her back rooms."

Kelmartin eyed me speculatively. "So?" he said.

"So," I said, "until you finish cataloguing the collection no one really has any idea as to what is or isn't in it. And it seems to me that under those circumstances the way is clear for a couple of clever men to make a nice little profit for themselves."

Kelmartin didn't say anything, just continued to study me.

"Suppose," I went on, "a really valuable painting were to be found hidden in the collection. The honest thing to do, of course, would be to list it in the assets of the estate. Which would make the heirs happy, but since they're second or third cousins and already stand to inherit more money than they can spend during the rest of their lives, their lot would hardly be improved. On the other hand, the painting could be quietly sold to a third party and the money diverted to far more deserving individuals."

"Such as you and me," Kelmartin said drily.

"Precisely," I said.

Kelmartin nodded curtly and turned back to the papers on his desk. "Unfortunately, Mr. Lang," he said, "for your little scheme to work it would be necessary that the Magruder collection contain at least one valuable painting. Let me assure you it does not. Bernice Magruder's tastes were as execrable as they were eccentric. I ought to know. I sold her most of the junk she had. And even if there were a pearl in all that dross I certainly wouldn't need you to help me dispose of it. So, good day, Mr. Lang." He picked up a pencil and began to make notes on the margin of one of his papers.

I didn't move. "No," I said, "you wouldn't need me. But because there isn't anything valuable in the collection you *do* need me. I can supply the painting."

Kelmartin paused in his writing and looked up at me over the edge of his glasses.

"I work partners with a man named Lovell," I said. "Now, Lovell has his little peculiarities, as who doesn't? He's as jumpy as a bean on a string and a real kook about the food he eats. But more importantly he's an artist with a very real if somewhat specialized talent. He can forge a painting by any artist living or dead and do it so well that only a spectroscopic or electro-luminescent examination can distinguish his copy from the artist's genuine work.

"Most recently he's been concentrating on the French artist Lamartine, because at one point in his development Lamartine did a whole series of paintings of wheatfields. According to Lovell, Lamartine was experimenting with light and shadow effects and didn't consider the paintings to be of any value. So he gave them to his friends and creditors pretty indiscriminately."

"Yes," Kelmartin said thoughtfully, "he did. Some of them have turned up in the oddest places over the years, and I doubt if Lamartine himself knew how many he'd given away or who had them."

"So," I said, "would it be so unbelievable for one to turn up in the Magruder collection?"

"No," Kelmartin said, steepling his fingers before his face and rubbing his thin lips along them. "And with the way Lamartine's reputation has been growing since his death, it would be a valuable painting indeed." He paused and glanced up at me obliquely. "Still it would have to be a very good forgery, and all I have is your word for how good your partner is."

"Judge for yourself," I said. "I've got the painting out in my car right now. I would have brought it in with me except that I didn't think it would be wise to let your girl see me carrying it."

Kelmartin looked at me for a long moment. "You're very sure of yourself, aren't you, Mr. Lang?" he said at last.

"If I am," I said, "it's because I do my homework and know my man before I approach him."

Kelmartin nodded soberly. "Very wise of you," he said, "I'm sure." He got up and opened the door to the outer office. "Miss Jones," he said, "I ordered some supplies from Bartlett's this morning. They're supposed to deliver them, but I find I can't wait. Would you mind running over and picking them up?" It was phrased as a request but his voice made it clear that she had better not mind, and the stocky girl got up with something near to alacrity.

As soon as the outer door had closed after her, Kelmartin turned back to me. "All right," he said. "now let's see that painting of yours."

He spent a good half hour examining the painting in both artificial and natural light. Finally he set it and his magnifying glass down. "There are a couple of flaws, I think," he said, removing his octagonal glasses and rubbing his hand across his eyes. "But that may only be because I know it's a forgery. It's hard to say how I'd react if I came across it cold." He sighed and put his glasses back on. "All in all, though, I'd say your partner is almost as good as you claim he is."

"Then it's a deal?" I said.

"That would depend on the deal," Kelmartin said drily.

"Well," I said, "a Lamartine ordinarily goes for $50,000 to $60,000. Under the circumstances, though, a buyer would expect a real bargain. So I'd say we ask $20,000 and go partners, splitting it down the middle—$10,000 apiece."

Kelmartin hesitated. "It's tempting," he said. "Still, we'd have to approach a prospective buyer and that could be risky."

"No problem," I said. "I already have a prospective buyer in mind."

Kelmartin raised his eyes. "Who?" he said.

"You wouldn't know him," I said. "He's more of a speculator than an art collector, interested primarily in picking up something he thinks he can turn around and make a quick profit on."

"I see," Kelmartin said. He chewed thoughtfully on his lip for a moment, then nodded. "All right," he said. "Bring your buyer around here tonight after everyone else has gone." He permitted himself a bleak, wintry smile. "Partner."

I smiled too and left.

It was a little after 7:00 and just beginning to turn dark when I rang Kelmartin's bell. With me this time was a tall heavyset man named Hasso. He stood slightly behind me and looked on impassively, his hands stuck deep in his topcoat pockets against the slight evening chill. With his balding forehead, bulbous nose, and drooping lower lip he resembled nothing so much as a grownup version of the grumpy dwarf in *Snow White*.

When there was no motion from within I rang the bell again, more insistently. This time Kelmartin came to the door, peeked out around the drawn shade, and when he saw who it was opened up to let us in.

"Mr. Kelmartin," I said, making the necessary introduction, "this is Mr. Hasso. I'd like him to see the painting we discussed this afternoon."

Kelmartin's eyes flicked suspiciously from me to Hasso.

"It's all right," I said reassuringly. "Mr. Hasso understands the need for discretion."

Kelmartin continued to study Hasso for a moment, then still without uttering a word turned and led us back to his office. Leaving us there, he disappeared into his showroom only to return a few minutes later with the Lamartine. He'd added to the authenticity of our story by fitting it into an ornate and timeworn oak frame.

Hasso took the painting in both hands and studied it silently, his thick lips pursed and a reflective frown creasing his forehead. "What's so great about this?" he said finally. "It's just a picture of a cornfield."

"Wheatfield," Kelmartin corrected. "And as for what's so great about it, nothing really. It's the reputation of the artist that makes it valuable."

"How valuable?" Hasso demanded.

"In today's market?" Kelmartin said, shrugging. "I'd say upward of $50,000."

"Then how come you are willing to sell it for $20,000?" Hasso said harshly. His eyes caught and held the art dealer's. Kelmartin clearly hadn't expected this bluntness and he opened his mouth somewhat like a startled fish.

"As I told you, Mr. Hasso—" I began.

Hasso shot a quick glance at me and jerked his head in Kelmartin's direction. "I want to hear it from him," he said.

By now Kelmartin had recovered his composure. "Let's just say," he intoned smoothly, "that there are certain irregularities about the transaction that make it inadvisable for me to give a bill of sale or offer my usual guarantee. So I've adjusted my price accordingly."

"Sure," Hasso said, "let's say that." He looked back at the painting. "How do I know this thing is genuine, though?"

"I know something about these things, Mr. Hasso," I put in. "I can vouch for its authenticity. And I'm the one taking the risk. All I want you to do is lend me the money to buy it."

"Um-hmm," Hasso said. He looked straight at Kelmartin. "What if I asked to have an expert of my own examine this?"

Kelmartin thought that over for a few moments. "It would be risky," he said. "But I suppose it would be all right—as long as he didn't know where the painting came from and agreed to examine it on the premises here." That last part was a touch of genius. It insured that Hasso's expert wouldn't be able to make an examination scientific enough to expose the forgery.

Hasso nodded his satisfaction. "That's good enough for me," he said. "If you're willing to risk an independent check, there's no reason to insist on one."

"Then you'll lend me the money?" I said eagerly.

Hasso shook his head. "No," he said. "I'll buy it myself."

"Now wait a minute," I began.

Hasso ignored me and turned to Kelmartin. "You wouldn't have any objection to selling to somebody other than Lang?"

"Of course not," Kelmartin said. "Money's money, not matter where it comes from."

"Exactly what I say myself," Hasso said. "I assume you don't want a check."

"Under the circumstances," Kelmartin said, "I think it would be best to keep this a cash transaction."

Hasso pursed his lips and nodded. "It'll take me a day or two to get the cash together," he said. "You'll hold the painting for me?"

Kelmartin opened his mouth to agree, but I cut him off. "Don't make any promises," I said. "At least give me a chance to raise the money somewhere else."

Kelmartin hesitated, then nodded. "All right," he said. "I'll sell to whoever shows up first with the money."

"Fair enough," Hasso said. He set the painting down and grinned at me. "I'm not worried, Lang," he said. "If you could have gotten the money from someone else, you'd never have come to me." He turned back to Kelmartin. "Be seeing you," he said, and left.

As soon as I heard the front door close after him I grinned at Kelmartin. "That went very well, I'd say."

"Perhaps," Kelmartin said. "But I expected your man would have the money with him."

I shrugged. "Hasso's not as rich as he likes to pretend. He'll have to arrange a loan to come up with the money. But his reputation's good with the money boys and he'll get it. And since he thinks he's got competition he won't dawdle or try to beat the price down."

"I hope you're right," Kelmartin said.

"I am," I said. I picked up the painting from where Hasso had put it down and looked for something to wrap it in.

Kelmartin frowned. "What are you doing?" he said.

"Taking this with me," I said. I found a copy of the afternoon paper in Kelmartin's wastebasket, smoothed it out on his desk and began folding it around the painting. "I have one standing rule," I said. "Never trust a partner. And as long as I hold onto this I'm sure you won't make a private deal and cut me out."

"How very prudent of you," Kelmartin said drily. "Perhaps I should insist on similar insurance from you."

"You already have it," I said. "Hasso thinks I'm a rival for the painting. He'd be suspicious as hell if I suddenly showed up trying to sell it."

"Perhaps," Kelmartin said. "But I prefer more concrete insurance." He opened a drawer to his desk and flicked a switch. There was a hum and then a tape recorder began to play back our conversation of that afternoon. Kelmartin let it play about halfway through, then switched it off.

"If you do try to cheat me," he said, "I'll see that this tape gets to your friend Hasso." He smiled his humorless smile. "Somehow I don't think he's the kind of man who would take lightly to having been swindled. And I'm willing to gamble that he'd vent his ire on you, not me."

I inclined my head in acknowledgment of his thrust. "Well, partner," I said, "we seem to be well matched."

"It *would* appear that way, wouldn't it?" Kelmartin said quietly. "And now, good night, Mr. Lang. I'll call you at your hotel when Hasso has the money ready."

I spent the next day loafing around the hotel, reading and catching up on my sleep, while Lovell kept running in and out, easing his nervousness by indulging in yogurt sundaes. Then on the second day Kelmartin called.

"Bring the painting," he said. "It's settlement day."

Lovell looked at me anxiously as I set down the phone. I winked at him. "Right on schedule," I said.

I found Kelmartin alone in his office, the stocky girl having probably been sent on some other fool's errand. He snatched the painting away from me, unwrapped it, and set it up against the back of his desk with solicitous care.

"When's Hasso coming?" I said.

"This afternoon," Kelmartin said, tearing his eyes away from the painting. "But the more I think about it, the more convinced I am that it wouldn't be wise for you to be here when he comes."

I started to protest.

"Don't worry," Kelmartin cut in half irritably. "I have your money for you." He took an envelope from his desk and handed it to me. "You can count it if you like," he said.

I took him at his word and counted it. It came to $10,000 right on the nose. I slipped the envelope into my jacket pocket.

"If you don't mind," I said, "I'd like that tape too."

"Of course," Kelmartin said. He played enough of the tape to prove to me it was the right one, then handed it over.

"Well," I said, "it's been a pleasure doing business with you. If the occasion ever comes up again—"

"Of course, of course," Kelmartin said and ushered me out so hurriedly that if I had been a more sensitive soul I might have suspected that he was trying to get rid of me.

Hasso was waiting where my car was parked two blocks away. "You have something for me, I trust," he said.

I reached into my pocket for an envelope—not the one Kelmartin had given me but another one—and handed it to him. "As agreed," I said, "$1000."

Hasso stuck the envelope in his own pocket.

"Better count it," I said.

"Naw," Hasso said. "I know you wouldn't cheat me." He looked at me quizzically. "Tell me one thing, though, Harry. How did you get Kelmartin to pay you off before he collected himself?"

"Well," I said, clearing my throat, "unfortunately not everybody in this business is as trustworthy as you and me. So when Kelmartin was approached by a second prospect who offered $30,000 for the painting he saw no reason to split the extra $10,000 with his partner. The only trouble was he couldn't collect until he delivered the painting. And I had the painting. So"—I smiled innocently—"he had to pay me off first."

"I see," Hasso said. "Only who's going to pay him $30,000 for that thing?"

"As a matter of fact," I said, "nobody. His second prospect was Lovell."

The Kidnaped Painting

The blonde at the receptionist's desk gave me a brilliantly false smile and when I told her my reason for being there she pointed to a door marked "Neil Savarin, Chief Adjuster." I went on through without knocking, thinking that another girl would be on guard behind it; but instead it was Savarin's private office, and he blinked up at me curiously from behind his desk.

"My name's Harry Lang, Mr. Savarin," I explained. "The girl outside said you were expecting me."

"Oh, yes," he said, rising. "Yes." He was a short balding man with a round shiny face, a wise guy's mouth, and eyes that kept sliding away from you. "It was good of you to come."

I smiled wryly. "Your note promising a financial reward if I did was too tempting to ignore," I said. "But, frankly, I didn't expect an insurance company. So if it was just a gimmick to get me here so you could sell me a policy, I'm afraid we've both wasted our time."

Savarin smiled back and shook his head. "No," he said, "I'm not selling. I'm buying—works of art. Or one particular work of art, at least. And I understand that you can—uh—supply them on demand."

That was a rather neat way of putting what Lovell and I did. Lovell was my partner. And if he was kind of a nut about some things, particularly the food he ate, he also had a large although somewhat specialized talent. He could forge a painting by any artist living or dead and do it so well that most of the time the original artist himself would swear it was genuine. I was the outside man, specializing in selling the finished product to gullible art collectors.

But now, rather than give anything away, I studied Savarin warily. "Where did you pick up that bit of information?" I said.

Savarin shrugged. "From a mutual friend," he said. "A Miss Horgan. I believe you and she have had dealings together in the past."

I relaxed slightly and nodded. "Yes," I said. "And I guess if she vouches for you, you're all right."

"Then there's no reason we can't do business, is there?" Savarin said, smiling.

"That depends on what the business is," I said.

"I'm sure you'll find it agreeable," Savarin said. He waved me into a chair. Then he sat down behind his desk again, leaned back and folded his hands across his stomach.

"What do you know about Hollingsworth's Leda and the Swan?" he said.

"Nothing," I said, "except that I assume it's a painting."

"It is," Savarin said. "And I'm surprised you haven't heard of it, because in its way it's a rather famous one. Charles the Second commissioned it in 1672 as a present for a young lady who'd caught his eye. The swan being a royal bird in England, the girl couldn't fail to understand and be flattered. But heavy-handed symbolism or not, the painting came to be considered something of a minor masterpiece. It was in the girl's family for generations—until the late 1950's, in fact, when it was finally sold to meet death duties. Since then it's changed hands several times. Most recently it was purchased by a man named August Wilding, who brought it to this country. Mr. Wilding, unfortunately, is our client."

"Unfortunately?" I said.

Savarin nodded. "Six months ago the painting was stolen. It was insured for a quarter of a million dollars, and needless to say, the prospect of having to pay out that much money doesn't make the company happy at all—particularly since it now appears that the painting was overvalued for insurance purposes."

"How did that happen?" I said. "Didn't the company have its own expert appraise the painting?"*

Savarin cleared his throat. "Yes," he said. "As a matter of fact, *I* examined the painting and it was on my recommendation that the policy was issued. It seemed safe enough at the time, but—let's just say that I made an error in judgment."

I nodded, knowing just what Savarin meant by an "error in judgment." He and the salesman had conspired to inflate the value of the painting and then had split the additional commission.

"I've been able to stall off a settlement so far," Savarin said, "because normally paintings this valuable aren't stolen so much as kidnaped and held for ransom. The pattern never varies. Someone 'finds' the painting and the insurance company pays a suitable 'ransom' for its return. Nobody's fooled, of course, but we aren't policemen. Our job is to get the painting back and save the company money.

"In this case, though, the painting's been missing too long. Six months and not a murmur about what's happened to it!" Savarin sounded genuinely aggrieved and for a moment his eyes actually held mine. Then they slipped away again. "Time's running out and I've got to come up with the painting soon." He paused significantly. "One way or the other."

I smiled. "In other words," I said, "if you can't find the original, a duplicate will do."

"Precisely," Savarin said. "Then everybody would be happy. The client, because for all he knew he had the original painting back. The company, because it had paid out only a fraction of the policy amount. Me, because there'd be no need to bring my original error out into the open. And last but not least, you, because I'd arrange for you to collect the 'ransom.' In this case, $25,000." He looked down modestly. "Less, of course, a small commission for me."

"Just how small is 'small'?" I said.

Savarin shrugged. "I'm not greedy," he said. "$5000 would do me quite nicely."

"I'm sure it would," I said, "but let's say $2500 instead, since all the risks and expenses are ours."

I expected Savarin to argue but instead he nodded quickly and said, "All right, but only if the painting's ready by the end of the month."

"It will be," I said. "We will need something to work from, though. Lovell's the artist, but I gather when you don't have the original to work from, there's some difficulty in getting the proportions and other details exactly right."

"No problem there," Savarin said. "The company has an exact description of the painting in its files plus some excellent color photos to scale. I'll give them to you."

"Then you've got yourself a deal," I said. We shook on it and I left. His hand left my own feeling slightly clammy. But $22,500 was $22,500, and nobody said you had to like the people you worked with.

I called Savarin two days before his end-of-the-month deadline ran out to tell him the painting was ready and to arrange delivery. Rather than risk being seen at his office too often, this time I picked him up a block away and drove around while he sat in the back seat comparing Lovell's duplicate Leda with his office records which I'd returned to be put back into the files.

He sat silently for a long time, and I was beginning to think he had some reservations. But when he did speak it was to say, "If I didn't know better I'd swear this was the original."

"Good," I said. "Let's hope the owner feels the same way. Since we didn't have the original to work from, we can't guarantee there aren't some minute differences. This painting should stand up, though, as long as it isn't compared with the original."

"No danger of that," Savarin said. "The original has long since disappeared into some other collection. And even if it hadn't, I doubt that Wilding would notice any differences. He's an art snob who buys paintings because other people have decided they're valuable. I doubt if he's looked at any of his acquisitions a dozen times except to show them off."

"Then all that needs to be done is for you to hand over the 'ransom' and I'll be on my way."

"That's not quite all," Savarin said. "First I have to call Wilding, tell him I've been contacted by the thief, and arrange for the three of us to meet."

"Now wait a minute," I said. "That wasn't part of the deal."

"Yes, it was, Harry," Savarin said. "You just weren't listening closely enough. Because if you want that 'ransom,' the deal has to look right. And that means it has to follow the usual pattern: contact, inspection, payoff."

I grumbled some more but in the end let myself be persuaded—although considering that Savarin held all trumps as far as the payoff was concerned, "persuaded" may be the wrong word. In any case, as soon as we were agreed, I dropped Savarin off near his office and returned to the studio that Lovell and I had rented, taking the painting back with me.

Savarin called me there about thirty minutes later. "It's all set," he said. "I just talked to Wilding and he's anxious to settle. Bring the painting to Room 415 of the Hotel Continental at four. That 'ransom' is as good as yours."

"It better be," I said.

I arranged to get to the hotel first, but hung around the edge of the lobby until I saw Savarin and an older, taller man with a flushed heavy-browed face cross to the elevators and go up. I gave them another ten minutes to get settled, then followed them.

Savarin opened the door at my knock with such alacrity that he must have been waiting just inside it. He frowned when he saw my empty hands. "Where's the painting?" he demanded.

"You didn't actually think I'd bring it with me, did you?" I said mildly, stepping into the room. "For all I knew, this place could have been crawling with cops."

Savarin gave me a disgusted look, apparently feeling you could carry realism too far. "Well, you can see for yourself it isn't."

"So I can," I said in the same mild tone. "Now. Did you bring the reward?"

Savarin took an envelope from his breast pocket and counted out the contents. There was exactly $22,000, which meant that he'd cut himself in for an extra $500. But this wasn't the time to quibble about that. I crossed to the phone and dialed the desk. "This is Room 415," I said. "Will you have someone bring up the suitcase I checked with you a little while ago?"

As I hung up, Wilding smiled ruefully from the bed where he'd been sitting quietly all this time. "You don't take anything for granted, do you, young man?" he said.

"I try not to," I said. "It's my way of staying healthy, wealthy, and out of jail."

Wilding continued to smile and watch me thoughtfully until a few minutes later a bellboy brought the suitcase up. I let Savarin tip him while I opened the suitcase and placed the painting on the bed for inspection.

"Well," Savarin said heartily, "that's the Leda all right. But just for the record, Mr. Wilding, will you please identify it?"

Wilding had risen and now he bent, frowning, over the painting. "I'm just not sure," he said.

"What?" Savarin said. "Don't you know your own painting?"

"Of course I do," Wilding said irritably. "But—" He frowned down at the painting again. "I wish the light were better here," he said.

"If it'll make you feel better," I said, "we can submit the painting for spectroscopic examination. That should prove whether it's genuine or not."

I ignored the startled glance Savarin cast over Wilding's back and concentrated on meeting Wilding's own steady gaze. After a long moment he said, "You'd be willing to submit this for scientific examination?"

"Of course," I said. Wilding's eyes held mine for another second or two. Then he glanced back down at the painting, picked it up, and moved to the window with it. After studying it a while longer he said, "No, that won't be necessary. I can identify this as my painting."

"Fine," Savarin said, rubbing his hands together. "Then it's all settled." Beaming broadly, he handed over the envelope. I checked the contents swiftly just to make sure he hadn't pulled a switch on me, then slipped it into my coat pocket.

"Well, gentlemen," I said, "it's been a pleasure doing business with you. Now, if you'll excuse me—"

"Ahh," Savarin said, "I will need a receipt from you for that reward." He smiled at Wilding. "There's no need for you to stay around, though, Mr. Wilding. I'll bring the papers for you to sign to your office tomorrow."

Wilding put the painting in its suitcase, shook hands with Savarin, nodded briefly to me, and left.

"Whew!" Savarin said after the door had closed after Wilding. "That was close."

"Not really," I said.

He raised his eyebrows.

"No?" he said. "What would you have done if he'd taken you up on that offer to have a spectroscopic examination?"

"It wouldn't have made any difference," I said. "There was a spectrograph in those records you gave me, made at the time the painting was insured. I took the precaution of replacing it with one made from a scraping taken off the copy. Any test would produce an exact duplicate—and 'prove' the copy was the original."

Savarin grinned appreciatively. "You really don't take anything for granted, do you?"

"Like I told the man," I said, "I try not to. Now, you said you wanted a receipt."

Savarin produced a form—for $25,000. I signed it and left, after promising to keep in touch in case any additional opportunities to work together came up.

My car was parked two blocks from the hotel. I went to it, drove around the block a couple of times to make sure I wasn't followed, then cut straight out to Wilding's estate.

He was waiting for me in his study, his tie loosened but otherwise dressed as he had been in the hotel room. Seated in an armchair across from him, her shapely legs crossed comfortably and with a drink in her hand, was Miss Horgan. She was an attractive girl, about 30 or so, with long blonde hair that looked as if it might be natural and an open, almost ingenuous expression concealing a devious and larcenous mind.

"Well," I said to her, "this is a surprise."

She smiled at me. "You didn't really think I'd miss the payoff, did you, Harry?"

"No," I said, "knowing you, I guess I didn't." I took out the envelope Savarin had given me, counted out $2000 as her share for having helped set him up, and divided the rest between Wilding and myself, $10,000 each.

He looked at it oddly. "Shouldn't there be $250 more for me?" he said.

"Savarin chiseled himself in for an extra $500," I said, "knowing I couldn't make an issue of it with you there."

Wilding nodded and stuffed his money in his pocket. Miss Horgan looked sympathetic. "That's just what I'd expect that creep to do," she said. "It was just too bad you had to give him anything."

I shrugged. "It couldn't be helped," I said. "But if it makes you feel any better he won't enjoy it long. Because in about two weeks Lovell will contact him and Mr. Wilding here with the *real* Leda. Savarin will claim it's a fraud, of course. But—" I smiled "—Mr. Wilding's doubts will be revived and he'll insist on a scientific examination. Which won't alarm Savarin since he thinks I switched spectrographs in the company records. But since I happened to lie about that, there won't be any difficulty at all establishing which is the real original. And the insurance company will find itself in the unenviable position of paying two 'rewards' for the same painting. You can imagine what will happen to Savarin after that."

"Beautiful," Miss Horgan said. "So that's why you needed the duplicate."

"Yes," Wilding said. "It isn't as profitable as faking a loss to collect the whole policy, but it is a lot safer. And, more importantly, I can collect and still continue to own the painting openly." He beamed at me. "You were a genius to dream this up, Harry, a genius," he said.

"I won't argue with that," I said. "Incidentally, you'd better let me take the original with me now. I'd rather not be seen coming here too often."

"Of course," Wilding said. He left the room, returning a few minutes later with the original Leda which he packed in my suitcase.

Miss Horgan smiled and raised her glass. "Well," she said, "here's to a successful job successfully carried out."

"I'll drink to that," I said.

Lovell was pacing nervously when I got back to the studio. He bit his thumb when he saw the painting. "So he gave you the original, did he?" he said.

"Of course," I said. "We're partners. So why wouldn't he?"

"I don't know," Lovell said. "But I was sort of hoping he wouldn't. I don't like this idea of recontacting the insurance company—I don't like it at all."

"To tell you the truth, Lovell," I said equably, "neither do I. So now that we've got the original, why don't we just move on? I'm sure we'll find somebody who'll pay us even more for it than we'd have gotten from the second 'ransom.'"

Hobson's Choice

The auction of "fine paintings and objets d'art" was almost over by the time I got to Hobson's Gallery—which, since I hadn't come to buy, didn't really bother me. What could pose something of a problem, though, was the small tastefully lettered sign hanging from a velvet rope stretched across the entrance to the auction room: *Private—Admittance by Invitation Only*. Because, of course, I hadn't been invited.

Still, there was no guard there to enforce the ban. So I simply unhooked the rope and went through.

Just inside, a girl wearing a smock-type jacket and clutching a handful of catalogues schoolgirl style under her bosom started away from the wall and opened her mouth to protest. I shushed her with a finger to my lips, then nodded forward to where the auction was in progress.

The girl hesitated, then acquiesced with a shrug as I slipped on past her and took the nearest empty seat.

The room was set up like an auditorium, with rows of folding chairs split by an aisle down the middle facing a raised platform at the far end of the room. Most of the chairs were occupied, which since it was a large room and the chairs set close together made for more than a fair-sized crowd. Hobson himself stood behind a lectern at the right-hand end of the platform.

He was a tall distinguished man with a long aristocratic face which he emphasized by brushing his silvering hair back from the forehead and temples in a straight pompadour. Beside him on an easel rested the painting he was currently engaged in auctioning. It was a medium-sized landscape done mostly in reds and greens, and from Lovell's previous description I had no difficulty identifying it as a Fragonard, with a value anywhere between $12,000 and $18,000 depending on how badly someone wanted it and how skillfully Hobson could play on that desire. And by all accounts, he was very skillful—which was what I had come to check out for myself.

Now, for just a moment, his eyes rested on me, shadowed by a flicker of annoyance. Then they moved on to rove over the audience once again. "I have a bid of $7000," he said, his voice quiet but carrying well. "Do I have 7500?"

No one in the audience spoke, but there was a ripple of anticipation and after a few moments Hobson nodded and said, "$7500 is bid." His eyes searched for more signals. "Do I have 8000?"

He got it quickly and then went on from there: 8500, 9000, 9500. After a while I lost interest in Hobson and joined the rest of the crowd in trying to spot the bidders. One was fairly obvious—a stocky, gray-haired man in a rumpled blue suit about halfway down on the aisle. He slouched expressionlessly in his chair, signaling his bids by a dip of an old-fashioned wooden pencil that he held upright on top of his crossed knees.

For a while I had one other spotted too, but he dropped out of the contest early. And the others must either have been hidden by the press of people or their signals were considerably more subtle, because I had no luck locating them at all.

When the bidding reached $15,000, Hobson paused to take a sip of water from the carafe on his lectern, then looked out over the room again. "I acknowledge the bid of 15,5 reported by my assistant in the rear of the room," he said. "Do I have 16?"

My eyes, along with a good many others, swiveled over to the man in the rumpled blue suit, because the $15,000 bid had been his and he had responded to every other challenge by upping his bid. But this time the pencil continued to point unmovingly toward the ceiling.

If this surprised Hobson, he didn't show it by as much as a flicker of an eyebrow. "Do I have $16,000?" he said. "No?" He picked up a gavel and rapped the lectern sharply. "Once at $15,500," he said. "Twice—"

He broke off, frowning, then took a deep breath and made a quick movement with his head and shoulders as if composing himself. "Please accept my apologies, ladies and gentlemen," he said, "but my assistant has just signaled me that she was mistaken about the 15,5 bid." Hobson glared back at the hapless assistant. "The proper bid," he said tightly, "is $15,000. Let us proceed from there."

He paused for a second, then said, "Do I have 15,5? No?" He rapped sharply with the gavel again. "Then once at $15,000, twice at $15,000—sold to Mr. Tate for $15,000."

Hobson smiled then and nodded toward the man in the rumpled blue suit, who permitted himself a curt nod in acknowledgement and then very deliberately put his pencil away in his inside pocket.

According to the catalogue, there were two more paintings to be disposed of, but they were lesser items and Hobson delegated the task to one of his assistants and left. I'd seen all I'd needed. So I left too, following him back to his private office.

The thin blonde, at the typist's desk outside his door gave me a sad smile. "I'm sorry," she said. "But Mr. Hobson gave definite instructions that he wasn't to be disturbed."

I smiled back. "I think he'll change his mind," I said, "when you tell him the man who bid $15,500 for the Fragonard is here."

She looked at me dubiously but finally rose, rapped on the door, and went inside, closing it after her. A moment later she was back, looking genuinely surprised. "He says you're to go right in."

Hobson received me standing behind his desk and glaring down his patrician nose. "Now just what is this nonsense?" he demanded as soon as the door had closed behind me. "You know as well as I do that there was no 15,5 bid on the Fragonard."

"That's right," I said equably. "But more importantly, there was no mistake by your assistant either. You simply announced a false bid to see if you couldn't jack the price up. And when it didn't work, you passed the buck to the most likely candidate."

All the bluster left Hobson's manner. "If this is a shakedown—" he began ominously.

I shook my head. "Just the opposite," I said. "I'm going to pay you money."

Hobson's eyes narrowed and he regarded me soberly for a long minute. "I don't believe I caught your name," he said at last.

"Lang," I said. "Harry Lang."

"And what is it you're going to pay me for, Mr. Lang?"

"It's rather complicated to explain," I said. "May I sit down?"

"Oh, please do," Hobson said drily. He waved his hand expansively to indicate any of the several clients' chairs scattered around the room, waited until I had picked one out, then sat down himself behind the desk. "All right, Mr. Lang," he said. "I'm all ears."

I leaned back and crossed my legs. "As I understand it," I said, "anyone offering a painting for sale at auction can specify a minimum price for it to be sold at."

"That's correct," Hobson said. "We call it a reserve price. If it's met or exceeded, the painting is sold. Otherwise, it's returned to the owner." He shrugged. "It's not an uncommon practice in any auction."

"No," I said. "What is uncommon, though, is that at an art auction the reserve price is never announced. In fact, the usual practice is for the auctioneer to start the bidding considerably below it and through use of shills or signals visible only to him build up to the reserve."

Hobson shrugged again. "So," he said, "what of it? Sometimes these little tricks are necessary to stimulate interest. But they're not illegal—or even unethical—since the painting wouldn't sell for less than the reserve in any case." He paused and fixed me with his eyes. "And now may I ask what all this is leading up to?"

"I thought that was obvious," I said. "I have a painting—a Fragonard landscape similar to the one you sold today, only from his 'blue' period—that I want to put up for auction. And I want to set a reserve of $20,000."

Hobson was silent for another long moment. Then he said slowly, "You saw what the Fragonard went for this afternoon, Mr. Lang. And I might add that the legitimate cross bidding ended at $12,000. So it wasn't merely a case of Tate seeing through my game and calling my bluff. $15,000 *was* his top price. And it's not out of line with what others would pay. All of which means, I'm afraid, that if you set a reserve of $20,000 your Fragonard would in all likelihood be returned unsold and you would have accomplished nothing."

"Not quite," I murmured. "Because the way the reserve system works, the published records of the auction would show only that the painting was knocked down for $20,000."

"Aha," Hobson said with satisfaction. "I knew there had to be more to it than met the eye. So what you really want is not a sale but the *record* of a sale."

"Right on the nose, Mr. Hobson," I said. "That's exactly what I want." I uncrossed my legs and leaned forward. "I'm going to be perfectly frank because I don't want any misunderstanding about what I'm trying to do or how you fit in cropping up later to spoil the deal."

Hobson nodded slowly. "I think I understand," he said. "What you have in mind isn't quite legal."

"Well, I suppose that depends on how you define 'legal'," I said. "But in any case, for the past several years I've worked partners with a man named Lovell. Now, Lovell has his little peculiarities. He's a real nut about the kind of food he lets himself eat and is as nervous as a cat in a roomful of fox terriers. But on the plus side he has a very large if somewhat specialized talent. He can forge a painting by any artist living or dead and do it so well that only a spectroscopic or electroluminescent examination can distinguish his copy from the artist's genuine work.

"I handle the outside end —the selling. Which isn't as easy as it may seem. Because you can't just walk up to someone and say, 'Hey, look, I've got this Old Master for sale,' unless, of course, you're prepared to answer a lot of questions about where and how you got it—and back up the answers with some sort of documentation.

"Up to now we've gotten around this by copying existing paintings and passing them off to unscrupulous collectors as stolen or otherwise illegally obtained. There are a couple of disadvantages to this, though. One, there aren't so many collectors of that kind around and for obvious reasons we have to be careful about repeat business. Two, we have to deal at bargain-basement rates. Sold under the counter, our Fragonard would bring at the most $5000, roughly one-third of what we'd get if we could sell it openly.

"What we need then is a means of 'legitimatizing' our paintings. And for that the reserve price seems made to order."

"So it does," Hobson said. "The question is, though, why should I agree to go along with your scheme?"

"Because," I said simply, "I'll pay you $1000 just to go through the motions of auctioning off a painting."

Hobson thought for a moment "Make it $2000," he said, "and you have a deal. Assuming, of course," he added, as I nodded agreement, "that the painting is as good as you say. When can I see it?"

"As soon as it's finished," I said. "In about two weeks."

"In that case I'll look forward to seeing you then." He spread his hands to indicate the papers on his desk. "And now if you'll excuse me—"

"Of course," I said and rose to let myself out.

Exactly two weeks later I was back with the completed painting carried for safety's sake in a rigid-sided suitcase which I set confidently before Hobson at his desk. He hesitated a few moments, then opened it and looked inside. After another moment he lifted the painting out and carried it to the window where the light was better and went over it with a magnifying glass, square inch by square inch. Finally he put both glass and painting down.

"If I didn't know better," he said, "I'd swear this was the real thing."

"I told you Lovell was good," I said.

"So you did," Hobson said. "Only now I believe you."

He came back to his desk, took a sheaf of blue-backed papers from the top drawer, and handed them to me. "You'll have to sign these," he said.

"What are they?"

"Just a standard contract. For my protection in case something goes wrong. For yours, too." He smiled easily. "To prevent me from stealing your painting before the auction. Not that anything like that would enter my mind, of course."

"Of course not," I said, signing. But I kept my copy of the papers.

Once the papers were signed, Hobson's usual routine took over, and six weeks later Lovell's Fragonard was offered at his scheduled auction.

The same smock-clad girl was on duty at the entrance, passing out catalogues to those who didn't already have them. She frowned slightly when she saw me, as if remembering how I'd crashed the gate before. But this time I had an invitation to show her and once again the frown gave way to an acquiescent shrug. I winked at her to show her I remembered too, then went on in to slip into a seat in the back row.

Shortly after I was settled, the high bidder from the previous auction, Mr. Tate, marched in and took his accustomed aisle seat and stared ahead as expressionlessly as before. And gradually the room filled up around us.

Hobson himself didn't show up until some fifteen minutes after the announced starting time. "Sorry to be late," he said, taking his place behind the lectern on the raised platform. "But I was delayed by the arrival of a distinguished visitor from the Municipal Museum of St. Louis, Dr. Morton Whitsett."

Hobson smiled and nodded in the direction of a tall harried-looking man who'd come in with him and was now in the process of easing himself into one of the few remaining seats.

"Dr. Whitsett and I have corresponded but this is his first visit here. Good to have you with us, Doctor," Hobson added. "Just how good, though, will depend of course on how much you buy."

He flashed another smile to show it was all in good sport and drew an appreciative laugh from his audience. The man to whom it had been directed just bobbed his head once quickly and squirmed down to make himself as inconspicuous as possible.

"And now," Hobson said, still in high good humor, "shall we proceed with business?"

The first item offered was a matched set of Eighteenth Century candlesticks in chased silver. There wasn't much interest in them and they were disposed of quickly. So was the second item—a poster-sized modern painting, all electric blues and yellows.

The third offering was Lovell's Fragonard.

"And now a real prize," Hobson said as his assistants set it up on its easel beside him. "Catalog Item Number Three, Landscape in Blue by Louis Pierre Fragonard. Note the careful attention to detail in the foreground and also the curious way in which the blue of the lake and sky seem to merge and yet still retain their individuality at the horizon line."

He paused to allow everyone time to admire both the painting and his cleverness in describing it, then said, "Shall we start the bidding at $5000 and follow our usual rule that bids must increase in multiples of $500?" He paused again and let his eyes wander over the audience. From where I sat there wasn't a discernible movement anywhere, but after a moment or two Hobson said, "Ah, thank you. I have $5000. Do I have $5500?"

Of course, it was only a matter of seconds before he had $5500 and then $6000 and so on as he ran the bidding up with consummate skill.

When he reached $20,000 Hobson paused for a drink from the carafe on his lectern—which he would never had done in a real auction since it would break up the rhythm of bid and counterbid. But in the present case, of course, it didn't make any difference, and otherwise his performance was flawless, right down to the final knockdown to me at $20,000.

I complimented him when I stopped by his office afterward to pick up the painting.

He had been admiring the Fragonard when I came in, having placed it on an easel by the window where the light would fall on it to best advantage. Now he sighed and turned to face me.

"It's very kind of you to say that, Mr. Lang," he said. "However, I'm afraid it wasn't all an act on my part. You see, as it turned out, there actually was a bidder for your painting. And he was willing to go as high as $19,500."

"Nineteen—" I began. "For God's sakes, who was it? Tate? That doctor from St. Louis?"

Hobson raised an eyebrow and looked at me coolly. "Does it really matter?" he said. "You couldn't sell to him in any case. He obviously won't match your price. And if you immediately offer to sell for less than you ostensibly paid, you'll really stir up questions. On the other hand—" Hobson smiled faintly and let his voice trail off.

"Go on," I said. "On the other hand?"

"On the other hand," he picked up smoothly, "*I* could simply announce that you had reneged on your $20,000 bid. It's not uncommon; people do get carried away at auctions and find afterwards that they can't honor their commitments. In which case, the next highest bid stands. So your Fragonard would automatically revert to the $19,500 bidder.

"But," Hobson added harshly, "*I'm* the only one who can do that. Just as only I have the reputation and standing to give the painting a believable provenance. But, of course, before I'd even consider it, it would have to be worth my while."

"How much?" I said.

Hobson waved a hand airily. "I'm not greedy," he said. "Shall we say one-third? $6500?"

I considered for a minute, then said, "All right. The balance is less than I'd anticipated, but I guess $13,000 in the hand is better than $16,000 or $17,000 in the bush a year or so from now."

"I knew you'd see it that way," Hobson said. "That's why I had the money ready." He handed me an unsealed envelope. "I assumed you'd prefer cash."

"You assumed correctly," I said, riffling through the bills for a fast count. When I finished, I frowned. "There's only $11,000 here," I said.

Hobson gave me a wide-eyed stare. "Surely you haven't forgotten my $2000 fee for conducting the auction, have you? It's common practice to deduct—"

"Hobson—" I began angrily.

"If you don't like the deal, Lang," he interrupted harshly, "I'll give you your painting back and you can find your own buyer. Of course, you should bear in mind that news travels fast and a few judiciously leaked facts could leave you with nothing but a worthless piece of junk."

"You don't give me much choice, do you?" I said.

"A Hobson's choice, if you like," Hobson said, "which is none at all really. But look at it this way. You had to meet somebody smarter sometime, and you *are* making twice as much as if you'd sold the Fragonard under the counter."

"So I am," I said, and put the envelope with the $11,000 in my jacket pocket.

"Good," Hobson said. "And now I do have things to do. So—" He let his voice trail off expectantly.

"Sure," I said and left.

His secretary flashed me a smile as I came out, but I strode past her, ignoring it. Once I was outside, though, and about half a block away I began to grin. People turned to stare, but I couldn't stop. Because I was wondering how smart Hobson would feel when he found his $19,500 bidder—the man he'd known as Dr. Whitsett—had disappeared. Because, of course, "Dr. Whitsett" was Lovell.

The Switcheroo

Cardwell leaned back in his chair behind the massive desk and carefully folded his hands over his ample stomach.

"I'm not sure I quite understand what your business is, Mr. Lang," he said. "Just what is it you want me to do?"

"Actually," I said, "it's more a case of my doing something for you."

Cardwell raised his eyebrows questioningly. "Mr. Lang," he said, "it took considerable effort on your part to get in to see me. And it's been my experience that people seldom go to that much trouble unless they see some advantage to themselves."

"Oh," I said, "of course. But what's wrong with that? As long as we both end up with something we want."

Cardwell permitted a bleak smile to play across his lips. "Not a thing," he said. "I assume what you want is money. Which I have. But what is it that you have that you think I might want?"

"A painting," I said. Cardwell shook his head. "I already have paintings, Mr. Lang," he said. "All I could reasonably want."

"Not quite," I said. "Some months ago you tried to buy a Van Erl Madonna to round out your collection of Seventeenth Century masters. You almost had it too, but then at the last minute it was sold out to a higher bidder. That's the painting I meant. Because if you still want it, I can get it for you. And for considerably less than you offered for it the first time around."

Cardwell dropped his pose of tolerant amusement and leaned forward to eye me grimly. "Morgan Reeves sent you, didn't he?" he said at last. "I was pretty sure he was overextending himself when he bought that painting away from me. And now he's got to get out from under, doesn't he? Well, he crossed me too many times in the past for me to be inclined to jump in and save him now. So you go back and tell Mr. Reeves I wouldn't buy from him if he were the last man on earth and if that Van Erl were the last painting."

"That's all very interesting," I said. "But also very much beside the point. Because Morgan Reeves didn't send me. And I never considered buying the painting. My plan is to steal it."

Cardwell stared at me. "Steal?" he said. Then he threw back his head and laughed harshly. "It seems I misjudged you, Mr. Lang," he said. "You are wasting my time after all."

"Why?" I said. "It wouldn't be the first time one collector stole from another. Of course, if you have moral objections—"

Cardwell shook his head. "Morals have nothing to do with it, Mr. Lang. As a matter of fact, I find the idea of stealing from Morgan Reeves very appealing—for a number of reasons. But, unfortunately, it's impossible. Morgan Reeves has a security system for the protection of his paintings that's the envy of art galleries the world over. You couldn't get within a mile of his collection, let alone hope to steal from it."

"That's right," I agreed. "*I* couldn't. But what if I could produce a man who could? Would you be interested then?"

Cardwell took a deep breath and thought about it for a minute. "That would depend on the man," he said finally, "and whether I believed he could pull it off."

"His name is Walter Evans," I said. "He's Morgan Reeves's curator, and all he has to do is walk in, lift the painting off the wall, then walk out with it. And nobody would question him. It's as simple as that."

"So it is," Cardwell said. "Except why would Evans want to do this?"

I shrugged. "Why do any of us do what we do? His income isn't adequate for his tastes. He wants money and this is his way of getting it."

"Then he's a fool," Cardwell said contemptuously. "And you're a bigger one for not realizing it. Don't you know that once that painting was discovered missing, Morgan Reeves would realize it had to be an inside job? And his curator would be the first one suspected. Knowing Reeves, I know the kind of pressure he'd bring to bear, too. Your man would break and he'd lead them right to you—and through you to me."

"No, he wouldn't," I said. "Because, you see, Mr. Cardwell, for the past several years I've worked partners with a man named Lovell. Now, Lovell is a real odd duck in a lot of ways. He won't eat ordinary food like you and me and he's as nervous as your Aunt Nellie at a strip-tease convention. But, offsetting all that, he's an artist with a very real if very specialized talent. He can forge a painting by any artist living or dead and do it so well that the original artist himself would be hard put to say it wasn't the real thing. In fact, the only way you can distinguish Lovell's copies from the original work is by spectroscopic or electroluminescent examination.

"That's why Evans came to me instead of approaching you directly. So that when he takes Reeves's painting down, he can put a perfect copy in its place."

I smiled and shook my head. "There won't be any suspicion or pressure, Mr. Cardwell, because Morgan Reeves will never know he's been robbed—unless you choose to tell him."

Cardwell pursed his lips thoughtfully. "You seem to have covered every conceivable angle, Mr. Lang," he said.

"I find it pays," I said.

"So do I," Cardwell said. "So do I." His lids drooped down to cover his eyes. "How much would you want?"

"$50,000," I said. "Half for Lovell and me, half for Evans."

"Fair enough," Cardwell said. "I offered twice that much when I tried to buy the Madonna legitimately, and God knows how much more Reeves had to pay."

"It's a deal then?" I said.

"Almost, Mr. Lang," Card-well said. "But there are still a couple of points that have to be cleared up. First, I would have to be convinced in my own mind that this Lovell's work is as good as you say it is—or at least good enough to deceive Morgan Reeves."

"No problem," I said. "I'll bring the copy over for you to inspect when it's completed. I promised Evans he could see it, too."

"Fine," Cardwell said. "And now for my second point. I would also want some assurances that you weren't simply foisting a copy off on me."

"Oh, I think you can trust us on that score," I said.

Cardwell allowed himself another of those bleak smiles. "Trust is all right in its place, Mr. Lang," he said. "Which may be a boy scout encampment but definitely isn't anywhere large sums of money are involved. Fortunately, however, the problem is not insoluble. It merely requires that a man I designate accompany Evans when he makes the substitution."

He looked over at me blandly, sensing my hesitation. "Does that cause you a problem, Mr. Lang?" he said.

I shrugged. "I don't know," I said. "It wasn't part of the deal I worked out with Evans. So I'll have to check with him to see if he has any objections."

"Do that," Cardwell said. "And if he does, I trust you'll be able to find a way to overcome them. Because if you don't, there is no deal."

And with that he smiled again and pressed the buzzer for his secretary to come in and usher me out.

A second person present when the paintings were switched was a complication I hadn't counted on. But necessity really is the mother of invention, and so I was able to call Cardwell early the following day to tell him his problem had been solved.

"Your problem," he reminded me, "not mine."

"Have it your way," I said, "but whoever's problem it was it's been taken care of. Evans will fake a short in an electrical connection some evening when Reeves is sure to be out and your man can come in disguised as an electrician."

"Hardly original," Cardwell said, "but it will serve. Now when will the copy be ready?"

"In about three weeks," I said.

"Fine," Cardwell said. "I'll look forward to seeing you then."

Actually it was closer to four weeks before I saw Cardwell again. Then I called at his home with a carefully wrapped painting under my arm.

It was late in the evening and Cardwell himself opened the door for me. "I took the precaution of giving the servants the evening off," he explained.

"Good idea," I said. "The fewer possible witnesses the better."

Cardwell gave me a long dry look. "Precisely," he said and led me back to a small book-lined study where he unwrapped the painting and placed it under a bright fluorescent light to study.

Finally he pushed back his chair and said, "It is an excellent copy."

"Perhaps a better one than you realize," I said. "Evans compared it to the original and he says there isn't a dime's worth of difference between them."

Cardwell looked up at me sharply. "Evans compared them? Were you present?"

"No," I said. "But—"

Cardwell wasn't listening, though. He had bent forward again and was peering intently at the painting.

"What's the matter?" I said.

"Perhaps nothing," Cardwell said. He ran his finger along the painting's wooden backing. "Tell me something, Mr. Lang," he said. "Was this copy ever framed?"

"No," I said, "of course not. There's no point in trying to duplicate a frame. It's simpler to pull the frame off the original painting and re-nail it to the copy. Besides, the original frame lends authenticity."

"Exactly," Cardwell said. "But you're wrong about this. It has been framed. You can see where nails were driven through the stretcher frame to hold the outer frame in place."

"What?" I said. I took the painting from Cardwell and turned it over. There were eight or nine holes angling through the backs and out the sides of the wooden framing holding the canvas taut where nails had obviously been driven and later withdrawn. "I don't understand this," I said. "This isn't the painting I gave Evans."

"Of course it isn't," Cardwell said. He smiled grimly. "Evans has already made his substitution. This is the original. And what he plans to do while my man watches is put this back in its rightful place while taking down the copy to pass on to me."

"I still don't understand," I said. "What's the point?"

"Think about it for a moment. Morgan Reeves is in financial difficulties. What better way to bail himself out without sacrificing any of his precious collection?"

"I'll be damned," I said. "That creep Evans, I'll wring his neck for him."

"Why be angry, Mr. Lang?" Cardwell said. "We're still both getting what we want. Me the painting and you your $25,000. All I have to do is keep this and pay you."

"Won't Evans and Reeves cause trouble?" I said.

"They may try," Cardwell said. "But primarily it will be a matter of my word against theirs since I assume by then you and your friend Lovell will be well out of reach. And in any case I doubt they'll push it too far. Otherwise, they may find that they've convicted themselves of conspiracy to defraud." He smiled, genuinely happy for once. "So how about it, Mr. Lang? Is it a deal? A new deal?"

I hesitated, then nodded. "All right," I said. "But no checks. Cash only."

"Of course," Cardwell said. He swung open a section of one bookshelf to reveal a wall safe, opened it, and took out a packet of bills which he handed to me.

I made a quick count to be sure it was all there, then stuck the money in my pocket. "It's been a pleasure doing business with you," I said.

"So it has," he said. "I doubt, however, that it will ever be repeated." He picked up the painting and looked at it fondly. "And now do you think you could find your own way out?"

I said I could and did. Outside, Lovell was waiting for me in the car.

"For God's sakes," he said anxiously, "how did it go?"

"Like a dream, Lovell," I said. "Like a dream."

Lovell sighed and mopped his brow. "I've been so worried," he said. "What if he didn't notice those nail holes?"

"In that case," I said, "I would have found some way of calling them to his attention. However, despite what he says, Cardwell is bound to expect some reaction from Reeves and Evans. And when none is forthcoming, it's going to raise some ugly suspicions in his mind that anybody can drive a nail into a painting to make it look like it's been pulled from its frame. He may even realize that the whole substitution plot and 'doublecross' existed solely in his mind. So I think the smartest thing for us to do is follow Cardwell's advice and be well out of reach well before that happens."

Lang and Lovell Go Legit

As always as I came in, I stopped for a moment out on the street to admire the display window with the neat gold lettering down in the lower left corner: *L and L Galleries—Showings by Appointment*. It was the first thing of any permanence I'd ever owned and even after all these months I still couldn't quite get over it.

This morning, though, I had company. A bulky man in a gray suit that was just a little too small for his shoulders stood in front of the window, frowning as if he couldn't quite figure it out either. But then he spotted me and his face broke out in a slow malicious grin. I remembered the grin well. Him too. His name was Peterson. He was a detective sergeant assigned to Fraud-Bunco, and needless to say most of our prior meetings hadn't been all that pleasant. For either of us.

"Well, well," he said, "as I live and breathe, Harry Lang." His smile turned almost happy. "They told me I'd find something interesting if I came down here and I sure did. What's the scam this time, Harry? Or do I have to ask?"

"No scam," I said. "I'm a legitimate businessman. I even pay taxes."

"On an art gallery?" His voice was heavy.

"Why not?"

"A better question is why? What do you know about art anyway?"

"More than you might think," I said. "And anyway I have a partner to handle that end of it. I just take care of the business and selling part."

"I'll bet you do," Peterson said. He tapped me twice on the shoulder. "Well, you just keep it legit, because after all these years I'd sure hate like hell to haul you in."

"Sure you would," I said. "That's why you came running down here," and watched his back disappear around the corner.

Lovell was waiting for me inside the gallery, even more ready than usual to bounce up to the ceiling at the slightest provocation. Even at the best of times Lovell is as jumpy as a cat in a roomful of fox terriers. He is also an absolute nut about the kind of food he will allow himself to eat. More importantly, though, from the partnership standpoint, he is also an artist with a very great if somewhat specialized talent.

He can forge the work of any artist living or dead and do it so well that even the original artist himself would be hard put to tell the difference, and it was by exploiting that talent that we earned enough money to buy the gallery and go legitimate—or as legitimate, anyway, as anybody trying to break into the art business can afford to be these days.

Now, as he saw me come in, Lovell blinked twice and swallowed hard. "You're late," he said.

"Unavoidable delay," I said. "Our old friend from Fraud-Bunco, Sergeant Peterson, was outside nosing around."

"Oh, lord," Lovell said. He actually wrung his hands. "Why today?"

"Any reason why *not* today?"

Lovell nodded. "Mr. Vincent called," he said. "Finally. He's coming over this afternoon for a private showing. If he sees a cop—"

"We'll tell him he's here to guard the premises," I said. "Don't worry. It couldn't be better." And with that I left him still blinking and went back to my office to get ready for the day.

I'd been angling to get Vincent into the gallery almost since we'd opened it, and to be sure I didn't muff it I set the showing up in a small room just off the main gallery, placing the paintings he had come to see one at a time on a single easel. There were eight in all, watercolors mostly, depicting the scenes around the artist's native White Mountains. They weren't everybody's cup of tea, but Vincent seemed to like them. He sat in the room's only chair, nodding only to indicate when he was ready for the next.

"Lovely," he said at last. He was a tall lean man with a long aristocratic face and a deceptively languid air. His family was one of the oldest in this part of the country, but by the time he'd come along there was little left to inherit except the name. Before he was 30, though, he'd made the name a force to be reckoned with in the then-booming electronics field.

He'd spent the next ten years milking it for all it was worth, then had sold out at enormous profit just before the bust and settled down to lead the life his upbringing had prepared him for—which included, of course, patronizing the arts. Considering the size and scope of the collection he had built up, just getting him into the gallery was a minor triumph.

"Lovely," he said again. "What's the provenance?"

"They're from the Dieckmann estate," I said. "The widow has to sell to meet the inheritance taxes. Otherwise they would have gone to the Art Institute with the rest of the collection."

"Of course," Vincent said. He looked at the painting instead of me. "Quite a coup your landing them," he said, "instead of one of the more established galleries."

I nodded agreement. "Yes, it was, and frankly the only way I could do it was to offer to rebate half of my commission."

Vincent raised an elegant eyebrow. "To Mrs. Dieckmann?"

I shook my head. "To her attorney," I said. I shrugged. "I don't like it, but—well, you have to do a lot of things you don't like when you're trying to get a business established."

Vincent smiled faintly; it was a subject he knew something about. "Yes, I suppose you do." He looked back at the painting on the easel. "Although," he murmured, "sometimes private arrangements can be worked out that even attorneys don't know about—if the price is right."

"I know," I said, "but unfortunately in this case the contract specifies a public auction."

"Too bad," Vincent said in the same soft voice. He looked as if he intended to say more, but before he got the chance the door from the main gallery opened and a short dumpy woman in the green print dress and short scruffy topcoat stuck her head into the room. She looked 50 if a day and carried a flat, brown paper wrapped package under her arm as if it were a shield.

"Hey," she said, "either of you two work here?"

Vincent looked at her with mild curiosity.

"How about it?" the woman said. "I've been looking all over and there's not a soul in the joint."

"It's not a joint," I said. "It's an art gallery and this is a private showing. You—"

She ignored me and went on speaking to Vincent. "Look," she said, "I won't take a minute. I just want to ask a question."

Without waiting for a response she started ripping the paper off her package, revealing a painting about a foot high by a foot and a half long. It was a landscape of some sort, but details were hard to make out because the entire surface was covered with blotches of varying hues and densities.

Vincent made a face. "Good lord," he said, "what did you do? Pour ink over it?"

The woman shuffled apologetically. "It was stored under some blankets in an attic," she said, "but the roof leaked and the colors ran. It wasn't me that did it," she added. "It was my sister. She didn't really care for it. She only took it to keep me from having it. You know how that is."

"Yes," I said. "Mrs.—?"

"Ferris," the woman said. "Anyway, after she finally did give it to me, somebody said maybe you could do something about cleaning it up. I don't want to pay too much if I don't have to, but my father brought it back from France after World War One and I grew up with it and I would like to have it back like it used to be if I could."

"I understand," I said, easing her back toward the door, "but that's really something you have to talk to my partner about. If you'll just go down the hallway until you come to the girl at the desk, she'll see that you're taken care of."

I closed the door after her and turned back to Vincent. He raised an eyebrow inquisitively.

"It's like I told you," I said. "You have to do a lot of things you don't like when you're trying to get a business established."

He laughed.

When he had finally seen enough of the paintings he had come for, I took him out through the rear exit past my office. Mrs. Ferris had apparently just finished her business and gone, because Lovell was still standing beside the secretary's desk looking down ruefully at the blotched painting.

"You haven't met my partner, have you?" I said to Vincent.

"No," he said. They shook hands.

"I see you accepted our insistent caller's challenge," Vincent said, looking down at the painting himself and grimacing again. "You have your work cut out for you."

"Not really," Lovell said. Jumpy as he is, the quality of his work is still the one thing you can't shake him on. "There's a coat of varnish over the paint. All I have to do is clean the mess off that and revarnish. Then a little wood filler where they cracked the stretcher nailing it to the frame and the whole thing will be as good as new. Maybe even better."

"I'm sure it will be," Vincent said. He began pulling on his gloves, smoothing them out carefully one finger at a time. "About those watercolors," he said to me, "you won't forget to notify me when the auction is to be held."

"Of course not," I said as if it was the farthest thing from my mind.

As it turned out, though, there wasn't any auction. The lawyer handling the Dieckmann estate called less than a week later to withdraw the watercolors from sale. I wasn't too surprised. Vincent hadn't got where he was by missing any tricks. He'd simply gone around me to make his own deal with the attorney, picking up the paintings for a good deal less—even counting the kickback—than they'd have gone for at the auction. I could afford to write it off, though, and in any case I hadn't seen the last of Vincent. Or, for that matter, of Mrs. Ferris.

She was back shortly after the first of the following month, carrying the same flat, wrapped package under her arm. This time, though, she wasn't alone. Peterson came with her.

"I'm disappointed in you, Harry," he said. "You told me you'd gone legitimate and I told you to keep it that way. And then what's the next thing I hear but that you've gone right back to your old tricks."

"Oh?" I said. "And just what am I supposed to be doing?"

"You know darn good and well what you're doing," Mrs. Ferris burst in. "I left a valuable painting here for your partner to clean up and now the two of you are trying to steal it."

"Oh, come on," I said. "You got your painting back—and in better shape than you brought it in."

"That's what you say," she said. "I say I got *a* picture back but not the same one I brought in. And don't try to tell me it just looks different because it's been cleaned. You might fool most people that way but I used to study that picture for hours when I was a girl and this one *is* different.

"That's not all either. After she saw it all cleaned up, my sister started talking about how we ought to have it appraised. It was just her way of trying to get it back, but anyway I took it over to one of the professors at the university who's supposed to know about these things. And, boy, did he get excited when he saw it. He even got a book out to show me what it was—one of the lost landscapes by a painter named Augustus Milverton.

"It seems this Milverton didn't get famous until after he died, which was around 1930 or so, and by then a lot of his paintings had disappeared, because he'd been selling them off to everybody and anybody just for money to live. Anyway, that's the kind of painting he said I had. But then he ran some tests just to make sure and afterwards he said he was sorry but he'd been wrong. All I had was a copy done in Milverton's style. Which sort of made sense because my father hadn't paid very much for it even if he did always say he'd bought it from the painter himself. It could have been the painter who made the copy.

"But afterwards I got to thinking. Why would somebody make a copy of another artist's picture twelve or fifteen years *before* that other artist got famous? It didn't make any sense. And that's when I really began to realize something funny was going on, and it had to be you that was doing it because the only time that painting's been out of my family's hands was when you had it. So I want my picture back."

"I don't have your picture," I said.

"Then I want the money it's worth—or I want you in jail."

"What about it, Harry?" Peterson said.

I shrugged. "It's her word against mine," I said. "If you want to go to the State's Attorney with that, be my guest. But I think we both know what his reaction will be."

"Yeah," Peterson said, "except maybe it isn't just her word against yours." He smiled his tight, happy little malicious smile. "Mrs. Ferris says there was another man here when she brought in her picture besides you and your partner—and that he'll back her up that this one she has now is different."

"That's ridiculous."

"You mean there wasn't another man?" Peterson said quietly.

"No, there was all right. But he saw that painting for less than a minute. He's not going to be able to tell you anything. He won't thank you either if you go wasting his time."

Peterson's face turned beet-red. "You ought to know better than that, Harry," he said. "I don't waste people's time—not when I'm conducting an official investigation. So who was he? And don't think you can run in a ringer. Mrs. Ferris will recognize him when she sees him even if she never did hear his name."

I hesitated then shrugged. "Arthur Vincent," I said. "He lives over on Belmont Terrace."

"Fine," Peterson said, smiling again. "So why don't we just run over there and see what he can or can't tell us?"

"You mean right now?"

"Why not?" Peterson said. He pointed his finger at me. "You may be just as legitimate as you say—now. But I remember you from the bad old days and the only way I can be sure you won't hop on the phone like a bunny to tell Mr. Vincent just what to say is to take you along. Any objections?"

"No. Of course not."

"Fine," Peterson said again. "Get your hat then."

Taking no chances, Peterson left me out in the car with a police driver while he and Mrs. Ferris went up to Vincent's apartment. It was a long half hour. Finally, though, they came back out. Peterson looked grim, Mrs. Ferris agitated.

"They're in it together," she was saying. "They have to be."

"Sure," Peterson said. He pulled the car door open and jerked his thumb up. "Out," he said. He meant me.

"I don't expect an apology," I said, "but you could at least take me back where you found me."

"Out!" Peterson said again.

I got out. They both got in, Peterson moving the other cop over so he could drive himself. I closed his door for him. He didn't say anything, but he left a half inch of rubber on the street.

I waited until they were out of sight, then went over into the building and rode the elevator up to Vincent's apartment. It filled the entire top floor, but Vincent himself answered my ring. He was wearing a pale-gray dressing gown with a scarf at the throat.

"I just wanted to say I'm sorry," I said. "I tried to prevent their coming but I'm afraid Peterson wasn't in a mood to listen."

Vincent smiled. "No, he wasn't, was he?" he said. "But do come in. I was just about to call you anyway."

He closed the door after me and moved back into the room, leaving me to follow.

"An unfortunate situation," he said. "One can't help but feel sorry for the poor woman—although I must admit I told her that since she had failed to register the painting with the International Art Registry or any of the other identification services, however much logic might be on her side she really stood very little chance of proving that the painting she had now wasn't the same one she'd had before. I trust you appreciate that."

"Well, of course," I said, "but under the circumstances there really wasn't much else you could say."

"Wasn't there?" Vincent said. He smiled faintly. "I won't pretend I remember the painting in any detail," he said, "but I do remember your painter's remark about repairing some cracks in the stretcher with wood filler. So naturally I checked the stretcher on the painting that poor Mrs. Ferris showed me this afternoon. And what to my surprise did I find? An absence of cracks of any kind, repaired or otherwise.

"I suppose you could argue that you simply replaced the stretcher. But that would seem to be a lot of trouble and expense for a relatively worthless painting. Unless, of course, it wasn't so worthless."

He looked at me searchingly. "Opportunities like that are rare, aren't they Mr. Lang, and when they come along they're much too good to pass up. It was an original Milverton, wasn't it? And you did switch pictures on her."

"You're quite a detective," I said. "Why didn't you tell all this to Peterson and Mrs. Ferris?"

Vincent's smile broadened. "Because, like you, Mr. Lang, I'm not one to let such a golden opportunity pass. I want the painting. I won't rob you, of course. Shall we say $15,000 just to insure that the deal remains our secret?"

"That's less than one-third of what it's worth," I said.

"True," Vincent said. "But I suggest you take it. Otherwise I might have to call Mrs. Ferris—and that detective—and explain what I had just 'remembered'."

He looked at me blandly until finally I shrugged. "I'll want the money in cash," I said.

"Of course," Vincent said. "Just as soon as the painting's delivered." He escorted me to the door. "Shall we say this afternoon? I find the sooner these affairs are settled the better."

"So do I," I said, and left.

When I got back to the gallery Mrs. Ferris was waiting for me in my office. She sat behind my desk, eating an apple and looking very much at home. She tossed the core into my wastebasket. "How did it go?" she said.

"Fine, Maude," I said. "Just fine." I opened the wall safe and got out her money. "$1000," I said handing it to her, "as agreed. You can count it if you like."

"Naw," she said. "You wouldn't cheat me." She stuffed the money into her purse. "There is one thing, though, if you don't mind my asking. Why did you go to all this trouble just to unload that painting? What I mean is, I appreciate the money and the chance to earn it, but if that picture was as good a fake as you said it was, why didn't you just stick it up on the wall and let somebody buy it legitimately?"

"Provenance," I said.

"Huh?"

"Too many people have been stung buying phony paintings in the past," I said, "and everybody knows it. So the smart collectors—the ones with the big money—won't buy anything these days until they've checked and double-checked where it came from and who owned it before back to the year one—unless, of course," I added, smiling, "you offer them a dealt that's just too good to pass up."

Quit When You're Ahead

Daniell carried the painting over to his office window where the light was better and studied it for several long minutes "A very fine example of its type," he said at last. He was a tall spare man in his mid- to late-fifties with a pale thin-lipped face that seemed set in a permanent expression of petulant disapproval. Despite the frosty manner—or perhaps because of it—h was one of the most successful art auctioneers in the city. He was also, if my research was right, one of the least scrupulous.

"Although," he added waspishly, "late Nineteenth Century Romanticism isn't quite everyone's taste these days." He gave the painting one last look, then replaced it on its easel and came back to sit at his desk across from me. "The real question, though, Mr. Lang, is why you brought it to me. You have your own gallery. Why not offer it there?"

I smiled wryly. "If I could I would," I said. "The problem is that it's a forgery. It was painted less than six months ago by my partner."

Daniell's eyes flickered but otherwise his expression didn't change. "He does very good work," he said.

"He'd be the first to agree with you," I said. "Lovell has a very great if somewhat specialized talent. He's as nervous as six cats and a real nut about the food he eats. But on the plus side he can forge the work of any artist living or dead and do it so well that the original artist himself—assuming he ever got to see the painting—would be hard put to deny it was his, short of subjecting it to spectographic or electroluminescent analysis. The only problem is establishing the painting's provenance. And that's where you can help us. According to the paper, over the next month or so you're going to be auctioning off a number of paintings from several large collections. Nobody would really notice if one more—from a separate collection—was quietly slipped in."

Daniell regarded me dispassionately. "Perhaps not," he said. "But I don't know that it would work particularly to your advantage. To protect myself—leaving aside the moral and ethical considerations, of course, and assuming that I would agree to your suggestion in the first place—I would have to present your painting as a very fine but unfortunately unauthenticated work from an unpopular period. Under those circumstances I doubt very much that an auction would bring much more than you would get by offering it on the same basis yourself. People do overbid, but not that much."

"I realize that," I said. "On the other hand, it's not unusual, is it, for owners of paintings offered for auction to set a minimum price below which they won't sell?"

"No. In fact, it's fairly common. It's called a reserve."

"And," I went on, "as I understand it, the way the system works, the reserve is never announced at the sale or afterwards. Even if the painting is returned to the owner, the record only shows that it was knocked down for a certain price."

Daniell looked at me for another long moment, then nodded. "That's right," he said. "To protect the owner's interests."

"To maintain the price," I said. "But whatever the reason, the system provides an almost tailor-made solution to my problem. All I have to do is set a reserve high enough to make sure the painting won't sell. Then afterwards I have what I need—a legitimate record ostensibly establishing where the painting came from. Later I may have to sell for less than I supposedly paid, but"—I grinned—"sometimes there's an advantage to letting the other guy think he's getting the better of you."

Daniell didn't smile back. "Sometimes," he agreed. He was silent for a brief moment. "There is one problem, however," he said, "that you may have overlooked. You can't just set the reserve as high as you like. The auctioneer—ah—has a certain obligation to make sure that it isn't unduly out of line with the painting's true value. Since the one you have is a forgery—" He looked at me inquiringly.

I smiled. "Only you and I know that," I said. "And to keep it that way I'm willing to pay you considerably more than you'd make on a normal reserve transaction. $5000 to be exact." I took the check from my pocket and placed it on the desk between us. "In advance."

Daniell considered the check. "The girl will give you a receipt for your painting on the way out," he said at last. "Tell her the reserve we agreed on."

"Which is?"

"I'm sure you'll set a reasonable one," he said. He picked up the check.

Most people think of auctions as noisy affairs. Tobacco auctions may be. Art auctions are not. Bidding is usually by prearranged signal, which does make for a high degree of decorum. On the other hand, since the signals are generally recognized only by the auctioneer and his assistants, the bidder generally has no real idea whom he's bidding against—or even if he's bidding against anyone other than himself.

This was no exception. It was a week later—time enough for my check to clear—and Daniell had just knocked Lovell's forged Nineteenth Century Romantic down for its reserve price. As far as I could tell the one legitimate bidder had dropped off a good $3000 earlier, but Daniell had blandly continued to accept bids and counterbids for another ten minutes until finally he declared the painting sold and moved on to the next item in the catalogue.

Afterward, when the gallery had cleared, I went around to his office. He was at his desk fixing up the final sale records. Without looking up he said, "You don't believe in wasting time, do you, Mr. Lang? Come to reclaim your painting?"

"And deliver another," I said. I put the package I'd brought on the desk. Daniell looked at me curiously.

"As you say," I said, "I don't believe in wasting time."

"Obviously," Daniell said. He removed the wrapping and studied the painting inside. "You also go from one extreme to another. Italian. Early Seventeenth Century, I'd say at a guess."

"Late Sixteenth. Donato Delvecchio, to be precise."

Daniell looked back at the painting. "Perhaps," he said at last. "You'd have a better case if there were a signature—not to mention a tremendously more valuable painting. Or can't your friend do signatures?"

"Of course he can," I said. "But can you imagine a *signed* Delvecchio lying unrecognized all these years? Or not creating the kind of stir that would lead to all sorts of embarrassing questions if we tried to claim it had?" I shook my head. "No, thanks. I learned a long time ago it's better to settle for what you can get safely."

"Of course," Daniell said. "And how much do you think you can get?"

"I'm setting a reserve of $50,000," I said.

"As you wish. Our terms are the same as before, I presume."

"I don't see any reason to change. Do you?"

"None whatsoever." He turned back to his ledger. As I started to rise he added without looking back up, "It *was* payment in advance, wasn't it?"

I smiled wryly. "Yes, it was," I said. "Your check will be in the mail tonight."

Daniell nodded. "I'll look for it," he said.

Actually I had two envelopes to put in the mail that evening. One, as I had promised, contained a signed check made out to Daniell Galleries for $5000, the other a letter addressed to a Foster Richards in Huntington, New York, reporting that I had finally found the painting he had been searching for and expected to have it in my possession within a few days. Unfortunately, the painting was unsigned but since it matched exactly a work in progress described in a letter Delvecchio had written Archbishop Ponzi in 1569 there should be no difficulty proving its authenticity. What I wanted now, I wrote, was confirmation of the price agreed on—$150,000.

Daniell called me two days later. "Your check hasn't cleared yet," he said, "but I see no reason why we can't proceed with the auction anyway. Would this afternoon be convenient—or have you changed your mind about not wanting to waste time?"

"No. This afternoon's fine."

"Good. I'll see you at one then. Be prompt."

He rang off and I went down the hall to tell Lovell. Then, since I had less than half an hour to follow Daniell's advice and be prompt, I got my hat and went outside—and ran immediately into an old acquaintance from less prosperous days—Detective Sergeant Peterson from Fraud/Bunco.

His grin broadened when he saw me. "Well, well," he said, "just the man I was coming to see. Saves me the trouble of going inside and rousting you out."

"Some other time, Peterson, all right?" I said. "Normally I'd be overjoyed to let you harass me, but right now I happen to be in a hurry."

Peterson stopped smiling and put his hand on my chest. "Not any more you aren't," he said. "You're under arrest."

I stepped back and looked at him unbelievingly. "You can't be serious," I said. "What for?"

Peterson started to grin again. "Why, conspiracy to defraud," he said. "What else?"

We drove down to the police station in Peterson's car, Peterson and me in back, his partner up front behind the wheel.

"You know, Harry," Peterson said expansively once we were under way, "you guys never change, do you?"

"Some of us don't," I said.

"Yeah," Peterson said, "that's what I mean. Guys like you keep on thinking you're so much smarter and better than everybody else that you just can't quit when you're ahead. So sooner or later you always trip up and that's when I'm waiting." He looked at me almost wistfully. "To tell you the truth, though, I never thought you'd pull such a bonehead play as postdating a bum check."

"Neither did I," I said. "In fact, I never did."

"Sure," Peterson said. "Next thing you'll be telling me is that you never heard of a woman named Natalie Warwick."

"You guessed it."

"Yeah? The trouble is Mrs. Warwick says different. She says you bought a couple of pictures from her, paying her with a postdated check so you could have time to transfer funds from one account to another. Only she says when she went to the bank after the check came due you didn't even have an account there. And you know what? I believe her over you. But if you want to do it the hard way, okay. We'll have her come down and pick you out of a lineup. How's that sound?"

"Like a very interesting experience," I said.

When we got to the station they put me in a small room furnished with a wooden table and two chairs and left me alone. Around two o'clock a uniformed officer brought me a cup of lukewarm vending-machine coffee. It was pretty bad and I left most of it. Finally, shortly after four, Peterson came back, accompanied by a taller, older man, and told me I could go. "Just like that," I said.

"Just like that," Peterson said. He wouldn't meet my eyes.

"You pull me off the street," I said. "You make me miss an important business appointment, not to mention the embarrassment, and then—"

"Ah, Mr. Lang," the older man said. "I'm Lieutenant Driscoll." He tried to smile reassuringly. "And it—ah—appears that you—and the police department—have been the victims of a particularly cruel practical joke. As Sergeant Peterson informed you, a woman identifying herself as Natalie Warwick did file a complaint against you and—ah—obviously, you know, we had to act on it. Unfortunately, when we attempted subsequently to contact her at the address she gave—"

"Nobody knew anything about her," I said.

"It was a vacant lot," Driscoll admitted unhappily.

"It's a pity," I said, "Peterson here was in such a hurry to pin something on me that he couldn't have checked that out first."

"It won't happen again," Driscoll said.

"I hope not," I said. "I'd hate to have to bring a suit for false arrest."

Driscoll looked at Peterson and Peterson looked very unhappy.

Driscoll offered to have a car take me back to where I'd been picked up. I turned him down and caught a cab to Daniell's gallery. It was close to five when I got there and it was empty except for Daniell working alone in his office.

"I expected you earlier," he said.

"I expected me earlier too," I said. "But you know how it is with the best laid plans."

"Yes," Daniell said drily. "I was somewhat at a loss," he added, "when you failed to show up on time. However, since I had advertised the sale it seemed best to proceed rather than risk comment by calling it off at the last moment."

"I agree," I said.

"Do you? Good, I'm glad. I'm afraid I have to advise you, though, that there was a legitimate bidder for your Delvecchio." His eyes met mine blandly. "He exceeded your stated reserve by $500."

Daniell looked down and picked up an envelope. "In your absence and without instructions covering such an eventuality I again had no choice but to do as I thought best." He handed me the envelope. Inside was a certified check for $45,500. "I allowed the sale," Daniell said. "That represents the proceeds—less, of course, my fee."

"Your fee was paid in advance," I said.

His eyes flicked away. "Your earlier check will be returned to you," he said.

"Sure," I said, "but we'll argue about that later. Right now the question is how do I get in touch with the buyer."

Daniell sighed. "I was afraid that would be your reaction," he said. "I'd advise against it, but if you persist I imagine a resale could be arranged—for $150,000."

For the second time that day I found myself staring at someone unbelievingly and saying the same words I'd used before: "You can't be serious."

"Why not?" Daniell said. "Isn't that the price you quoted Foster Richards?"

"How do you know about Richards?"

"You told me," Daniell said. He smiled, a brief, bleak movement of the lips. "Yesterday in the mail instead of a check I received a very interesting letter. It wasn't addressed to me, but I'm afraid I read it anyway." He looked at me mockingly. "You see what happens when you get in too much of a hurry, Mr. Lang. You make mistakes. In any case, Mr. Richards is well known as a collector and I took the liberty of calling him. He's out of the country for the rest of the month, but I was able to speak to his secretary. I'm afraid I identified myself as you, explained that there had been an apparent mixup, and asked if Mr. Richards had received a check intended for Daniell Galleries. He confirmed that Mr. Richards had." Daniell smiled again. "I assumed you'd stop payment on it as soon as you realized what had happened. So I told him to return it to you. You should have it in a matter of days."

"Sure," I said. "And that's why you moved the auction up. To have everything settled before that check came back. You even set me up with the police so I couldn't be here to stop you, didn't you?"

Daniell shrugged. "And if I did? Would you have acted differently in my place? I think not. In any case, I'm afraid it's a little late now for you to do anything about it except—how did you phrase it—'settle for what you can get.' And now"—he picked up his pen—"if you'll excuse me I do have this to finish. Unless, of course, you're still interested in buying the painting back."

"No," I said. I put the envelope and check in my pocket and left.

Once I was outside I started to grin. I wondered how Daniell would feel when Richards didn't rise to his bait, because, of course, there was no letter from Delvecchio describing a work in progress anything like the one Lovell had painted. For that matter, the check and letter hadn't been placed in the wrong envelopes by mistake either. So all in all, it looked as if Daniell was going to be the one who was going to have to settle for what he could get; and it wouldn't be all that much, since by the time he found out what happened, his check would have long since been cashed and the money put where it would do the most good—for Lang and Lovell.

The Canadian Caper

The girl who manned the reception desk in the front showroom had said that a customer had asked for me personally. But of course the slim blonde I found gazing raptly at a medium good watercolor was no customer. She still wore her hair at shoulder length to emphasize the little-girl innocence of her soft round face and wide-spaced blue eyes, but the smile she gave me—as far as I could tell anyway—was genuinely happy. "Hello, Pauline," I said.

"Harry!" Pauline Morgan said. "How long as it been? Five years? Six?"

"Closer to eight," I said.

"That's right. Not since that thing with the three panels. What was it you called it?"

"A triptych."

"Of course. And what do you suppose that terrible little man you sold it to did when he came back and found I was gone?"

"Took his loss like the gentleman he was, I suppose," I said. "I never went back to find out."

"Nor did I." She put her hands on my shoulders and studied me appraisingly. "My, but you look good, Harry. And to think I wouldn't even have known you were in town if it wasn't for that awful detective, what's his name?"

"Peterson," I said.

"That's right. Why can I never remember that? Anyway, I had this little misunderstanding in Cleveland and someone must have wired ahead, because when I got off the bus he was waiting for me. Of course, it was all straightened out in next to no time, but at one point he practically accused me of coming over here just to pull something off with you." She paused and looked at me earnestly. "That man doesn't like you, Harry," she said.

"So naturally," I said, "the first thing you did when you got free was head straight here."

"Oh, *please*," Pauline said. "Give me some credit. That was three days ago and nobody would follow little old me for three days—not without my knowing it anyway. Besides, the last time he saw me I was on a bus headed for St. Louis and points south."

"Put you on it, did he?"

She nodded ruefully.

"But of course you got off at the first stop and came back. Why, Pauline? What is it you want from me?"

She smiled brightly. "Lunch," she said. "For a start."

I took her to a small Italian place down the street. It was a little early for the usual lunch-hour rush, so we had no trouble finding a corner booth that promised a maximum of privacy.

"I just can't get over how well you're doing," Pauline said after the waitress had taken our order and gone off. "Your own gallery even." Her wide-set eyes reflected admiration. "Still working partners with Lovell?"

I nodded. Lovell is, of course, the key element in our partnership—although I'm not sure he realizes it or that it would matter to him if he did. Lovell is an artist in the real sense of the word, although his talent is limited to forging paintings of any style, period, or artist to a degree of perfection that only the most detailed scientific examination can distinguish from the original artist's work, and the technical end—the actual painting and associated craftsmanship—is all he cares about. Which leaves me free to concentrate on what I do best, which, of course, is disposing of the paintings to our mutual profit.

It was in the course of one of these transactions that we'd previously run into Pauline. A less than scrupulous art dealer had contracted for us to forge the missing third panel to a triptych that a not-too-bright client of his was desperate to buy. The whole thing was a set-up, of course. The not-too-bright client was Pauline and as soon as we had our money the three of us had split to go our separate ways. Until now, that is. And Pauline, I knew, wouldn't have come back after having been escorted out of town just to say hello or gush over old times.

"You were going to tell me what else you wanted," I said.

"Same old Harry," Pauline said. "Always business. But yes, I was." She looked at me earnestly. "Have you ever been in Toronto, Harry?"

"Not that I recall."

"Beautiful city," she said. "But cold. It helps if you like snow. But anyway I was there about a year ago. Sheila Tynan and I were working a modified version of the old magic wallet trick and doing very well at it until Sheila met this dreamboat with a farm with ninety-nine oil wells or uranium mines or something on it. In any case, the combination was too much to resist. So while Sheila went off west to live a life of unearned ease, I was left with nothing to do but look around for something to tide me over until I could find a new partner. It wasn't easy, Harry, but finally I ended up taking a job with a man named Oliver Wendell Horton. Ever hear of him?"

I shook my head. "I don't think so."

"Dominion Development? Northwest Territories Unlimited?"

I continued to shake my head. "No. What is it? Real estate?"

"Hardly," Pauline said. "Oliver Wendell is a corporate promoter or a manufacturer's representative or foreign sales rep or whatever else the fancy strikes him to call it. What he does—or promises to do—is represent U.S. firms that want to expand into the Canadian market."

She smiled ruefully. "You'd be surprised at how many there are. Small companies mostly that want to get bigger but don't have the organization or distribution setup to go up against the big boys in the U.S. So when Oliver Wendell comes in with his talk of the vast undeveloped potential of our neighbor to the north they jump in with both feet, sure this is the ground-floor, low-competition area they've been looking for all their lives.

"Anyway, if Oliver Wendell thinks the company is promising enough—and he particularly likes specialty bakers and convenience-food processors—he'll contract to push its products in Canada in return for a percentage of the net he brings in. Then after a reasonable period of time he'll write back with the good news: one of Canada's largest chains is ecstatic about the product and wants to pilot it in its Toronto outlets. How soon can the company fill the order?

"How soon? You guess, Harry. Will yesterday be all right? Ninety-nine times out of a hundred the company will break its collective backs getting the order out. You can guess what happens next."

"There's a snag," I said.

"Give the man a dollar," Pauline said. "As soon as the shipment hits the border, customs impounds it and Oliver Wendell wires down that they won't release it until the duties are paid. Of course, this is all news to the company because usually they've never done any international shipping before and Oliver sure as hell never mentioned anything about it. But anyway suddenly, there they are, faced with a bill that can run as high as a couple of thousand dollars. Of course, that's only a fraction of what they stand to make if the deal goes through—or lose if it falls flat. So almost invariably they panic—particularly the food people who can just *see* the whole shipment going stale or spoiling—and send the money off by return wire."

"To Oliver, I assume."

"Another dollar," Pauline said.

"And equally naturally," I said, "that's the last they ever hear from him."

"Not always," Pauline said. "Sometimes if Oliver thinks the traffic will bear it, there may be an additional delay or expense or two—but basically that's it."

"How did you fit in?"

"I was Oliver's secretary. I sent out the letters and wires, answered the phone, stalled clients when he was 'in conference'. It wasn't that I didn't know what I was getting into. Even if Oliver Wendell hadn't been upfront about it, you get so after a while that you can smell a scam a mile off. And I was upfront with him too. What irks, Harry, is that even after all that, he stiffed me.

"It was all boom or bust, he said. Once the money started coming in, everything would be fine, but until then all he could afford to pay was pocket money—he'd have to owe me the rest."

"Oh, Pauline!" I said.

"I know," she said, "I should have smelled it. But what else was I to do? Besides, I was handling the books and all the mail, wasn't I? I'd *know* when the money arrived. And sure enough, as soon as it did he wrote me a check for the full amount. The only thing he asked was that I wait a couple of days for the sucker's check to clear before cashing it."

"And did you?"

"Of course not. As soon as it was my lunch hour I practically ran to the bank."

"Only to find he'd beaten you and already closed out the account."

"Worse. He'd never even had one. The check was solid rubber through and through. And of course when I got back to the office, he was gone.

"He'd overlooked one thing, though, and that's that when you're in the business yourself it's not too hard if you put your mind to it to track somebody who sticks to the same line of work. And Oliver Wendell's too old to change. He's here in the city right now, recruiting business for his next go-round.

"And that's the real reason I came here from Cleveland. He owes me, Harry. And I want it."

"Good luck," I said.

"You better wish yourself that, Harry," Pauline said. "I had mine when I ran into Peterson and he told me about you. Because I knew that if anybody could get that money back for me it would be you. No, don't shake your head, you're going to do it—because if you don't, I'll hate myself but I'll just have to tell that nice Sergeant Peterson all about that triptych deal."

"I see," I said. I nodded thoughtfully. "All right, Pauline," I said finally, "hate yourself. Tell him."

"What?"

"Tell Peterson," I said. "I don't care. Neither will he, because it wasn't his jurisdiction—and even if it was he still couldn't prosecute. It's been eight years, remember? The statute runs out in seven."

"You mean you aren't going to help me?"

"That's exactly what I mean," I said. "Vengeance I leave to the Lord, if for no other reason than because it butters no parsnips."

"You rat."

I shrugged. "Rats have a bad name," I said, "but they've managed to survive for a long time."

"So have cockroaches."

"I see we understand each other," I said. "On the other hand, I might have a use for Horton. You put me in touch with him and, who knows, there just might be something in it for you too?"

"I expected better of you, Harry," she said reproachfully. But she gave me the address anyway.

There was somebody in with Horton when I arrived for my interview at the hotel suite he'd rented. The girl he'd hired to handle the phone was apologetic. "Gee," she said, "I'm sorry, but when you called I thought sure he'd be free by now. If you like, I can give you another appointment later."

"How long do these interviews usually last?"

The girl shrugged. "It varies," she said. "He allows an hour and a half, but some of them are like, you know, over in less than twenty minutes. So it kind of evens out."

She was eighteen and a gum chewer, and I wondered briefly whether Horton planned to stiff her the way he had Pauline. He probably didn't, I decided, because it would be foolish to risk any repercussions at this end that could queer the whole deal. It was only after the money had come in and he was ready to run anyway that squawks didn't matter.

In any case, I told her I'd wait and sat down. Fifteen minutes later, Horton finished his interview and it was my turn.

He was an older man than I'd expected, mid-sixtyish at the least, with a pale bony face, a hawklike high-bridged nose, and the quick fluttery gestures of a nervous sparrow.

"L and L Galleries," he said, studying the business card I'd given him. "Fine Art and Paintings. Oh, dear, not my usual line at all. On the other hand, there's nothing, I always say, that aggressive merchandising can't sell. In fact, I believe Sears tried just such a scheme with art works several years back. I'm not quite sure how that worked out, but what's to say it isn't an idea whose time has come—particularly in an untapped market area that's crying for culture?"

"What indeed?" I said. "But before we go any further, there are a couple of things I should make clear. One is that original works of art, including paintings, are not generally subject to customs duties."

"Ah," Horton said carefully, and I had the distinct feeling he was deciding this was going to be one of those interviews that evened the schedule out and was just trying to think of a way to break it to me more or less gently. To forestall him I added: "The other is that it was a mutual acquaintance who recommended you to me." His eyebrows went up questioningly. "Pauline Morgan."

"Oh, dear," Horton said. He looked at me apprehensively. "You aren't a violent person, are you, Mr. Lang?"

"Not at all," I said.

Horton looked relieved. "Nor am I," he said. "I trust then that we can discuss this in a civilized manner. It was really, as you might imagine, a most unfortunate situation, and I'm sure Pauline has told you some terrible things about me. But let me assure you, Mr. Lang, that they are simply not true. Simply not true at all."

"That's too bad."

"I beg your pardon?"

"I said it's too bad they're not true—because, frankly, Mr. Horton, it was those terrible things that interested me in you."

"I see," Horton said. He sat back and regarded me carefully again. This time the look was calculating, and while he still had the same fluttery mannerisms they seemed just that now—mannerisms. "What is it you want from me?" he said.

For answer I passed over a large folded sheet of paper. Horton looked at it curiously. "What's this?"

"A hot sheet," I said. "Otherwise known as an Interpol Bulletin. It's a list of the twelve most wanted stolen or missing works of art. The one

I'd like to call your particular attention to is number eleven, Eilmeyer's *Girl with Bouquet*."

"I see it. What about it?"

"I have it," I said. "At the gallery." I smiled wryly. "It's what you might call another 'unfortunate situation.' I had a client who wanted the painting and wasn't too particular about how he got it. So I made a deal with a servant of one of the owners. We'd bring the painting here while the owner was on extended vacation so my partner could copy it, then return the copy and sell the original. Unless the original owner submitted the copy for scientific examination—which wasn't likely—he'd never know the difference and everybody would be happy. What we couldn't foresee was that the owner would break his leg skiing and come back early—before we could get the copy in place.

"Fortunately, his man was able to convince him there must have been a break-in while the house was untenanted and that the painting was stolen then. That took him off the hook, but it does nothing to solve *my* problem."

"I don't see where you have a problem," Horton said. "Not if your client really doesn't care how he obtains the painting."

"Oh, he doesn't," I said. "In fact, he wants it worse than ever and is willing to pay even more now. These real nut collectors are like that. I don't dare sell to him, though, because with all the publicity if that painting ever surfaces again it's bound to be recognized and the trail will lead straight back to me. My best bet would be to burn the painting and be done with it, but that's too much like burning money and I can't bring myself to do it."

Horton nodded sympathetically. Burning money was something I imagined he would find difficult to do himself.

"Which leaves me with the next best," I said, "which is to get it out of the country and sell it someplace where it isn't quite so hot. That's where you come in. I'll pay you a thousand dollars to smuggle it into Canada for me."

"Oh, dear," Horton said. "That's hardly my line of work, Mr. Lang."

"I realize that," I said, "but I'm not looking for a professional smuggler. The painting's small and light and fits very neatly behind a false side in a suitcase I've already set up. All you have to do is pack your clothes in it and carry it across the border. I'd do it myself except that as a known art dealer I automatically fall in the area of suspicion, and if I start going back and forth into another country for no apparent reason people are going to start asking questions.

"You, on the other hand, have no known connection with the art world. You're simply a Canadian citizen returning to your own country after a legitimate—" I smiled "—or at least apparently legitimate visit to this one. Nobody will think a thing. And once you're in Canada, I'll take over again. So you're clear on that end too."

"There still would be an element of risk."

"Of course," I said. I knew what he was thinking. As long as he kept his victims on one side of the border and himself on the other, he was practically untouchable. But a hassle with the Canadian customs authorities on his own turf would be another matter altogether. "That's why I'm offering a thousand. But, look, if you're worried, do this: come down to the gallery tomorrow to check out the suitcase and decide for yourself whether it's worth it to you or not. To make it worth your while, I'll pay you a hundred just for showing up. If you decide to go along, it'll be an advance on the thousand. If you don't, it's still yours to keep. Fair enough?"

Horton looked at me thoughtfully. "There must be a lot of money involved."

"That's not your concern," I said. "Nor is what happens to the painting after it's in Canada. I'll take over from there again."

"I see." Horton smiled briefly. "Well, I don't see where it would hurt me to look at it. Would noon be all right?"

I told him noon would be fine. We shook on it and I left.

Outside, the girl gave me a sad smile. I had been one of the shorter interviews, after all. I winked at her, which didn't tell her anything except maybe that sometimes it wasn't really the length of an interview that mattered.

There were two people with me in my office when Horton arrived the following day. One was Lovell. The other was a short, stocky man in his mid-fifties who kept an unlighted cigar clamped aggressively in one corner of his mouth as if to tell the world he wasn't about to take any nonsense from anyone. After another ten minutes I told him I couldn't keep Horton waiting any longer and escorted him out through the front office, where Horton was sitting looking aggrieved.

The stocky man didn't bother to spare him a glance. "I'll go another five thousand," he said to me. "That's top dollar. You won't do half that good anyplace else."

"It's not a question of money, Mr. Carrdock," I said.

"It's always a question of money," he said. "You think about it. I'll be at the Sheraton this afternoon from three on. You can get in touch with me there when you change your mind."

"I won't," I said.

He smiled faintly, shifting the cigar. "You think about it anyway," he said and left.

Horton frowned after him. "Who was that?"

"Just a customer," I told him. "Nobody you need worry about."

"If you say so," Horton said, but he continued to look back over his shoulder as I took him into my office.

Lovell was still standing where I'd left him. I introduced him to Horton, then got a medium-sized suitcase from its niche and placed it on my desk. Horton looked at it curiously but made no move toward it.

"There was to be a payment," he said, "for my time."

"So there was," I agreed. I got $100 from the safe and counted it out for him. Lovell frowned and shifted his weight from foot to foot. Horton didn't appear to notice. Smiling his satisfaction, he put the money away and bent to examine the suitcase. Several minutes later he looked back up.

"The interior dimensions seem to be the same on both sides," he said.

"Of course they do," I said. "I told you it wasn't an amateur job. And filled with clothes it'll look even more natural. But the painting's there all right. Look."

I undid the concealed clips and lifted out the false panel to reveal the painting fitted neatly underneath. Horton looked at it appraisingly. "How much is it worth?" he said.

I shrugged. "Like most things," I said, "whatever you can get somebody to pay for it."

"And that would depend on who you were selling to," he said, "and where." He bit his lip thoughtfully. "A thousand isn't enough," he said. "Make it five thousand and you've got a deal."

Lovell frowned. "I told you he'd try to hold us up," he said. "We could get a professional smuggler for half that."

"But you don't want a professional smuggler," Horton said. "You said so yourself. You want me. Someone above suspicion, you said. I won't be greedy, though. I'll settle for the twenty-five hundred—plus, of course, a bill of sale."

"A what?"

"A bill of sale," Horton said, "*and* an affidavit stating that the picture is yours to sell and that you obtained it by legitimate means." He smiled. "Just a little added insurance. As you so correctly point out, I have no known connection with the art world, and with a receipt if customs do catch me I can reasonably claim not to have known there was no duty. I'm sure they'd be considerably more lenient with someone trying to beat a nonexistent tax even if—to his great consternation—the object was later discovered to have been stolen."

"Covering all bases, are you?" I said.

Horton nodded smugly. "I find it's generally a good policy."

"That cuts two ways," Lovell said. "I don't like this, Harry. He gets everything while we take all the risks. How do we know we can trust him? He might try to pull the same kind of stunt on us as he did on Pauline."

"That's ridiculous," Horton said. "Even if I was tempted, how could I betray you without contacts or information as to who would buy? A stolen painting's hardly the kind of thing you can hawk on a street corner. Or would you suggest I put an ad in the papers? I'm hardly that foolish."

"You could turn it in for the reward."

Horton sniffed. "I wasn't aware there might be one. Even so, the time to have decided you couldn't trust me was before you started."

"He's right," I said. "He knows enough to blow the whistle any time he wants."

"Not that I would, of course," Horton said. "But it does appear you have no real alternative but to go ahead as planned."

"Maybe not," I said. "But Lovell's right, covering all bases does cut both ways. And so I think we're entitled to a little insurance too. So here's the deal. You get your bill of sale and affidavit. In return you put up an amount equal to the reward as a guarantee the temptation to cash in won't turn out to be too great."

"And how much would that be?"

"Ten percent of the painting's value," I said. "Twenty-five thousand. As soon as the painting's delivered to our man in Canada, you get it back plus the twenty-five hundred. And we get the bill of sale and affidavit back too."

Horton worried his lower lip. "I hadn't counted on any investment," he said. "I'd want to think about it."

"Not too long."

"No," he said. "I'll call you tonight. And," he added, "the fee has just gone up to five thousand. Definitely no less."

Nervous as ever, Lovell was sure we'd seen the last of our hundred bucks, but, true to his word, Horton called a little after five to say he'd decided to go along with the deal. The money would be transferred down from his bank in Canada by Friday and we arranged to make the exchange then.

I asked Pauline to lunch that day and we were just getting back when Horton arrived to pick up the painting. To avoid an explosion I stashed her in a back room while I dealt with him in my office.

"I trust everything is ready for me," he said.

"Ready and waiting," I said. I showed him the bill of sale and affidavit, then put them back in their envelope. "But if you don't mind, I think I'll have a look at the money first."

"Of course," Horton said. He opened the briefcase he'd brought with him to reveal $25,000 in neat packages. "And while you're counting that, since we're speaking of trust, perhaps you wouldn't mind if I just verified that the painting really is inside that suitcase as well."

"Be my guest," I said.

Horton opened the case, removed the panel, and gazed lovingly at the painting inside, then replaced it and closed the case.

"I would say we're in business," he said.

"So would I," I said. I handed him the envelope and accepted the briefcase and money in return. "Our man in Canada will expect to hear from you," I said.

"Of course," Horton said. He moved to the door, clutching the suitcase under his arm. "Perhaps I shouldn't mention this," he said, "but there's an alternative to getting the painting out of the country. And that is to get out of the country yourself *after* selling it. I'm afraid I put two and two together and deduced that the importunate Mr. Carrdock was your mysterious American client. In any case, I took the liberty of contacting him at his hotel afterwards to verify the fact. Needless to say, his offer was considerably more than any paltry reward. So I'm afraid you'd better tell your man in Canada not to wait too long for my call."

He was gone before I could move.

Pauline burst in from the other room. "I told you that man was a crook, Harry," she said.

"Heard it all, did you?" I said.

"Every word. You wouldn't listen, though, would you? You were so smart. Well, I hope you're satisfied."

"Reasonably," I said. "And if I'm not, you should be." I took a packet of bills from Horton's briefcase. "How much did you say he owed you?"

"Five thousand."

"That's funny," I said. "When I asked Horton about it the other day, he said it was two."

"That liar!" she burst out. "I worked for him thirteen weeks if it was a day, and at three hundred a week that's—" She broke off and smiled sheepishly.

"Thirty-nine hundred," I said. "But take the five thousand anyway. You deserve at least a little interest for your time and trouble."

Pauline looked at me suspiciously. "You're too cheerful," she said. Suddenly comprehension flooded her face. "Harry, that painting—it was one of Lovell's forgeries, wasn't it?"

"Of course," I said. "There's a real *Girl with Bouquet*, and it was stolen just like the circular said. But by whom or for what purpose is beyond me. Lovell and I sure didn't have anything to do with it."

"So when Oliver Wendell goes to contact this man Carrdock—"

"He'll find him long gone, taken off for sunnier climes with the five hundred I paid him for a sterling performance. I suppose Horton could try to recoup by claiming the reward, but the insurance companies are pretty wary these days. The painting's good—all Lovell's work is—but it'll never stand up to the sophisticated scientific examination they'll give it."

"Beautiful!" Pauline said. "But—oh, Lord, he has that bill of sale! Won't he use that to cause trouble?"

"Hardly," I said. "While he was checking out the painting I took the liberty—as he would say—of switching envelopes on him. The one he has now contains a bill of sale for a *copy* of the *Girl with Bouquet*, and there's nothing illegal about copying any painting as long as it's so labeled."

"Harry," Pauline said, "I'll say it again—you're a real rat. But I love you." She put the money in her purse. "I'd love to stay too, but after all this I've had enough snow and cold for a while, and that sunnier-climes bit sounds very appealing. So I think I'll follow your Mr. Carrdock's example and be on my way."

"Don't let me stop you," I said. "Have a nice trip and goodbye."

"*Au revoir*," Pauline said.

The Bellman Portrait

The big man with the battered face and hulking shoulders barely constrained by the tight-fitting suit looked slightly ill-at-ease, as if he would have been more at home in a fight ring than an expensive near-north art gallery. So would his smaller fox-faced companion—but only on the other side of the ropes, angling for the fast bucks earned by somebody else's blood and sweat. There was nothing ill-at-ease about him, though—and, to show it, he flashed me a quick, false smile as I came in from my office at the back.

"Nice place you got here, Harry," he said.

"I like it," I said. "Am I supposed to know you?"

Fox-face continued to grin and shook his head. "Not particularly," he said. "But we have what you might call an acquaintance in common. Frank Douglas. You remember Frank, of course."

"Sure," I said. Like I'd remember an attack of measles or a broken leg. "Has his health improved any since that Senate committee was trying to subpoena him?"

He laughed. "You can ask him yourself. He's got a little party planned up at his place this weekend. He wants you to come. You and your partner both."

"And if we can't make it?"

The big man moved then, a shambling lurch to the right that brought him into contact with a small table and set the vase on it teetering dangerously. Fox-face moved swiftly to steady it.

"Careful there, you big ox!" He gave me another example of his insincere grin. "You got to watch this guy every minute," he said. "He's a regular walking disaster-zone even when he isn't trying to be. Now what was that you were saying?"

"Does Frank always send you two around to deliver his invitations?" I said.

Fox-face continued to grin. "Only when he wants to be sure the message really gets across. Friday night. Around seven, he said. Don't forget."

"I'll make a note of it."

"Yeah, you do that." Fox-face turned then and went out, followed by the lumbering man, who managed to make it out the front door without bumping into anything else.

Lovell stood beside his easel in the skylighted room he used as a studio, shifting uneasily from foot to foot. "What if we just didn't go?" he suggested.

"Then I imagine our two friends would come back and turn this place into a shambles on purpose. Even if they didn't, it would only postpone the inevitable. Frank wants something and we're going to have to find out what it is, and better sooner than later."

Lovell wrung his hands together. "Why did we ever get involved with him in the first place?"

The answer to that wasn't simple. Lovell has been my partner for a number of years now. He's as nervous as the proverbial long-tailed cat in a room full of rocking chairs and an absolute nut about his health and the kind of food he'll let himself eat. But he has one great redeeming quality. He can forge paintings of any style, period, or school and do it so well that only an expert scientific or spectrographic examination can tell them from the real thing. That talent of his coupled with my flair for what you might call "salesmanship" is what earned us the money to set up this gallery.

The idea, of course, was that once we had it, we'd go legitimate. But things don't always work out quite the way they're planned. There were times when money was short, and others when opportunities came up that were just too good to miss. Lovell's involvement with the Bellman restoration was one of the latter—or seemed at the time.

Bellman is a story in itself. Shortly after the Civil War, an enterprising young businessman named Harvey Bellman set up a factory on the prairie south of the city to manufacture rolling stock for the then booming railroad industry. He was close to the materials he needed, but in order to attract workers he had to provide housing. Company towns were nothing new, but Bellman was smart enough to realize that the better the housing, the better the worker he'd draw, so instead of setting up an instant slum he called in a team of architects to design a model community, with churches, a business district, even a hotel and a community center for dances and Chautauqua-type lectures. I don't know what his fellow industrialists thought—probably that he was a lunatic—but any number of international sanitary and architectural organizations showered awards on Bellman for what in fact was a showplace, and when John Barlow Singer painted his portrait he hung it proudly in the hotel lobby.

The problem was that while Bellman was ahead of his time in some respects he wasn't in others, and so when hard times hit toward the end of the century, it seemed to him it was just good business to cut wages. It wasn't good business to cut rents, though—so he didn't. The result was rioting and a long bloody strike, during which the painting disappeared—a loss that was felt heavily by art lovers because it was the only Singer portrait for which no copy existed.

Eventually, of course, the strike ended, but things were never the same. Bellman died. The city grew south, swallowing up the town, which became just another blue-collar neighborhood sliding into a slum. But then, two or three wars later, it was "rediscovered," like Georgetown in Washington, and suddenly it became fashionable to own a house in Bellman and restore it. Lovell joined in, primarily to provide his artistic energies an outlet. But when a stack of old paintings was found in a long-sealed storage room in the old hotel basement, the opportunity was just too good to pass up.

Like most do-gooders, the restoration-project director was only too willing to let himself be persuaded that the end justified the means, and for a half share in the profits to be ploughed back into the project he agreed to support our claim that one of those found was indeed the lost Singer. It was no big deal for Lovell to paint the portrait using known photos of Bellman as a guide, then age it and dirty it up the way it would have been if it had in fact lain neglected in a basement for eighty-odd years. The problem was that since it wasn't exactly clear who really owned the painting—the Bellman family or the city as successor to the town but definitely not us—we couldn't sell it openly. I made a couple of tentative approaches to potential buyers with no success. And then one day, without warning, Frank Douglas approached me.

Frank was an ex-mobster—or as ex as you can be once you've mixed with the organization—but not an ordinary one. He'd gone into crime from college the way other grads had gone into law or banking, as a promising field in which to carve out a successful career. And now that he had, he was determined to live the life of the cultured gentleman of leisure he'd always considered himself to be. There were those uncharitable enough to suggest that he'd originally gone into collecting art simply as a means of laundering dirty money. But whatever his reason, it wasn't long before the collecting mania had taken hold full force and whatever Frank wanted Frank had to have. And what Frank wanted now was the Singer Bellman.

There was no way I could have refused to sell to him even if I'd wanted to. I took his money, he took the painting, and that was that. Until now.

Douglas lived northwest of the city, almost at the county line, and if the area lacked the old money cachet of the north shore, at least it was the last place around where there was still enough open land for a truly spacious estate—a fact I suspected that Douglas had capitalized on as much for security reasons as for personal preference. His house was a sprawling brick Tudor with fake half timbering on the upper stories, screened from the highway by a well tended stand of pine and approached by a narrow road that turned into a looping drive at the end. There were three cars parked along the far curve when Lovell and I drew up that Friday night.

Fox-face met us at the door. "Well," he said, "the prodigals at last. We were beginning to think something must have happened to you. Like an accident, you know what I mean?"

"No accident," I said. "It's just farther out than I realized."

"It's farther out than a lot of people realize," Fox-face said. He held out his hand. "If you'll let me have your keys, I'll see your car gets put away."

I hesitated a fraction of a second, then handed him my car keys. If it was Douglas's way of insuring I didn't leave before he wanted me to, at least it was a relatively polite method. And there was no point in making an issue of it since there was a second set of keys taped well back under the hood of the car.

Fox-face grinned maliciously, then, putting the keys in his pocket, led us inside and over to a large reception room that opened off to the left of the foyer.

Douglas was standing at the far end with two other men, from whom he broke away when he saw us and came over. He reached out and pressed my hand between both of his. "Harry," he said. "Glad you could make it." He wasn't a tall man, but he kept himself in trim and his knobby, almost handsome face was deeply tanned despite the season. Alone of the group, he was dressed formally, in a wine-red dinner jacket tailored so that it fit his slightly uneven shoulders smoothly without a hint of a wrinkle.

"You had us worried there for a while," he told me. "You don't want to do that."

I shrugged. "You had me worried there for a while, too, Frank. Maybe you don't want to do that, either."

For a moment something flickered behind Douglas's eyes, but then the amusement was back. "Same old Harry," he said, dropping my hand and clapping me on the shoulder. He turned to Fox-face. "McCarthy, why don't you show Mr. Lovell his room while Harry and I get reacquainted. You two *are* going to be able to stay the weekend, aren't you?"

"If that's what's planned," I said. "Your boys weren't too clear on the point."

"I'll have to talk to them about that," Douglas said. "But don't worry. Anything you didn't bring, we'll have. McCarthy?"

McCarthy nodded. "All in hand," he said. He touched Lovell on the shoulder. "You want to come with me?"

Lovell threw me a despairing glance and allowed himself to be led away. Douglas watched them go almost fondly. "Good boy, that," he said. "I don't know what I'd do without him."

"Or somebody like him," I said. "What happened to the other boy you used to have?"

Douglas sighed. "What happens to us all, Harry?" he said. "The world doesn't stand still. You move up or you move out. But you don't want to talk about that. Let me introduce you around. You know Coombs and Bissel, I think."

Arthur Coombs was a tall man in his mid- to late-sixties with a thin, patrician face and thinning hair of a startling whiteness. At one time he had had a fairly respectable collection of mid-Nineteenth Century masters, and in fact he was even one of those to whom I had tentatively offered the Bellman portrait. But more recently I'd heard that although he still kept up the facade, his actual collection had been quietly disposed of years before. I could believe it, watching him now refilling his glass at the bar with the exaggeratedly careful motion of a man already gone over his limit.

I was more surprised to see Bissel there. Or maybe concerned is the word. Bissel was the Bellman restoration director. He was standing almost directly opposite Coombs, an expression like apprehension on his pale, triangular face.

The third and last guest was a stranger to me. Douglas introduced him as George Strother. He was a slightly built man with a thin mouth continuously trembling on the verge of a nervous smile and eyes that never seemed to rest for long on any one subject.

"I think you two will find you have a lot in common," Douglas said, "but I'm afraid we'll have to leave that for later. I hate to rush you, Harry, when you just got here, but my cook said eight-thirty and that means eight-thirty on the dot." He put his arm around my shoulders and turned to guide me out of the room. "You won't believe what that woman can do with food."

Actually, Douglas's cook was probably every bit as good as he claimed. Lovell looked dubiously at the veal with cheese sauce being served, but when his own plate arrived, it contained only vegetables.

"All organically grown," Douglas told him, grinning. "You see, I do my homework." He let his eyes wander around the table and almost as if on cue Bissel leaned forward and said in a rushed voice, as if he'd been rehearsing the words and was hurrying to get them out before he changed his mind:

"Mr. Douglas, I came here this evening under the impression it was to discuss a donation to the Bellman restoration project. Instead I find—"

"You find what?" Douglas said, still smiling. "A group of people gathered for a friendly meal. Don't worry. You'll get your donation. But later. After all, why spoil good food talking business? Right, Harry?"

"Sure," I said. "Eat, drink, and be merry."

Douglas laughed. "That's what I like about you, Harry. Your mind works the way mine does."

He continued to ramble on expansively throughout the meal, ignoring or oblivious to the fact that our responses were short. Coombs continued to punish the bottle. Bissel ate grudgingly, his eyes remaining wary. Strother, if anything, was more nervous than Lovell.

Finally, it was over. Douglas lounged back in his chair and instructed McCarthy to tell the cook she could go home and clean up in the morning.

"Business time?" I said.

Douglas nodded. "Why not?" he said, "Business is what makes the world go round. It's what brought us together in the first place. You sold me a painting. Remember? When was that? Five years ago?"

"Closer to six," I said.

Douglas shook his head. "Time flies. I was just starting my collection then, and there were a lot of people—private collectors, mostly—who wouldn't sell to me. Oh, they always had a good reason—some prior commitment, or they wanted to make the painting available to a wider audience—but you and I know, Harry, that what it really boiled down to was that they didn't much approve of me. I wasn't their kind and no way were they going to let me join the club. What I like about you, Harry, is that you weren't like that. Maybe, though, I should have asked myself why."

I shrugged. "No big secret," I said. "I wanted to sell, you wanted to buy. That's the way most deals are made. Besides," I added, "knowing you, I didn't think it'd do any good to say no."

Douglas laughed. "You're right, Harry," he said. "It wouldn't have. Just as in the end it didn't do those others any good, either. They wouldn't sell to me—well, I just went out and found somebody they would sell to. One of their own kind." He looked at Coombs, who took another long pull from his glass and refused to meet anyone's eyes.

"I always wondered how you found out about the painting," I said.

"Now you know," Douglas said. "I haven't done much buying lately, but Coombs still does me a small service now and then like letting me know when Strother here showed up one day to ask him, as an expert in the field, if this old painting he said he'd bought at an estate sale was worth anything. What made Coombs think I'd be interested was that the painting Strother showed him was the Singer Bellman—the same painting I bought from you, when was it you said, Harry—close to six years ago?"

He waved a hand negligently. "Naturally, I had to check into it. And I almost hate to tell you this, Harry, but Mr. Strother's story checks out. He is what he says he is—a little man trying to make some big bucks—and he did buy some paintings at an estate sale not long ago just as he says he did."

"Including the painting he's trying to sell you now?"

Douglas grinned. "There you go," he said. "That's the problem. All I've got is his word for that—just as all I've got for that painting you sold me is your word you found it where you say you did. Yours and Mr. Bissel." He glanced over at Bissel, who looked steadfastly down at his plate.

"Mr. Douglas," Strother cut in, "I—"

Douglas, no longer grinning, spared him a brief, hard look. Strother sank back on his chair, took out a handkerchief, and wiped his face.

"What it boils down to then," Douglas said, turning back to me, "is that there are two Bellman portraits, identical as the proverbial two peas in a pod. But only one of them can be the original. The question is which one."

"The only way you'll know that for sure is to send them off to a lab," I said.

"Possibly," Douglas said. "And if I have to, that's just what I'll do. But of course that could create some complications of its own, particularly if somebody started raising questions of legal title. So I'm hoping there's another way." He looked down at McCarthy at the foot of the table. "Everything set up?"

McCarthy nodded.

"Fine," Douglas said. "Well, gentlemen, shall we proceed to the next step?" He rose and, still playing the genial host, ushered us back to the reception room—unchanged, except for a large covered easel set up at one end. Douglas moved past us toward it, and with a dramatic gesture threw back the covering to reveal the two Bellman portraits—neither of them framed.

"There you are, gentlemen," he said. "Before I removed the frames, I marked the back of each canvas to indicate which is the Strother Bellman and which, shall we say, is the restoration."

Coombs began to laugh, a high-pitched giggle that threatened to go out of control. "Gentlemen," he said, holding up the glass he'd brought with him from the table, "let me salute our host, the ultimate collector. Two paintings and he has to *mark* them to tell which is his." He steadied himself with an effort and regarded Douglas scornfully. "Tell me, Douglas, do you ever *look* at what you own—enjoy the colors, marvel at the technique? Or do you just gloat over your possessions the way a miser gloats over gold he's afraid to take out of a bag for fear some of it will melt in the light?"

Douglas was silent for a long moment, his eyes never leaving Coombs. When he did speak, it was in a surprisingly mild tone. "I know what I paid for," he said, "and that's what I intend to have."

After a pause he added: "I thought I knew what I was paying for when I bought you, too. Are you going to prove me wrong?"

Coombs continued to meet his eyes for another few seconds, then abruptly drained his glass and lurched off toward the bar.

"As I was saying—" Douglas turned back to the paintings "—they have been marked. And I'd like to have you tell me which is the original." He let his eyes wander over our little group. "I know you're no expert,

Harry. Your partner is, but if you don't mind I think I'd like a more impartial opinion. You, Mr. Bissel."

Bissel looked around, flustered. "Not me," he said. "I'm an architect, not a painter."

"No," Douglas agreed, "but architects and painters have instincts in common. I'd like to hear what those instincts say."

Bissel hesitated, then, wetting his lips, stepped forward to study the paintings. Finally he shook his head. I can't tell," he said. "They both look the same to me."

Douglas shrugged and looked at Lovell. "Well, Mr. Lovell," he said, "I guess I have to rely on you, after all."

For a long time, Lovell did nothing but look at the paintings. Then he moved closer and ran his hand carefully over the surface of first one, then the other. After another long moment, he repeated the gesture, then stepped back and indicated the one to the left.

Douglas leaned forward intently. "Why that one?"

"The surface," Lovell said. "It would take an X-ray to be sure, but on the one you can sense the ridges where the artist layered paint to build up his effects. The other's too smooth. That's characteristic of a copy where only the surface appearance is important."

"That's interesting," Douglas said. "Especially since the painting you picked as authentic is the one Strother's been trying to sell me."

For a minute I was afraid Lovell was going to do something stupid. His jaw dropped a figurative foot, but then he caught hold of himself, closed his mouth firmly, and simply stood watching Douglas.

"Can't think of anything to say?" Douglas asked him. "How about *you*, Harry? No? Well, I'm sure you'll both think of something sooner or later." He broke off and cocked his head as a sudden sharp rattle of rain against the window announced that the storm that had been threatening all day had finally broken. He grinned. "It's a good thing you were planning to stay over, gentlemen. There's no way I'd let you go out on a night like this."

My room was a pleasant one on the second floor facing the back, with a connecting door to Lovell's adjoining room. He joined me after Douglas had adjourned his party and sent us all up to bed.

"He's lying, Harry," Lovell said. "There's no way that painting could be Strother's."

"You couldn't be wrong?"

"Of course not. Even if they were close—which they're not—I'd know my own work."

"Yeah, well, for God's sake, don't tell *that* to Douglas. In fact, don't tell Douglas anything. Just keep your mouth shut and follow my lead."

"Of course," Lovell said. But being Lovell, of course, that didn't stop him worrying. "But what about Bissel?"

"He could be a problem," I admitted. "But right now I think he's too worried about his precious reputation to do more than curl up into a ball if anybody looks at him suspiciously. I'll leave it to you to see he gets the message to keep it that way. This is one time confession is *not* good for the soul."

"Whatever you say." Lovell paused with his hand on the door to his room. "What's Douglas trying to prove here anyway, Harry? Why doesn't he just do whatever he's going to and get it over with?"

"For the same reason he insisted on going through that charade of a dinner before springing his little surprise. He knows that the more people sweat the more likely they are to panic and make a mistake. Just make sure you don't."

Lovell nodded nervously and went out, and for a long time I stood by the window looking out at the rain. Something nagged at the back of my mind—something Douglas had said to me or I had said to him earlier in the evening. But I couldn't remember quite what it was, or why it bothered me. Finally I gave it up and went to bed.

I must have slept, because I woke suddenly to darkness. Something—a noise, I thought, just beyond the edge of my consciousness—had disturbed me. Not a usual household noise, either, I was sure as I reached for the lamp switch. Apparently, though, the storm had knocked out the electricity because it didn't work. I pulled on a robe and went out to the hallway.

And was hit full in the face by a flashlight beam.

"Lose something?" McCarthy said.

"I thought I heard a noise."

"Like what?"

"That's the problem. I don't know."

McCarthy snorted. "It must have been the ghosts," he said. "Douglas had them brought over specially from England to give the place class."

"Funny, I thought that was why he kept you around."

"That, too," McCarthy said. "Now if I was you, I'd go back to bed. Mr. Douglas wouldn't like it if you got yourself hurt wandering around in the dark."

"I'll bet he wouldn't," I said and did go back to bed. Eventually I slept again.

It was full light the second time I awoke. The storm had blown over and the landscape outside my window sparkled under a bright sun. I dressed and went downstairs to find Lovell in the kitchen preparing his own breakfast. A stout, grey-haired woman in an apron watched him with a mixture of amusement and exasperation.

"I suppose you want to make your own, too," she said to me.

"No," I said. "I'm not fussy. I'll take whatever's offered."

"Good," the woman said. "Go back to the dining room and as soon as I get my stove back I'll bring you something."

I did as she said. Bissel and Strother were already there, seated at opposite ends of the table and each doing his best to pretend he was alone. Neither said anything as I sat down midway between them. A few minutes later, Coombs came in. His eyes were a network of blotchy red lines but otherwise he seemed to bear no ill effects from the alcohol he'd downed the night before. He gave me a wry smile. "I hope you'll excuse me for my behavior last night."

"You didn't do anything needing to be excused," I said.

His smile turned a little more genuine. "I'm glad to hear that. I find there are days when I forget, so I've made it a habit to apologize as a matter of principle." He sat down across from me. "I trust there's coffee."

McCarthy came in and after a quick, frowning look around the room demanded: "Where's your partner?"

"You mean Lovell? In the kitchen," I said. "Why?"

For answer, McCarthy continued to stand glowering where he was—then, as Lovell pushed through the door leading from the kitchen, he drew a gun from under his coat and pointed it at him. Somehow Lovell managed to keep from dropping his tray. McCarthy gestured with the gun. "Over there," he said. "Beside your partner. No, you just stay where you are, Harry," he added quickly, moving to cover me as well. "And keep your hands where I can see them."

"What's this supposed to mean, McCarthy?" I said. "Another of Douglas's little jokes?"

"No joke," McCarthy said. "Douglas is dead. You two killed him."

"That's ridiculous," Lovell said.

"See if the cops think so when they find out about that phony painting you sold him and how he caught you out." He half turned and looked down at Coombs. "You sober?" he said, and when Coombs nodded he handed him the gun. "Make sure these two don't go anywhere while I make the call." He went out.

Coombs smiled as if embarrassed and held the gun limply pointing at nothing in particular. "Is Douglas really dead?" he said.

"You heard the same thing I did," I said.

Coombs smiled again. "Yes," he said. "It's funny in a way, you know. Ironic. The times I wished that man dead, and now here I sit guarding his alleged murderers."

"Thanks for the benefit of the doubt," I said.

"My pleasure," Coombs said. "Under slightly different circumstances, you might very well be holding the gun on me, but fortunately I continued to—ah—indulge after the rest of you left last night to the point where McCarthy had to put me to bed. So I'm afraid I wasn't in any condition to murder anyone. Although I suppose in a sense I can take some small credit for the act. If I hadn't told Douglas about Strother's painting, none of this would have happened, would it?"

"That's right," I said. "You told him about both paintings."

Coombs nodded. "It was pure spite the second time," he said. "He had everything I valued or wanted and they might have been so many matchbook covers for all he knew or cared. If you want to leave, go ahead. I won't stop you."

I shook my head. "It wouldn't solve anything."

McCarthy came back and took back the gun. He looked at us suspiciously. "What's been going on here?" he said.

"Just talk," I said. "Coombs was wondering if Douglas was really dead."

"Oh, he's dead all right," McCarthy said. "Shot twice with a .22. The gun's still where you dropped it."

"That was kind of stupid of me, wasn't it?" I said. "Kill a man, leave the gun right there where it's sure to be found, and then wait around to be arrested."

McCarthy shook his head. "You talk good," he said. "But it's all bluff. It's not going to work this time, though. You and Lovell were the only ones with any reason to kill Douglas. All the talk in the world isn't going to change that."

"I wouldn't be so sure if I were you," I said. "That was the other thing we were talking about just now—how badly Coombs wanted Douglas dead. He says he was too drunk last night, but was he really? Or does he just want us to think he was? Or, for that matter, don't forget Bissel—he was part of the original sale, too. He'd have as much, if not more, to lose as the rest of us."

Bissel gasped. "How dare you—"

McCarthy grinned. "See what I mean?" he said. "Bluff. If you're smart, Harry, you'll save your stuff for the cops. They'll be here soon enough."

They were. McCarthy had barely finished speaking when two blue caps and a team of paramedics pounded in.

The paramedics confirmed McCarthy's diagnosis that Douglas was dead. Other cops began arriving in shifts: homicide detectives, technicians of all kinds, medical examiner's men. There was a lot of bustle and noise and comings and goings, a good part of which I suspected had less to do with the murder investigation than with a police attempt to cash in on a heaven-sent opportunity to find out something of what was going on in the mob these days. Eventually a uniformed officer came into the library where we'd all been herded and escorted McCarthy out. Twenty minutes later he came back without McCarthy, asked which of us was Harry Lang, and when I said I was beckoned me to follow.

He took me down a short hallway to what I assume was Douglas's study. It was a small, dark paneled room dominated by a large oak desk at which a grey-haired beefy-faced man in a rumpled blue suit sat leafing through some papers. His credentials, spread out faceup in front of him, identified him as Detective Sergeant Joseph Driscoll. A younger, sprucer detective sat off to one side armed with a steno pad and a pencil.

The first thing Driscoll did after telling me to sit down and verifying that I was Harry Lang was to toss aside the papers and read me my rights in a rapid monotone. It was hardly an encouraging beginning, but then it wasn't intended to be. When I had nodded that yes, I understood, he leaned back in his chair and studied me. Finally he said: "Why don't you just tell us what happened here last night?"

"Starting when?"

"Say when you first got here."

There was no point holding anything back. He'd already heard McCarthy's version. I told him as briefly and factually as I could what had happened from the time Lovell and I arrived until the party broke up for the night.

"And then?"

"I went to bed."

"All night?"

"No. Something woke me. I went out in the hall to investigate, ran into McCarthy, and went back to bed—this time for all night. Or what was left of it."

"Yeah," Driscoll said, "McCarthy said he found you wandering around the halls. About what time was this?"

"I have no idea. The power was off and I didn't look at my watch. Incidentally, if anybody was wandering the halls, it was McCarthy. He was the one with the flashlight. I never went more than two feet from the door to my room."

"I asked him what he was doing in the hall when he encountered you." Driscoll nodded. "He said the same as you—that he heard a noise and went out to see what it was. He thinks it was you, and now you're saying you think it was him. Of course, it's possible both of you are telling the truth and it was some third party that made whatever noise it was—the assumption being it was the shot that killed Douglas. A .22 isn't very loud—maybe not much louder than a door slamming. In that case, you'd both be in the clear. But, frankly, if I had to bet one of you is lying, I'd bet it's you."

"Why? Because I allegedly sold Douglas a copy of a painting for an original six years ago?"

Driscoll laughed. "That's the first time I ever heard anybody use the word 'alleged' in connection with his own statement. But, yeah, because of that."

"Except that I never said I sold Douglas a copy. All I said—and all that can be established despite what anybody says—is that Douglas claimed the painting my partner identified as the original was the one Strother has been trying to sell."

"It seems to me that comes to the same thing," Driscoll said.

"Not really. Douglas could have been mistaken. Or lying."

"Now why would he do that?"

"I have no idea," I said, "and I don't claim he *did* lie. Only that he could have. But for the sake of argument, let's assume he didn't. And let's agree, too, that the chances of two paintings so similar being produced independently of each other are so small as to be virtually nonexistent.

But all this talk about which is the original and which is the copy only draws attention from the really important question. Which is *when* was the copy made?"

"Yeah? What's so important about that?"

"Everything. Think about it for a minute—like I did all that time you had us waiting in the library. We know from the record that no copy was made before the painting was lost. Obviously none was made while it was lost, either. Which leaves only two reasonable alternatives: one, that Lovell and I made the copy at the time we discovered the original, or, two, that it was made after we'd sold it."

"Are you trying to tell me now that Douglas would have copied his own painting?"

"It's not out of the realm of possibility," I said. "It might have appealed to his sense of humor to pass a fake off onto one of those upright collectors who piously refused to sell to him. But there's one big stumbling block: Coombs. Coombs is—or rather, was—Douglas's man. Douglas might have used him as a front, but he never would have sent Strother to him with a story that Coombs, knowing all he did about what had gone before, would be bound to recognize as phony."

"Which seems to put the finger right back on you," Driscoll said.

I shook my head. "No, same stumbling block. Lovell and I couldn't re-approach the people we'd contacted before with a different story about the painting's origins any more than Douglas could. Even more importantly, we wouldn't dare. There was too much chance that whoever had leaked the story to Douglas before would do it again—which, in fact, is exactly what happened.

"So it really all boils down to somebody else with access to Douglas's collection. Coombs? Not likely. By both his and Douglas's admission, there's been no contact between them for years. Bissel? No. Strother? Definitely not. I suppose it could be the cook, but when you check into it I think you'll find the only one who really fits the bill is McCarthy.

"I have an advantage, of course. I *know* that Lovell and I didn't make the copy—but what I can reason out, so can others. I think Douglas had already pretty well narrowed it down to McCarthy, too. In which case, the whole business of pressuring Lovell and me to come, the menace just below the surface and all the rest of it was just smokescreen to keep McCarthy from guessing his real purpose—which was to find out just how badly he was being burned. If McCarthy and his assumed partner, Strother, were selling the copies they made, that was one thing, and probably the worst Douglas would have done was cut himself in for most of the pie. But when Lovell picked the one Strother was selling as the original—well, you can figure that out yourself."

Driscoll looked at me thoughtfully. "Very pretty," he said. "Except for one thing. Working for Douglas, McCarthy would have known about the connection with Coombs, too."

"Not necessarily," I said. "McCarthy didn't start working for Douglas until fairly recently—until after he'd bought the Bellman portrait. But there's an easy way for you to check it out. Why don't you call Strother in and tell him that Lovell and I routinely X-ray all paintings that come into our possession and that I'm insisting that the two present paintings be X-rayed now and the results compared with the plate made at the time we sold ours to Douglas?"

Driscoll gave me another long, thoughtful stare. Then he called back the policeman who'd brought me in. "Put this bird where he won't bother anybody," he said. "Then bring me the one called Strother."

I spent the next several hours in the bedroom I'd spent the night in, this time with a cop outside the door. I tried the connecting door once out of curiosity. It was locked.

Finally, there was a slight shuffling outside, the door opened, and Driscoll entered.

"You can go," he said.

"Just like that?"

"Sure. What else do you want?"

"Well, for a start you might tell me what happened with Strother."

The detective shrugged. "Sure, why not? It'll all come out in the papers. It was all pretty much the way you figured it. Strother and McCarthy had a nice little racket going, substituting copies for Douglas's pictures and selling the originals secretly. Strother says it was really his brother-in-law and McCarthy's idea, his brother-in-law being the artist who did the actual painting. According to Strother, they just brought him in as front man and probable fall guy. He's particularly bitter nobody bothered to tell him Coombs used to work for Douglas. He says the killing was all McCarthy's work, too. He didn't know anything about it until this morning and was shocked when he heard. He claims he thought it was you or your partner until he heard about the X-rays." Driscoll looked at me speculatively. "You really have them?"

"No," I said.

Driscoll nodded. "I didn't think so. But your bluff worked and you're home free. Before you start thinking yourself the next Sherlock Holmes, though, there's one thing you ought to know. I got two years' night law school and one of the first things they teach you is that you can't prove a negative fact. So if Strother had stuck to his story about buying the original at an estate auction, there's no way you could have proved the one you found wasn't a copy that, despite what the records say, had to have been made when the original was still hanging in the Bellman hotel. In which case, there would have been nobody left to take the heat but you."

He was wrong there, because if worse had come to worst there was a way we could have proven Strother's painting had to have been made after ours. "But," as I commented to Lovell later as we were driving back to the city, "that would have meant admitting we had forged the 'original' in the first place. That was the problem right from the beginning—proving what we knew had to have happened without giving away how we knew."

"What will happen now?" Lovell asked.

I shrugged. "I imagine justice will run its course. But that's the cops' and the court's problem, not ours."

"I meant about the painting. Will there be any trouble about our selling it without title?"

"If there is, it'll be a civil action, not criminal. I don't think it's too likely there will be, though. I suspect Douglas's heirs aren't going to want any more publicity or poking around in his affairs and will settle the matter by quietly donating it to one of the city museums, or maybe to the restoration project itself." I laughed, "That'll put Bissel in a nice fix, won't it?"

Lovell shook his head. "I don't know, Harry," he said. "This has taught me one thing. Never again. I mean it. From now on, we're strictly legitimate."

"Well, of course," I said. "After all, that's been the idea all along, hasn't it?"

I said it with a straight face, too.

Bread Upon the Waters

The first time I met the Major I was in jail, serving out a $100 fine for disturbing the peace at the time-honored rate of $1 a day. I understand inflation has played havoc with that as it has with all things these days, and the judges now trade the time you have for the money you haven't at the rate of $3 or even $4 a day. But be that as it may, it was $1 a day then. And by my reckoning I still had 72 days to go when the turnkey lumbered down the corridor, unlocked my cell, and jerked his thumb up to motion me to my feet.

"Vacation's over," he said. "It's back to the cold cruel world for you."

"Now?" I said. "Just when the chef is learning to make hash the way I like it?"

The turnkey gave me a sour look. "You want to lay there and crack wise," he said, "or do you want to get out?"

I really didn't have to give that much thought. "I want to get out," I said.

I was curious, though, and at the entrance to the cell block I asked the bored clerk who passed over the envelope containing my meager personal possessions, "How come I'm being sprung?"

"Ask the man at the front desk," he said without looking up.

Which I did. "Your fine's been paid," he said. "By your friend over there," he added, nodding his head to indicate a short barrel-chested man with a square ruddy face, full gray mustache, and close-cropped hair of the same gray color. The man was standing near the door.

His face lit up as soon as he caught me looking at him curiously, and he advanced with his hand outstretched to grasp mine. "Ah, James," he said. "Thought I recognized you from your picture. Sorry not to have got here sooner, but I only just learned your whereabouts this morning. Still, better late than never, eh?"

"If you say so," I said, "although—"

"I have the advantage of you, eh? Of course. But let me rectify that." He drew himself to his full five-foot-five and thrust out his chest even farther. "Major Henry T. McDonlevy, late U.S. Army. And the world's greatest adjutant until some bureaucratic mixup got me passed over for promotion and forced my retirement. Still," he added cheerfully, "the Army's loss is your gain. Because if I hadn't retired I wouldn't have been your fellow lodger at Mrs. Peters' and therefore wouldn't have heard about your plight."

"Yes," I said, "that's all very interesting. But—"

"But you don't want to hang around a jailhouse discussing it. Of course not." He took my arm and guided me out through the double doors. "On a beautiful day like this," he went on, "a young man—and even an old one—can find better things to do."

I let him take me a couple of steps down the street. Then I carefully disengaged my arm. "I don't want to appear ungrateful," I said, "but I can't help wondering just why you'd plunk down $100 for a total stranger, fellow lodger or not."

The Major's face sobered and he nodded thoughtfully. "Yes," he said, "I suppose it does seem a little odd. But," he continued, taking my arm again and pulling me with him down the street, "you see, my boy, I try to guide my life by the Good Book."

"You mean 'Do unto others' and that sort of thing?" I asked.

"No," the Major said, dragging the word out. "As a matter of fact, I had a different text in mind. Ecclesiastes ten, twenty: 'Cast thy bread upon the waters.'"

"Now," I said, "I do see. But if you're looking for a thousandfold return from me, I'm afraid you're in for a disappointment. If I had any money, Major, or any prospects of getting any, I'd have paid that fine myself."

"I think you'll find the exact text is 'for thou shalt find it after many days,'" the Major said unperturbed. "Although I must admit most people would have it your way and I myself have found that my investments generally result in a tidy profit.

"As for your prospects. Well"—he coughed delicately into his cupped hand—"I'm afraid I overstated the case somewhat when I said we were fellow lodgers. Actually, I rented your room after you—ah—vacated it. Apparently, however, the postman wasn't aware of the change and this morning he delivered this."

He took an envelope from his breast pocket and handed it to me. "I'm afraid I opened it—inadvertently, of course—before I noticed the name of the addressee."

"Of course," I said drily, opening the letter. It was three months old, having kicked around a bit before catching up with me, and it was clearly addressed to Thomas James.

"Dear Mr. James (it read), I regret to inform you that your great-uncle Arthur Wallace passed away on the 15th of last month, naming you as his sole heir. If you will call at my office with proper proof of identity I will arrange transfer to you of his estate, said estate consisting of 750 acres in the heart of Michigan's vacationland."

It was signed Byron Swope, Administrator of the Estate of Arthur Wallace, Appleby, Michigan.

I glanced up from reading and as my eyes met the Major's he smiled brightly. "I took the liberty of doing a little research on your behalf," he said. "And the area is booming, summer cottages being a big thing right at the moment."

I refolded the letter and stuck it in my pocket. "All right, Major," I said. "Fair's fair. I'll see you get your money back plus a reasonable profit."

"Fine," the Major said. He puffed out his chest and strutted along beside me. "We can discuss what constitutes 'reasonable' later, after the extent of my services has been determined. For now, though, let's concentrate on getting you to Michigan. And since one should never undertake a journey of that magnitude alone, I'll just trot along—if you don't mind."

Actually, whether I minded was something of a moot question. If I was going to get to Michigan at all, somebody was going to have to pay for the trip. And the Major was as good a prospect as any.

I'd never been to Appleby, Michigan, but I had a pretty good idea of what the town was like from my mother's description of her childhood—a wide spot on the road somewhere between Tawas and Traverse City. As far as I could tell from my admittedly limited knowledge, about the only thing that had been added since her day was a sign at the edge of town proclaiming it "The Heart of Michigan's Vacationland."

I remarked as much to the Major as we drove past in the car we'd rented when we'd found that the only public transportation north from Saginaw was a bus.

"Tush, tush, my boy," he said. "Nobody's asking you to live here. We simply realize our profit and move on to greener pastures, as agreed."

"And the sooner the better," I said, surveying the weathering storefronts that made up Main Street. The area might be booming as the Major had said, but the town certainly wasn't being ostentatious about it.

Swope's office turned out to be a narrow book-and-paper-cluttered cubicle on the second floor above the town's only restaurant. And Swope himself was a tall spare individual in his mid to late sixties with small glittering eyes in a long narrow face and a tight, almost lipless mouth.

"Well," he said, as the Major and I presented ourselves, "this *is* something of a surprise. After all these months I'd just about decided you didn't intend to claim your inheritance."

That should have alerted me. What I mean is, people just don't *not* claim inheritances. Unless, of course, there's some reason not to. But to tell the truth, in the last several days I'd sort of got used to letting the Major make the decisions. So I just stood there and let him take charge now.

"No mystery," he said bluffly. "The lad had simply moved and I didn't manage to track him down with the news until just recently."

Swope favored the Major with a long cool glance, then turned back to me. "I suppose you've brought your birth certificate," he said.

"I did," I said and passed it over.

Swope examined it briefly, then nodded. "Seems to be in order," he said. "Now all we have to do is transfer the land formally to you. Let's see now I've got one of those forms around here somewhere." He rummaged through his desk and the cabinets surrounding it, finally coming up with a legal-sized document which he began to fill in with a ballpoint pen, the only modern touch as far as I could see in the entire office.

"I should warn you, though," Swope said, "that this is going to cost you some money."

"I knew it," I said. I took hold of the Major's arm. "Come on, Major, Let's go."

But McDonlevy held back. "Not so fast," he said. "First let's find out how much."

"Well," Swope said, scratching behind his ear with the click button end of the ballpoint, "as I recollect, the taxes are paid through the end of this year and there was enough in Arthur's bank account to cover my fee as an administrator." His face brightened. "So all you have to pay is the standard recorder's fee of $20."

"Well," the Major said heartily, "I think we can afford that." He took two $10 bills from his wallet. "I assume we pay this to you," he said to Swope.

"That's right," Swope said, deftly lifting the bills from the Major's hand and stuffing them into his own pocket. "Among other things I'm deputy clerk of the court here and the recorder."

Swope set about finishing filling in the form, stamped it with an official-looking seal, and handed it to the Major who passed it on to me. I looked at it briefly, then folded it and put in in my coat pocket.

"Now that that's out of the way," the Major said, "my young friend and I would like to see the property. You can tell us how to find it, I assume."

"Sure," Swope said. "It's about five miles northeast of town. You can't miss it. It's the only slue land anywhere close by."

The Major looked blank. "I don't think I'm familiar with the term," he said. "Slue land?"

"I am," I said. I looked hard at Swope. "Do you mean to tell me that what I've traveled so far to inherit is nothing but a swamp?"

"Well," Swope said, "swamp is probably too strong a word. But it is wet. Except in the winter, of course, when it freezes."

"Sure, though, man," the Major said, "it must be worth something?"

"It would be," Swope admitted, "if you could find a buyer. Which isn't too likely, I'm afraid, unless you can figure out how to drain it. About eight, ten years ago Arthur had some engineers up from Bay City. They said it wasn't 'feasible.' That means you can do it, but it'd cost more than the land's worth."

"I know what it means," I said. "Tell me, though, If the land's so worthless why did you bother to write me in the first place?"

"Had to," Swope said. "The law says the heir has to be notified." He smiled tightly. "I suppose I could have told you before you paid the transfer fee. But to tell the truth it never occurred to me."

"I'll bet," I said and left, followed by the Major.

"Sorry," I said to him outside, "but it looks as if you cast your bread on the wrong waters this time."

"Perhaps," he said. "But if I may mix metaphors—no battle's lost until the last shot's been fired."

"And just what shots do you plan to fire in this particular battle?"

"Who knows?" he said cheerfully. "But surely it wouldn't hurt to spend one night in the hostelry here, would it?"

I agreed it probably wouldn't. But I wasn't so sure when I saw the room they gave me. Still, I'd learned in jail that you can sleep anywhere and on anything when you're tired enough. And that's just what I was preparing to do—sleep—when the Major popped in. "Come, come, my boy," he said, "moping alone is no good. Let's be out where the action is."

"Action?" I said. "In Appleby, Michigan?"

"There's action everywhere, my boy," the Major said. "All it requires is a nose to ferret it out."

The particular action the Major's nose had ferreted out this time was a poker game at—of all places—Swope's bachelor quarters. Besides Swope there were two others present—a frail looking, much younger man named Forbus who taught English at the local high school and a stolid hulk of a man named Mitchell whom I took to be a farmer.

"Good of you to help us out, Major," Swope said. "The man who usually fills in the fourth chair had to go out of town and we don't like to play three-handed."

"My pleasure," the Major said, settling into the fourth chair.

Swope picked up the deck and began to shuffle. "Seven card stud all right with everybody?" he said.

Forbus and Mitchell nodded, and so did the Major after a moment. "I'm more partial to draw," he said. "But when in Rome, you know."

Swope gave the Major another of his long cool looks. "Yes, of course," he said, finished shuffling and began to deal.

Everybody seemed to take it for granted that I was just there to kibbitz. Which was fine with me, because seven card stud is a game I try to avoid even when I'm flush. On the surface, it's a deceptively simple game. You're dealt two cards face down, then four more face up and another face down in rotation. Best poker hand based on any five cards wins. The kicker is that you bet after *every* card except the first two. In other words, there are five bets (six if there's a raise along the way) to be met on each hand. Compared with regular draw poker, stud is a real plunger's game where you can lose a lot of money in a very short time if you're not careful. Sometimes even if you are.

Partial to the game or not, the Major knew his way around a card table, and it soon became apparent—at least to me—that he and Swope were the only real poker players present. Forbus was the eternal optimist, always hoping for a miracle and consequently always staying with a hand too long. Mitchell, on the other hand, was an out-and-out bluffer who hadn't learned that bluffing works only when it's the exception to the rule.

Poker isn't entirely a game of skill, though. Luck enters into it as it does in everything else, and the other two couldn't help but win a pot now and then. And since both the Major and Swope played especially tight games, dropping out unless the third or fourth card showed strength, that wasn't as infrequent as you might expect.

So it began to look like the Major's "action" was just what it appeared to be on the surface—a friendly, not too exciting game in which not enough money was going to change hands to make or break anybody. Until 11:30, that is.

At 11:30 Forbus glanced nervously up at the clock on the mantlepiece as he passed his cards back to the dealer—Swope again—at the end of a hand. "Half an hour to go," he said.

"So it is," Swope said mildly. "We always make it a rule," he explained to the Major as he shuffled and reshuffled the cards, "to quit exactly at twelve. Saves argument and embarrassment. But," he added, "for the last half hour we pull out all the stops and play no limit. We find it makes a more interesting evening."

"I'm sure it does," the Major murmured. He straightened in his chair and put his hands flat on the table before him.

Something flickered momentarily behind Swope's eyes. Then he finished shuffling and began to deal the cards. The Major's first face-up card was an ace. Swope showed a king, Forbus a three, and Mitchell an eight. "Your bet, Major," Swope said.

The Major sat quietly for a moment, his fingers toying with a stack of white chips. "When a man says 'no limit'," he said at last, "I have to assume he means just that." He pushed the stack of chips forward into the pot. "Fifty dollars," he said.

That was exactly twenty-five times the highest bet made up to that moment, and it effectively served to separate the men from the boys. Forbus and Mitchell pushed their hands in and for all practical purposes joined the kibbitzers' circle, leaving the game to the Major and Swope.

With only two hands to deal, the game went faster than before. And by the time the large and small hands on the clock met at twelve, the Major owed Swope slightly over $900.

"I assume you'll accept my check," the Major said, reaching inside his jacket for his check book.

Swope's eyes went bleaker than usual.

"And," the Major added, "give me a chance to win it back before I leave town."

Swope's eyes brightened. "Planning on staying around for a while, are you, Major?" he said. "In that case, I'll be glad to take your check *and* honor your request."

He accepted the check the Major dashed off and, holding it loosely in his hand, walked with us to the door. "Same time tomorrow night then?" he said.

"Looking forward to it," the Major said.

I waited until we were about half a block away from the house. Then I said, "Operating on the assumption that that check is going to bounce back faster than a tennis ball, I suggest we just keep on going and not even bother stopping at the hotel. That Swope looks like a mean enemy and this is his town, not ours."

"Nonsense, my boy," the Major said. "All I did tonight was cast a little more bread on the waters and it would be foolish to leave before we found it again. But if it bothers you, reflect on this: it will be Monday morning—two days from now—before friend Swope can present that check at any bank and several days more before it clears to the bank it's drawn on. Surely that should give us ample grace period to do what we have to do and leave—even if, as you assume, the check is no good."

"Well, maybe," I admitted. The Major slapped my shoulder heartily. "Of course it does," he said.

"Now have a good sleep. Things will look better in the morning."

Actually, they looked worse. Because when I stopped by the Major's room on my way to breakfast, he was gone and his bed hadn't been slept in.

It took about a minute for the realization to sink in. Then I spent another minute swearing silently at him before settling down to figure out what to do. Instinct told me to cut out, too. Because even if technically only the Major stood to fall on the bad-check charge, small town justice has the regrettable tendency to overlook technicalities and settle for the bird in hand. And if they wanted a peg to hang a case on, there was the small matter of a hotel bill I couldn't pay.

Unfortunately, getting out of town wasn't going to be that easy. The Major had taken the car and hitchhiking meant at least a ten-mile walk down to the main highway since rural drivers are understandably skittish about picking up strangers in city clothes.

Of course, there are worse things than walking ten miles, and going to jail is one of them. But I felt I still had some grace period left. And when some unobtrusive checking around revealed that there was a bus at four that afternoon I opted for it, figuring I could slip on board just before it pulled out and be on my way before anybody realized what had happened.

What I failed to take into account, though, was just how fast and efficiently news spreads in small towns. Swope and Mitchell cornered me a half hour before the bus was due to leave. Mitchell had changed into his working clothes. And despite his farmerish appearance and willingness to break the laws against gambling, it turned out he was a deputy sheriff.

"Haven't seen much of your friend, the Major, today," Swope said conversationally.

"As a matter of fact," Mitchell put in more bluntly, "we haven't seen him at all."

"I'm not surprised," I said. "He said he was tired and was going to stick pretty close to his room."

"Now that's strange," Swope said, "because he isn't there now. And the chambermaid told the desk clerk the room looked as if not a thing had been touched."

"Well," I said, searching for something to say, "you know how it is with these military types. They spend so much time getting ready for inspection they forget how not to be neat."

"Perhaps," Swope said. "But his—shall we say, unavailability—does raise some questions. Particularly since I had our local banker call a banker friend of his in Detroit and neither one of them had ever heard of the bank your friend's check is drawn on."

"Now, look," I said. "That check is a matter strictly between you and the Major."

"It certainly is," a familiar clipped voice said, bringing all heads swiveling around.

The Major glowered at the doorway, hands locked behind his back and his barrel chest thrust out. "What's this all about, Swope?" he said.

"Just a little misunderstanding, Major," Swope said coolly.

"Hmph," the Major sniffed. "It seems to me that gentlemen don't misunderstand each other this way."

"Perhaps not," Swope agreed. "But then how would either of us know? He moved to the door, followed by Mitchell. "Same time tonight?"

"Of course," the Major said stiffly, stepping aside to let them pass. "Cheeky buzzards," he added in a mild, almost disinterested voice after they had disappeared down the hall.

"Maybe I'm one, too," I said. "Because I sure would like to know where you disappeared to today."

The Major's face brightened into a smile. "Just following the Good Book again, my boy," he said. "And now if you'll excuse me I'd better get some rest if I'm to be at my best tonight."

The same players as before were waiting for us at Swope's house that evening. No one made any references to the events of that afternoon. But, whether for effect or not, Mitchell had left on his deputy sheriff's uniform. The only thing lacking was for him to place his gun meaningfully on the table beside his cards.

"Seven card stud still all right, Major?" Swope said as the Major took his seat.

"It's your game," the Major said. "I do have one suggestion, though. Since I'm the big loser, how about giving me a chance to catch up by extending the no-limit period to—oh—an hour or two? Or even," he added a shade too casually, "to the whole game?"

Forbus and Mitchell both looked at Swope, who let the moment drag out before shaking his head. 'No,' he said. "A rule's a rule. And as you said yourself, 'When in Rome—'"

'Do as the Romans,' the Major finished. "Of course."

But it was apparent from the way he fidgeted in his seat and slapped his cards down that he was straining at the leash, impatient for the real game to begin. It wasn't long before Forbus began to fidget, too, and even Mitchell began to show signs of nervousness. Only Swope appeared unaffected, accepting his cards and playing them as unperturbedly as ever.

As for myself—well, I'd thought time had passed slowly in jail. But those days were sprints compared with tonight. And it was with a real sense of relief that I heard Swope announce: "Well, Major, half an hour to go. Now's your chance to get even—if you can."

As before, the game narrowed down immediately to Swope and the Major, and the cards and chips passed back and forth between them with such rapidity that it was impossible to keep track of who was winning. Still, when the dust settled at midnight, the Major was ahead.

"$800, I make it," he said, tallying his chips.

"So do I," Swope said equably, "and since you said you wanted a chance to win your check back, I saved it for you." He reached in his pocket and threw the now folded and crumpled check on the table between them. "I'll take my change in cash if you don't mind," he said. "$125, I make that."

He permitted himself a sly smile, and Forbus and Mitchell both grinned openly. The Major looked at them blankly for a moment. Then he smiled, although a bit wryly. "I have to hand it to you, Swope," he said. "You're a hard man to get the better of."

"I try to be," Swope said drily. He flicked his thumb rapidly over his fingers. "Now, I'll take my money, please."

"Of course," the Major said. He counted $125 out of his wallet, passed it over to Swope, then picked up the deck of cards and regarded it with the wry expression still on his face. "Perhaps from now on I should stick to parlor tricks." He grinned suddenly, fanned the deck, and offered it to Swope. "Go ahead," he said. "Pick a card."

Swope hesitated, then selected a card, showed it to Forbus, Mitchell and me, and put it back in the deck for the Major. The Major cut and recut swiftly, then began dealing cards, laying them out in neat rows. When he'd got about halfway through the deck, he stopped, his thumb just flicking up the edge of the top remaining card. "One last fling, Swope," he said. "My next half-year's income against your next half-year's fees of office that the next card I turn over is yours."

I started to open my mouth, because Swope's card—the four of Spades—lay about a third of the way back in the rows of cards already face up! But a heavy look from Mitchell killed whatever I had planned to say.

Swope's face was as impassive as ever. "You have a bet," he said.

Smiling faintly, the Major reached out and turned the four of Spades face down!

There was a moment of silence. Then Mitchell guffawed and slapped Swope hard across the shoulders. "By God, Byron, he took you that time," he said.

"So he did," Swope said mildly. His eyes came up to the Major's. "That was clever," he said. "Deliberately going past the card you knew was mine. It lured me into overlooking the first rule of gambling—never bet on another man's game.

"Still, maybe you haven't won as much as you thought. I make my living from law and real estate. I only took that job as deputy clerk and recorder for the political weight it carries. That $20 I got from you was the first fee I've collected in six months and the last I'm likely to collect in as many—unless, of course, you manage to find someone foolish enough to buy that worthless land your friend James inherited, in which case you'll be more than welcome to the $20 that sale will bring." And with that he laughed nastily. So did Forbus and Mitchell. They were still laughing when the Major and I let ourselves out.

"Satisfied now, Major?" I said after the door had closed behind us.

"Very much so," he said.

"Then let's get out of this town while we still have money to buy gas."

"Nonsense, my boy," the Major said. "It would be foolish to leave now when we're just about to find again the bread we've cast upon the waters." He took my arm and marched me along beside him. "Old Swope was right about one thing," he said. "You *can't* sell that land of yours. But you *can* give it away. Which, as your agent, is just what I proceeded to arrange for this afternoon.

"First thing Monday morning a reliable direct-mail firm in Detroit will begin releasing letters notifying the lucky 3000—selected at random from the telephone directories maintained at the excellent public library there—that they have each won a quarter of acre of land 'in the heart of Michigan's vacationland.' All that's required to confirm the prize is that the lucky winner record the deed and pay the standard $20 fee before the end of the month.

"Naturally, I wouldn't expect too many to come up and do that in person. So a convenient return envelope will be enclosed. And all we have to do as the letters come in is simply extract the money and pass the work on to Swope." He smiled benignly. "If experience is any guide, we can expect about fifty percent to respond, giving us a gross of $20 times 1500, or $30,000. Which isn't a bad return at all."

Nobody Can Win 'Em All

The small round-faced girl at the receptionist's desk just outside the railing that separated the executive offices from the rest of the bank looked up and gave me a bright professional smile. "Yes?" she said.

"My name is Thomas James," I said. "I'm supposed to meet a friend of mine here. A Major McDonlevy."

The girl's smile faded. "I don't believe—" she began dubiously.

I held my hand shoulder high. "Short," I said. "About five five and built something like a barrel on two legs."

"Oh," she said, the smile back in place, "that would be the gentleman with Mr. Andrews, Junior. Just a moment while I buzz them."

She picked up her phone with one hand and simultaneously dialed a three-digit number with the other; in a moment she spoke softly into the receiver, then set it back in its place as smoothly as she had picked it up. "You're to go right in," she said. "Third office on your left."

I gave her a smile and a wink for thanks and pushed through the swinging gate into officers' country. The entire rear wall was lined with office doors, but even without the girl's directions I would have had no difficulty locating Andrews, Junior's, because his door was one of three that had names printed on them in neat gilt letters. I rapped once, then went on in without waiting for a response.

They both looked up as I came in and the Major rose automatically in greeting. And after a hesitation Andrews rose too. He was a tall man with thinning fair hair, a pale undistinguished blur of a face and, in his late thirties or early forties, relatively young to be such a high-ranking bank executive—although the fact that one of those other lettered doors had borne the name Andrews, Senior may have had something to do with it.

"Ah, there you are, my boy," the Major said heartily. "Sorry to have gone off without you like that. But you know how it is with time and tide, and I see you got my message all right."

"Yes," I said.

"In your absence," the Major went on, "I took the liberty of going ahead and discussing with Mr. Andrews our interest in the old Easdale Shoe building."

"I see," I said. "And what decision did you come to?"

"Well, of course I haven't committed us to anything," the Major said. "But the property does sound extremely promising, and since Mr. Andrews has consented to drive us, I suggest we run out and take a good look at the place and then see if we can't come to a decision."

"Fine with me," I said. "I wouldn't want to inconvenience Mr. Andrews, though."

"No problem," Andrews said in a voice that tried for a hail-fellow-well-met heartiness. "Thursday afternoons are always slow. But I'd be glad to do it at any time."

I imagined he would. Because it wasn't every day that someone showed up to express an interest in acquiring a building that had lain idle since the previous owner had defaulted on his mortgage six years before. But rather than bring that up, I just smiled and said, "Offer accepted then."

"Good," Andrews said. He moved around from behind his desk. "If you'll just follow me," he said. "My car's right out back."

Andrews wasn't a fast driver. But he was a frightening one, given to swiveling his head and eyes away from the road as he talked in an attempt to include all his passengers in his conversation. As a result, he almost didn't see the gray coupe pulled off onto the narrow shoulder until it was almost too late. But his head jerked back as the Major and I cried out a warning in near unison, and he managed to swing the wheel away just in time to avoid a hard sideswipe.

"Damn fool," Andrews grumbled. "What's he doing parked out on the highway?"

"I think you'd better stop," the Major said.

"Why?" Andrews said, alarmed. "I didn't hit him, did I?"

"No," the Major said calmly. But *he* is a young lady, and *she* looks as if she were in distress."

"Oh," Andrews said. "Oh." He didn't look particularly happy about it, but he did pull over to the shoulder. As soon as he stopped, I got out and walked back to where a slim girl with long blonde hair framing a round, almost doll-like face stood beside the coupe.

"Trouble?" I said.

The girl looked at me apprehensively—which wasn't an entirely unnatural or unexpected reaction since this was a lonely road and she couldn't be sure I wasn't a wolf out to add to whatever trouble she already had. Her face brightened almost immediately, though, when she saw Andrews and the Major coming up behind me.

"Oh," she exclaimed, relieved. "Mr. Andrews."

Andrews frowned and peered at her. "I don't believe—" he said slowly.

"I'm Carol Ferguson," the girl said. "And, oh, of course you don't know me, but I've seen you several times when I've come to the bank on business for Mr. Robert Horsley."

"I see," Andrews said. "That explains it then."

The Major stepped forward between them, inclining his head gravely. "Permit me to introduce myself," he said. "Major Henry T. McDonlevy, formerly the U.S. Army's and hence the world's greatest adjutant, now retired and at your service."

The girl acknowledged his half bow with a smile.

"That young gentleman over there grinning like a jackass," he went on, "is my associate, Mr. Thomas James. Think we can help the young lady, Tom?"

"We can try," I said. I spoke to Miss Ferguson. "What seems to be the trouble?"

She smiled wryly. "I'm not sure," she said. "I pulled off the road to check my map for a turnoff and the motor stalled. And I haven't been able to get it started again."

"Let's take a look," I said. I lifted the hood, bent over the motor, and sniffed. The smell of gasoline was almost overpowering. "Just as I suspected. You flooded the carburetor. Do you have a screwdriver?"

"In the glove compartment, I think."

I got out the screwdriver, then went back to the motor and unscrewed the air filter to get at the choke underneath. Setting the filter to one side, I used the screwdriver to prop the choke closed. Then I got in behind the wheel, floored the gas pedal, and turned the ignition key. The motor ground once, then kicked over and settled down to a steady purr. I got out, retrieved the screwdriver, and replaced the air filter.

"See," I said, slamming the hood back down, "nothing to it."

Miss Ferguson clapped her hands in glee. "Oh," she cried, "I can't thank you enough. I might have been stuck here all day."

"No need to thank us at all, my dear," the Major said. "Glad to be of service."

"No," she said, sobering somewhat but still smiling. "One good turn deserves another. Do you plan to be around town very long, Major?"

"That depends on how our business goes," the Major said.

"Well," she said, "if you decide you've had enough business and want to relax for a while, you'll probably want to stop by Mr. Horsley's." She fumbled in her purse and brought out a business card which she handed to the Major. "Just show that and it'll open the way for you."

And with that she flashed me a bright "thank you" smile, got into her car, and pulled off onto the highway, giving us one last wave of her hand as she went past.

"Nice girl," the Major said, slipping the card into his breast pocket. "I'm glad we stopped to help her."

"I suppose," Andrews said.

The Major looked at him curiously. "That's an odd thing to say," he said.

"Maybe it is," Andrews said, "and I don't know anything about her personally. She does work for Mr. Horsley, though. And—well, I suppose I shouldn't talk against him since he is a depositor and his has always been a good account. But the fact of the matter is that Horsley runs a gambling den behind that restaurant of his."

"Really?" the Major said. "I didn't think gambling was legal in this state."

"It isn't," Andrews said drily. "But most of Horsley's customers are out-of-state people from across the river, and as long as there are no complaints locally, I guess the sheriff just looks the other way. Or lets himself be paid to."

"I see," the Major said. "Well, as Tom well knows, I try to live according to the precepts of the Good Book. And not being without sin myself, I hesitate to throw the first stone. But that's neither here nor there, I suppose. So shall we get on with the business we set out to do?"

"Just what I was going to propose myself, Major," Andrews said, and led us back to his car.

Whether as a result of the experience or not, Andrews did pay more attention to his driving and we made it the rest of the way to the building site without further incident.

The building itself was a long shedlike affair set well back from the highway on the crest of a low knoll. Unfortunately, in common with a lot of other factory buildings put up in this part of the country some 20 to 30 years ago, the lower half had been sided with corrugated metal sheeting and then left to fend for itself. It hadn't done too well. On the other hand, the upper stories were all glass—or would have been if the broken windows had been replaced. Those few that remained intact had weathered to an opaque gray that almost matched the color of the metal below.

We spent a full hour tramping around and studying the building from all angles, both outside and in. Or rather the Major did. Andrews and I both copped out early and went back to his car to wait.

"Unusual man, your friend, the Major," Andrews said.

"Yes, he is," I said. "Very unusual."

"He never did really make clear why you two were interested in this place," Andrews added casually.

I smiled. "To be perfectly frank with you, Mr. Andrews," I said, "I haven't the slightest idea either. But this I do know: the Major never does anything without a reason and he has a positive genius for making money out of the most unlikely situations. Take my worthless Michigan swampland, for example. We gave that away and made $20,000 in the process."

"Really?" Andrews said. He sounded more than a little interested.

"Really," I said.

"Very interesting," Andrews murmured and looked thoughtfully over at the old building.

Not long after that the Major finished his inspection and came back to join us.

"Well, Major," Andrews said, "what's your decision?"

The Major shrugged. "It's hard to say," he said. "The basic structure is sound, but it would take considerable work getting it in usable condition. And, of course," he added, smiling, "a lot would depend on the kind of financial arrangements that could be worked out. But perhaps we can discuss those over dinner this evening."

"With pleasure, Major," Andrews said and put the car in gear. You could almost see him rubbing his hands together.

At the Major's suggestion we ate at Horsley's Restaurant. As a gesture of courtesy to Carol Ferguson for giving us the card of admittance, he said. But I wasn't surprised—nor, I suspect, was Andrews—when after the meal the Major leaned back expansively and suggested we take a look in at the gambling room. "After all," he said, "you can't talk business forever. All work and no play, you know."

Andrews hesitated, then nodded. "I suppose it would be foolish," he said, "to have gotten this close and then go away without seeing what the place looks like."

"You've never been here before?" I said.

He gave me an oblique look and shook his head. "I'm no gambler," he said. "When I lay out money, I like the return to be calculated in advance."

Carol Ferguson's card admitted us into the gambling room without question. It was a standard layout, most of the action centered around a large craps table at one end of the room with a scattering of roulette wheels and other games occupying the rest of the room. Just for something to do, I bought a $10 stack of chips, lost it in fifteen minutes betting against the shooters at the craps table, then went over to rejoin Andrews and the Major watching the play at one of the roulette tables.

We were just about getting ready to leave when I spotted Carol Ferguson coming toward us. She was wearing a long hostess-type gown and had pinned her hair up in a stylish knot, but her smile was as friendly and bright as ever.

"Fancy meeting you here," she said. "Enjoying yourselves?"

"Well, yes," the Major said.

She caught the undertone in his voice and cocked her head to one side. "What's the matter?" she said. "Don't tell me they've wiped you out already?"

"No," the Major said. "But I was hoping you'd have some card tables. Poker's more my game than either dice or roulette."

"Sorry," she said. "We can't offer you poker. Not enough action for the house. All we have in the way of cards is faro."

The Major's head came up smartly. "All?" he said. "Why I didn't think anybody played faro anymore."

"We do here," she said. "It's Mr. Horsley's specialty."

"I don't think I've ever heard of the game," I said.

"Well, my boy, it's time you did," the Major said, "because faro's the Game That Won the West and even when I was a boy it was *the* game to play. So much so, it was practically an American institution. But then like the buffalo and the nickel cigar it just seemed to vanish. Until today. Oh, I tell you, my boy—Andrews—we just can't pass this by without giving it a whirl."

Miss Ferguson looked at him dubiously. "Maybe I shouldn't have mentioned it," she said. "It's a pretty high-stakes game and I wouldn't want you to get in over your head."

"Don't you worry about that, my dear," the Major said. "I learned to swim a long time ago just so I could go in over my head."

"Well, all right," she said. "They keep moving it from place to place for security. Tonight it's at Room 622 at the Madison House Hotel. I'll phone ahead to let them know you're coming."

"Fine," the Major said. He turned back to us, beaming. "Well, Tom—Andrews—shall we?"

Andrews shrugged. "I've come this far," he said. "I'll go all the way with you."

The door to Room 622 opened as far as the safety chain would permit and an eye and half a face peered through the crack. The Major held up Carol Ferguson's card for inspection. The man behind the door nodded, then opened up to let us enter.

It was a typical hotel room, except that the bed had been pushed to one side to make space for a table around which eight men were gathered. They all turned to give us a quick once-over as we came in and there was a flurry of mumbled introductions. But the only names that stuck were Jensen, the smooth-faced youth who had let us in, and Thorkill, the dealer.

The latter was a burly man in his late forties with the battered face and bulging muscles of the professional boxer. But for all his bulk there was no musclebound clumsiness about him. His thick-fingered hands cut and shuffled and dealt with surprising dexterity.

In some respects, though, his skill was wasted. Because, American institution or not, faro is really a simple game and, unless you're involved in the betting, about as interesting to watch as dominoes.

All thirteen spades from ace to king are laid out on the table and the players place their bets on them to indicate whether they think a specific card will win or lose. When all bets are down, the dealer deals two cards face up off the top of the deck. The first is a "loser," the second a "winner." The house pays those who bet against the loser or on the winner and collects all other bets. And then the whole thing starts all over again.

It has only one advantage—if advantage is the right word. It's fast and you can win or lose a lot of money in an extremely short time. As witness: it took the Major exactly fifteen minutes longer to lose the $300 in chips he bought than it had taken me to lose my $10 back at the main gambling room.

"Well," the Major said, pushing his chair back, "I'm afraid that cleans me out."

"Too bad," Thorkill said dispassionately. "But nobody goes away from my table with nothing to show for his time. Jensen, take the gentlemen downstairs and buy them a drink. Then come right back up. I need you to spell me while I run over to the main house."

"Yes, sir," Jensen said and ushered us out.

Riding down in the elevator, I said, "That was a pretty expensive exercise in nostalgia, Major."

"That it was, my boy," the Major said. "However, $300 won't break me—although I won't deny I'd rather have the money than the experience."

Jensen shifted his feet nervously. "I'm taking a chance by opening my mouth," he said. "But you did Carol a good turn this afternoon, and Carol and I—well I just can't stand by and see a friend of her cheated without saying something."

The elevator doors slid open and we stepped out into the lobby. "Cheated?" the Major said.

Jensen nodded. "Thorkill was palming cards. He cheated you blind."

"I see," the Major said. He sighed. "Well, thank you for telling me anyway."

"'Thank you for telling me'!" Andrews said. "Is that all you're going to do about it?"

"I'm afraid there's not much else I can do," the Major said. "If we try to face Thorkill with no more proof than we have, he'll simply laugh in our faces, and the net result will be to get our young friend here in trouble."

"That's exactly right," Jensen said. "And if you go to the law—well, Bob Horsley has the law in his back pocket and Thorkill is Horsley's right-hand man."

"So he gets away with it," Andrews said bitterly.

"Well, maybe not," Jensen said. "I can't just give you your money back, Major. But I can do this. When I go back up, I'm going to replace Thorkill as dealer, and I can palm cards with the best of 'em. You come and get back in the game after he leaves and I'll fix it so you can win your $300 back. After that, it's up to you. You can quit then or you can continue to play with the understanding that as long as I'm dealing it'll be an honest game after that."

"Major," I said, "don't do it. It sounds too much like a come-on."

Jensen flushed. "I made my offer," he said, "and it stands. But if you want to kiss your $300 goodbye, it's okay with me."

The Major was silent for a long moment. Then he said, "I'm afraid I'm out of cash. Would you accept a check?"

"Under the circumstances," Jensen said, "sure. But you'd better give it to me down here. I don't want to set a precedent by letting some of the others upstairs see it."

"Of course," the Major said. Then they went together to the hotel desk to ask for a blank check and stood there for a few moments while the Major filled it out. Then Jensen took the check and went over to the elevator. The Major came back to where Andrews and I had remained standing.

"You just made a big mistake, Major," I said.

"Perhaps so, my boy," the Major said. "But nothing ventured, nothing gained. And I think you can trust the old Major to look out for himself."

"I hope so," I said. "But you're sure not giving me much basis for trust."

He just gave me a smug smile for reply. And not long afterward the elevator came down and Thorkill got out and strode past us. The Major let him get clear out of the building, then headed toward the elevator.

I turned to Andrews and spread my hands helplessly. "I hope I'm wrong about this," I said. "But just in case I'm not, we'd better stick with him to make sure he doesn't get burned too badly."

Andrews nodded and followed the Major with me.

Jensen let us in as before, slipping the Major a stack of chips as he passed by. Then the Major took his former seat and play stared in earnest.

I made it a point to stand directly in back of the Major and to watch Jensen closely. He wasn't quite as good with cards as Thorkill, but he was good enough and if I hadn't been watching for them I never would have seen him palming the "winners" he slipped in.

When the Major's winnings reached the $300 mark, I tapped him on the shoulder. "Time to call it quits," I said.

"Nonsense, my boy," he said. "We've just gotten back to where we started and the way to go from there is upward and forward."

"All right," I said. "But I want you to promise me that you will quit as soon as you lose that $300 back."

The Major nodded. "Agreed," he said. "*If* I lose it back."

And he didn't. He won. Not every turn, of course. But consistently enough and for ever-increasing stakes so that when the game broke up shortly after 2:00 A.M. the pile of chips in front of him had grown to staggering proportions.

"Count it up for me, will you, my boy?" he said to Jensen.

Jensen's hands moved swiftly, stacking and tallying chips. "Over $35,000," he said when he had finished. "$35,310 to be exact."

An almost reverent hush fell over the room at the mention of that much money.

"That's a lot more than I can cover with what I've got on hand," Jensen said. "So I'll have to give you an I.O.U. on Horsley. You don't have to worry, though. Horsley never welches on a debt."

"I'm sure of that, my boy," the Major said, beaming. "But if you don't mind, I'll take my check back as part payment."

"What check?" a harsh voice said. It was Thorkill standing just inside the doorway and glowering into the room.

"My check, of course," the Major said. "The one the lad here was good enough to accept and let me get back into the game."

Thorkill advanced on Jensen who quailed before him. "What's wrong with you, Jensen? First you forget to chain the door so anybody could have busted in on you. And then you let some guy play with a check that could be just so much worthless paper."

"I resent that," the Major said.

"I'll bet you do," Thorkill said, swinging around on him. "But resent it or not, the rule's the rule. And we don't let guys play on checks."

"By George," the Major exclaimed, "I see what you're doing. You're using this as an excuse to bilk me out of my winnings."

"That's exactly what he's doing," Andrews chimed in. He thrust his pale face out at Thorkill. "Well, let me tell you, you're not going to get away with it. I'll see to it that your name and Horsley's will stink in this county."

Thorkill made little placating motions with his hands. "Now, everybody cool it," he said. "Nobody's trying to bilk anybody out of anything. I'm just not going to be four-flushed, that's all. You'll get your I.O.U. all right, Major. It'll be for the full amount *and* it'll be conditional on your check clearing through the banks without a hitch. Fair enough?"

The Major just stared at him stonily. Finally Andrews spoke. "I don't see how you can really object to that, Major," he said. "The man's only taking an elementary precaution."

"All right," the Major said shortly and accepted the I.O.U. that Thorkill offered him. Then the Major, Andrews and I left.

Once we were away from the building, the Major laughed wryly. "Well, easy come, easy go," he said and held up the I.O.U. as if to tear it in half.

"What are you doing?" Andrews cried, shocked. "That's worth over $35,000 when your check clears your bank."

"That's just the trouble," the Major said. "The check isn't going to clear. Because, like Tom, I suspected Jensen's offer might be just a come-on. So I covered myself by buying back into the game with a rubber check. But now it seems that all I did was outsmart myself."

"Maybe not," I said. "It's bound to take a couple of days for that check to clear the local banks. So all you have to do is get enough money into the bank you wrote it on to cover it before it gets there."

"I'm afraid that's not possible," the Major said, "because there is no such bank. I just wrote down the first name that occurred to me." He gave another short wry laugh. "Maybe there's a lesson to be learned here. Nobody can win 'em all."

"You can win this one, though, Major," Andrews said quietly.

"Can I, by George? How?"

"It's so simple I'm surprised you didn't think of it yourself. As I told you, Horsley has his account at my bank, and that's where he'll present your check."

"Of course," the Major exclaimed. "All you have to do is honor it and Horsley and Thorkill will have to pay off."

"Precisely," Andrews said.

"Andrews," the Major said, "if you'll do this for me—"

"I wasn't thinking of doing it for *you*, Major," Andrews said. "I was thinking of doing it for *us*. Shall we say a partnership? Fifty-fifty on your winnings."

"Fifty—" the Major began, then broke off and smiled. "Well," he said, "you're asking a lot, but I suppose half of something is better than all of nothing. You have a deal, sir."

"I thought you'd see it that way," Andrews said. "But just in case you're tempted to change your mind, *I'll* hold the I.O.U. until we go to cash it. You see," he added, smiling, "you're not the only one who knows how to protect himself."

"So it would seem," the Major said sadly, handing over the paper.

And on that we parted.

Shortly before noon the next day there was a knock on our hotel room door. I got up, trailing the newspaper I'd been reading, to answer it.

It was Thorkill. "Hi," he said and walked right past me.

"Ah, there you are," the Major said. "Any difficulty at the bank?"

"None whatsoever," Thorkill said. "Andrews boggled a little when he saw the check was for $5000, but in the end he paid over like the little gentleman he is. I took out $500 to cover paying off the others plus $1000 for myself. That leaves $3500 for you two."

"As agreed," the Major said, accepting the money Thorkill offered him. "how long do we have?"

"A couple of hours at least," Thorkill said. "Andrews wanted to know when you could cash the I.O.U. I said Horsley would be out of town until three this afternoon but to come out any time after that."

"In that case, my boy," the Major said to me, "I suggest we waste no time. Because as soon as our banker friend discovers that Horsley did not have a faro layout here at the hotel last night and in fact has never had one, he's bound to realize that everything from our interest in that disaster of a building to meeting Carol on the road to the faro room was simply a setup to get him to pay $5000 on a worthless check. And discretion would seem to dictate that we be a long way from here when that moment of truth hits him."

The Long Arm of the Law

The girl at the receptionist's desk looked over at me for perhaps the tenth time. "I'm sure someone else could help you," she said, "if—" She let her voice trail off. What she wanted, of course, was for me to tell her why I was there, but she was too well trained to come right out and ask. And, of course, I wasn't going to volunteer anything either. I shook my head.

"I'll wait," I said, and went back to watching the Major and Drexler through the glassed-in top to Drexler's office. The interview seemed to be going well. At least the Major was smiling, and Drexler for his part didn't look unhappy. Finally they both rose, shook hands across the desk, and the Major came out alone. He was a short, barrel-chested man with a square ruddy face, full gray mustache, and close-cropped hair, and as he strode past he gave me a brief, uncurious glance. I waited until he was well clear, then turned back to the receptionist.

"All right," I said, "now I'll talk to your Mr. Drexler."

She gave me a quick nervous smile, then scurried back to Drexler's office. I couldn't blame her; I would have scurried too if someone identifying himself as a special agent for the Federal Bureau of Investigation had just spent half the morning waiting for my boss.

Drexler spent a long time comparing my face with the photo on my I.D. He was a small slightly built man in his mid-60s with a pinch-featured face and thinning hair of no particular color. His suit was a wrinkled blue that would have been equally out of style any time after the 1930s.

Appearances aren't always deceiving, of course. But this time they were. If you went by his tax returns, he was worth well over $500,000, not to mention the assets of the bank he controlled. And if you could believe the rumors, he had at least twice that much squirreled away in lockboxes and negotiable securities that the Internal Revenue Service had never heard about.

Now, finally satisfied, he passed back my card. "This is something of an honor," he said. "Or is it? We don't usually see much of the F.B.I. around these parts."

I smiled. "I don't imagine you usually see much of people like Henry T. McDonlevy either," I said.

Drexler looked up cautiously. "What about Major McDonlevy?" he said.

"Nothing," I said. "except that he just happens to be one of the slickest con artists operating today. I know he doesn't look it, but three years ago he and a younger man named Tom James made over $20,000 in a phony land giveaway in Michigan. Shortly after that they took a Cincinnati banker for another $5,000 in a switch on the old faro-bank scam. Then they dropped out of sight. God knows where Tom James is, but six months ago the Major popped up again in Evansville with a fake stock offering. I've been on his trail ever since."

"I'm surprised you haven't arrested him."

"I wish I could," I said. "But knowing and proving are two different things. It's a rare man who'd be willing to get up and testify that he's been foolish and greedy and maybe a little bit dishonest as well. Not in open court anyway. That's why I changed my tactics and decided *not* to wait until after the victim had been stung."

"I see," Drexler said. He pursed his lips and stared thoughtfully at the wall. "Well, anyway," he said at last, "I thank you for the warning. You can rest assured I'll be extremely cautious in any future dealings with the Major."

I shook my head. "That's exactly what I *don't* want," I said. "I want you to go along with him."

Drexler raised his eyebrows and looked me full in the face. "To trap him, I suppose," he said.

"Exactly," I said, "and because it would be a trap you could testify to afterwards with no stigma."

Drexler nodded slightly. "So I could," he said, "if I chose to involve myself. On the other hand, the occasion might never arise. Ordinarily I don't discuss bank business with third parties. In this case, however, I don't mind telling you that Major McDonlevy is primarily interested in obtaining some land west of the city and is looking to the bank for help in financing the purchase. Whether or not we make the loan is largely dependent on the value of the security—in this case, the land itself. I know the area, and values are appreciating. So, frankly, I don't see how the bank could lose even if he were to default.—Of course," he added drily, "what the Major does with the property once he's acquired it is no concern of mine or the bank's."

"You mean you won't cooperate?" I said.

"I didn't say that," Drexler said. He made an irritable gesture with his hand. "I'm to meet McDonlevy for lunch tomorrow, then go out to inspect the property. If it develops that he does plan to bilk me in some way, well, then it will be my pleasure to see him behind bars. On the other hand"—he shrugged—"anyone else, it's their problem. Understood?"

"Perfectly," I said.

For a traveling man there was only one place in town for lunch and that was the Elk's Club. It was open to the public and crowded at noon, but a bill slipped to the waiter gave me a table within earshot of Drexler and the Major.

"Actually," the Major was saying as I settled in, "I could get by with only three of the lots. However, I try to guide my life by the Good Book, and so naturally I need the surrounding lots as well."

Drexler looked at him curiously. "I'm not sure I see the connection," he said.

"Love thy neighbor," the Major said. He smiled ingenuously. "I find it easier if I can insure he isn't competitive."

"Yes," Drexler said, "very wise." He looked down at his plate. "I don't think you've ever said, though, just what you have in mind."

"Haven't I? It's no secret, of course. Actually—" He stopped as a slight disturbance broke out nearby. A large harried-looking man had come in and was expostulating with a waiter. Moments later, followed by the now frowning waiter, the large man headed straight for the Major's table.

"It was this one," he said. "I know it." The waiter tried to shush him but he was already addressing Drexler and the Major. "You gentlemen didn't happen to find a wallet, did you? I had it here. I know I did because I paid with a credit card. But when I got back to the hotel—"

The Major leaned back in his chair and regarded the stranger evenly. "Perhaps we did find something," he said. "If it's yours I'm sure you won't mind describing it."

The stranger's face brightened. "Of course," he said. "It's a wallet. I said that, though, didn't I?" He tapped his jacket over his heart. "Breast pocket type. Brown leather."

"Any initials?"

"L.G.A.," the stranger said. "For Lester G. Arnold. Inside there was $51 plus credit cards."

The Major glanced over at Drexler and nodded. "I think that's sufficient," he said. He took a flat wallet from his jacket and handed it over to Arnold. "It was on the chair when we came in," he explained. "We were going to turn it over to the cashier when we left. But now, of course, you've saved us the trouble."

"Saved you the trouble?" Arnold said. He laughed a short barking laugh and sat down uninvited. The waiter gave him one last frowning look, but at the Major's nod the waiter drifted away.

"I was the one who was saved," Arnold said. "And I don't mean just the money either. I owe you a lot and I'm going to make it up to you."

"That's hardly necessary," the Major said.

"I think it is," Arnold said. "No, I mean it. I won't insult you by offering you money, but—well—is either of you a betting man?"

Drexler shook his head. "No," he said flatly.

"Well, I am," Arnold said. "I came to town for the races, and won't let you stop me. Part of whatever I bet this afternoon goes down for you. How about it?"

Drexler looked over at the Major who shrugged. "I suppose," the Major said, "if it would make you feel better—"

"It would," Arnold said earnestly. "Believe me, it would."

From where I sat it was impossible to judge Drexler's reaction. But the Major's was obvious. He sat back and smiled indulgently. Then, while they were exchanging introductions, I signaled the waiter I was ready to order.

Later that evening Drexler called me at my hotel, after he and the Major had returned from their inspection trip.

"I'm afraid it's beginning to look as if you may be right," he said.

"I thought you would feel that way," I said, "after that little act that was put on in the restaurant this afternoon."

"Yes," Drexler said. "That was an interesting coincidence. Even more interesting. Arnold called me not half an hour ago. It seems he won $100 for me today."

"You didn't expect him to lose, did you?"

"No," Drexler said, "I suppose not. However, Arnold has now offered me the option of taking the $100 or going with him to the track tomorrow to build it higher. Ordinarily I'd take the money, but under the circumstances it might be more interesting to go to the track and see what develops. I thought you might like to come along."

I smiled happily. "You better believe it," I said.

The ages were right; so Drexler introduced me as his nephew when Arnold came to pick him up the next afternoon.

"I hope you don't mind my asking the boy along," Drexler said.

"No, of course not," Arnold said. He turned to me. "Is this your first time too?"

"I'm afraid so," I said.

"Nothing to be ashamed of," Arnold said. "Everybody has to start sometime. And if I may say so myself, you and your uncle couldn't have picked a better teacher."

"I'm sure of it," I murmured.

Arnold let it pass, but the Major frowned. "I've seen you before, haven't I?" he said.

I nodded. "Probably at the bank," I said. "I was waiting for my uncle one day when you had business there."

"Of course!" The frown disappeared and we all went down to Arnold's car.

"There is one thing I ought to clear up," Arnold said as we got in. "We aren't going to the track itself."

"But you said—" Drexler began

"I know what I said. I said we were going to the races. And we are. The smart way." And he put the car in gear and started off.

It was a short ride, down through town and out to the fringes of the business district. Wholesalers predominated here and most of the buildings were closed for the weekend; but Arnold led the way to an unmarked side door, then up a short flight of steps and down a corridor to a second door, also unmarked. Inside was nothing less than an old-fashioned horse parlor complete with a wall blackboard and a cluster of desks festooned with telephones which rang incessantly.

"By George," the Major said, "I didn't think there were places like this anymore."

"Just a few," Arnold said smugly. He got us installed in chairs facing the one concession to changing times—a large TV set high up on one wall. Then he went to place his bets. When he came back, he looked even more like a proverbial cat. "All set," he said.

"What happens now?" Drexler said.

"We wait," Arnold said. He looked at his watch. "It shouldn't be long. If you'd like something to eat—or drink—there's a bar."

Drexler shook his head. "No," he said and folded his arms and settled back to watch the blank TV. A number of others drifted in to take places behind us and occasionally one of the desk men would come over to replace one set of numbers on the blackboard with another. Then finally the TV set switched on.

The horses were already lined up in the gate, the camera looking almost straight down at them.

"Closed circuit," Arnold whispered. "You can't get anything like this kind of view anywhere at the track."

A bell rang and the horses were off and running.

"Keep your eye on number three," Arnold said. "That's ours."

At the moment the horse was well back in the pack, but just before the far turn it began to move and after that there was no contest. It pulled ahead and stayed there, finishing a good three lengths ahead of its nearest competitor.

"By George!" the Major said. "We won."

"Of course," Arnold said calmly. He got out his copy of *Racing Form*. "Now in the next one," he said, "the one to watch is number six. King's Only."

Some of those behind us had got up and gone over to the desks to lay fresh bets. When Arnold didn't move, Drexler looked at him curiously. "Aren't you betting?" he said.

"Already take care of," Arnold said. "We'll just keep on parlaying our winnings."

"But suppose we lose?"

"We won't," Arnold said.

And they didn't. King's Only won in a romp. So did Raintree in the third and every other horse Arnold had picked. At the end of the seventh, though—a cliffhanger which saw a 5-to-1 outsider come galloping out of the pack at the last minute to streak across the finish line a nose ahead of the favorite—he folded his *Racing Form* and leaned back in his chair with an air of heavy finality.

"That's it for me," he said. "You two can take a fling on your own if you like, but I'm through for the day."

The Major hesitated. By now his stake—and Drexler's—had grown to $2500 each. Finally he shrugged. "No point in being greedy," he said. "How about it, Drexler? Shall we call it quits too?"

Drexler nodded slowly. "I see no reason to go on," he said. His eyes were small and thoughtful.

The trouble came as they were cashing in. One of the desk men took Drexler's and the Major's receipts and carefully counted out $2200 for each of them.

"You're $300 short," Drexler said sharply.

The desk man shrugged. "Service charge," he said.

The Major began to sputter. "I never heard of such a thing!" he said

"House rule," the desk man said. He picked up Arnold's receipts, looked at them for a long moment, then rose wordlessly and went through a doorway behind him. He was gone a few minutes and when he came back he was accompanied by a stocky balding man in shirt sleeves.

"That's the one, Mr. Gunderson," the desk man said, pointing to Arnold.

The stocky man looked at Arnold balefully. He held the stub of a cigar in one hand and Arnold's receipts in the other. "You won a lot of money from me these last couple of days, friend," he said, trying hard to sound indifferent and not quite succeeding.

Gunderson shook his head. "Not at all," he said, "if it's on the up and up. The problem is you did it all on credit and when I checked with the guys who recommended you, he said he couldn't vouch for you beyond a couple of hundred bucks." He cocked his head to one side and looked at Arnold suspiciously. "You went in way over your head, friend. What would have happened if you lost?"

"I would have paid up," Arnold said.

"Would you?" Gunderson said. "Well, suppose I gave you a chance to prove it. I don't mind paying off a couple of small bills on spec, but when somebody nicks me for $75,000 I like to know he's as serious about his end as I am about mine." He turned to the desk man. "What was his last bet?"

"$15,000."

"$15,000," Gunderson repeated, savoring it. He turned back to Arnold. "All right," he said, "this is what you're going to do if you want me to pay off. Cover the bet. Show me you've got $15,000. In cash."

Arnold swallowed hard. "You'll have to give me a couple of days—" he began.

"I'll give you nothing," Gunderson said. "I'll stop by your hotel after we close tonight. If you've got the money, fine. If not"—he stuffed the receipts into Arnold's breast pocket—"you can use these to paper your wall."

"You can't do this!" Arnold protested.

"Sue me," Gunderson said and turned on his heel to go back through the doorway through which he had come. The desk man just looked at Arnold dispassionately.

The Major was literally trembling with anger, but he held himself in until we were back in the hallway. "This is outrageous," he sputtered. "The man's no better than a thief."

Arnold shrugged despondently. "Sure," he said. "But I haven't got any muscle and he knows it."

"Good lord, man, you can't just give up. Call his bluff. Show him the $15,000. It would ruin him if he welshed then."

"I wish I could," Arnold said. "The trouble is I don't have the $15,000."

"Then you *were* betting money you didn't have."

"Of course," Arnold said. "In my place you would have done the same. Because for the first time in my life I had the real straight stuff. Those races were fixed. I couldn't lose—it was a sure thing." He managed a wry smile. "Or so it seemed."

The Major looked down at his hands, obviously embarrassed. "I'd help you if I could," he said, "and you're welcome to the $2200, of course. But, unfortunately, the bulk of my money is still tied up in the east."

"I'd make it worth your while," Arnold said. "You wouldn't have to lend me the money. Just show it to Gunderson and I'll cut you in for a full third. $25,000."

The Major continued to study his hands. Drexler glanced over at me. I gave him the faintest of perceptible nods. "I think we can work something out," Drexler said drily.

"I don't suppose by any chance it could be true," Drexler said. It was later and we were alone in Arnold's car on our way to pick up the money, Arnold and the Major having dropped off at their request to wait at Arnold's hotel in case Gunderson showed up early.

"You 'don't suppose' right," I said. "In the first place, horse parlors like that went out with World War Two. And even back then nobody but nobody was allowed to bet large amounts on spec until his credit had been checked out thoroughly."

"And yet he was able to pick the winners."

"Sure," I said. "In the old days there would have been a man on the other side of the wall with a microphone tied into a radio. Now all you have to do is set up a TV to play back a tape of an earlier race. You'll notice they were careful *not* to let us hear the start when the date and place would have been announced."

"That simple," Drexler murmured.

"It usually is," I said. "People like Arnold and the Major count on greed doing most of the work for them. Their next step most likely is to inveigle you into joining Arnold for a bet that will really take Gunderson for a bundle—which, of course, will lose."

"I see," Drexler said. "And if I don't play along?"

"Then we'll have done all this for nothing."

"Not quite," Drexler said. "I'll still have $2200 of their money."

"Look again," I said. "I think you'll find it's slush, funny money—counterfeit."

Drexler smiled bleakly. "They don't leave anything to chance, do they?"

"They try not to," I said. "But you've got a couple of things going for you that put you way ahead of them. One: you know what they're up to."

"And two?"

"Me," I said.

"Yes," Drexler admitted. He didn't say anything more until we reached his house. It was a large rambling structure half overgrown with ivy and surrounded by a high stone wall. All I saw of the inside was the ground-floor sitting room Drexler parked me in while he went off into the rear of the house. When we returned he was carrying a slim brown-leather attaché case.

"I imagine you'll want to count this," he said, "unless, of course, you're prepared to give me a receipt on my word alone."

"A receipt?"

"Of course," Drexler said. He smiled faintly. "This is your plan. I'm merely going along as a good citizen. And like a good citizen I expect the government to reimburse me if anything goes wrong."

He held out the case. I took it reluctantly. "You don't leave much to chance yourself either, do you?" I said.

"Not a thing," Drexler said and watched as I counted. There was $10,600 inside, just enough to bring the $4400 he and the Major had won to $15,000. I put the money back in the case and, using the case as a desk, wrote out Drexler's receipt. He accepted it gravely.

"If you don't mind," he said, "I'll just put this away in my safe and then we can be on our way."

"Whatever you say," I agreed. "I'll wait for you in the car." And I went outside, taking the attaché case with me. A few minutes later Drexler joined me, and we drove back downtown.

The Major was alone in Arnold's room when we got to the hotel.

"Where's Arnold?" I said.

"Downstairs. Didn't you see him?"

"No."

The Major frowned. "Gunderson was here," he said, "and when Arnold couldn't produce the cash he called off all bets. Arnold went down with him, hoping they'd run into you on the way. You must have just missed each other."

"What happens now?" Drexler said.

"I don't know," the Major said. "Perhaps—"

He never finished. The door opened and Arnold came in. He looked bitter—and angry. "Damn!" he said. "There you are."

"Gunderson wouldn't wait?" the Major said.

"Not a single damn minute," Arnold said. "But he hasn't seen anything yet! If he thinks he was stung today—" He broke off and looked around at the three of us. "How about it?" he said. "Are you still with me? Shall we *really* take him?"

Drexler regarded him calmly. "That would depend on what you have in mind," he said.

Arnold nodded. "There's a horse running tomorrow," he said. "Pleasant Fancy. If you look at *Racing Form* you'll see he's lost his last five starts. Not a good record at all, but what the *Form* doesn't show is that he was deliberately overmatched. It's an old trick that owners use to run the odds up. Then they race the horse well below his class, where he's sure to win, and bet as heavy as they can. Tomorrow the odds on Pleasant Fancy will go at least as high as 15-to-1, and the owner's set for a killing. We'll have to spread the bets out—maybe even hire a few stooges to place some for us to keep Gunderson from getting wise—but with $15,000 we can take him for over $200,000 easy." He looked directly at Drexler. "What do you say?"

Drexler's eyelids drooped slightly; then he nodded. "All right," he said.

Later, after the details of where and when we'd meet the next day had been worked out, Drexler and I rode down together in the elevator. If I hadn't still been holding the attaché case, I would have been rubbing my hands together gleefully.

"You don't mind going home alone, do you?" I said.

"Why? Where are you going?"

"To see the local police," I said, "and set up a raid on that 'bookie joint' now that I know it wasn't dismantled the minute we left. Plus arrange to have our good friends upstairs picked up." I handed him the attaché case. "We won't be needing this anymore," I said. "The TV setup plus your testimony should carry it from here. Especially after we pick up a tape showing Pleasant Fancy losing."

Drexler nodded, then, true to form, opened the case to check the money inside. By then, though, we'd reached the lobby and he had time for only a quick look before the elevator door slid open. The sight of money inside was enough to reassure him, so he closed the case with a decisive snap.

"You can count it when you get home," I suggested.

The sarcasm was lost on him. "Yes," he said.

"And while you're at it," I added, "don't forget to tear up that receipt I gave you."

This time he did smile. "Yes," he said again. "Of course."

I saw him safely in a taxi, then went down to where the car was parked, tipped the boy I'd asked to watch it, and drove back to the hotel. The Major and Arnold were waiting by the rear entrance. I pulled over to let them in the car.

"Where's the money?" Arnold said.

"In the trunk compartment," I said. "Where it's safe."

"I take it then," the Major said, leaning back comfortably, "you had no trouble making the switch."

"None at all," I said. "Drexler wouldn't put up the money without a receipt, then made the mistake of leaving me alone while he put the receipt in his safe."

"Very good," the Major said. "Very good indeed, but now I suggest we follow the Good Book once more and shake the dust of this town. I don't think it will remain so hospitable once our friend Mr. Drexler finds out that he's carried home only a small fraction of the money on top of stacks of cut paper—and realizes that his favorite F.B.I. man is none other than the Tom James he was so carefully warned against."

Sufficient Unto the Day

The girl at the receptionist's desk would have made a good model. At least she had the long slim lines and bony facial structure. Also the faintly aloof air.

"Yes?"

"Would you be so kind," the Major said, "as to tell Mr. Porterfield that Major McDonlevy and Mr. James are here to see him?"

The girl's expression didn't change. "Do you have an appointment?"

"Not exactly," the Major said, "but I believe he is expecting us."

"I'll see," the girl said. She rose langorously and went back through the door to the inner office, closing it behind her.

The Major looked around and rubbed his hands together briskly. "Very impressive," he said, "wouldn't you say?"

"The girl?"

"No, I meant the office." He smiled suddenly. He was a short man—barely five foot five—with a barrel chest, square ruddy face neatly bisected by a full gray mustache, and a bristle of close-cropped hair the same iron-gray color. Only his eyes didn't fit the military image. They were very blue and ingenuous—most of the time. "Although I must admit the girl does have her points as well. Nevertheless, I think you'll find that in this business it pays to keep your mind on the essentials."

"I'll try," I said, "but at the moment it seems to me that the really essential thing would be to get some money coming in."

"Of course," the Major said. "But then to make money is why we're here. I showed you the ad, didn't I?"

I nodded. The Major had met Porterfield earlier that week as a result of an ad that Porterfield had been running in the local papers offering investors an opportunity to double their money in 30 days. Even if we'd had money to invest, it still would have been too good to be true and I said as much now.

"Of course, my boy," the Major said, "but that's precisely what makes it so interesting." He broke off as the inner door opened. "Ah," he said, "and now unless I'm mistaken here's the young lady come back to tell us Mr. Porterfield will see us." He smiled beamingly at the girl. She looked expressionlessly back.

"You can go right in," she said.

Porterfield was a tall heavy-set man in his mid-to-late-fifties with a tanned, craggy face and tight curly hair just beginning to go gray. He went well with the office, which was large, carpeted, and paneled in dark expensive-looking oak. The back wall was lined with bookshelves except for the far right corner where space had been left for a door to the outside corridor. Porterfield rose easily now as the Major and I came in.

"Ah, Mr. McDonlevy," he said. "Good to see you again."

"Actually," the Major said, advancing into the room, "it's *Major* McDonlevy. Major Henry T. McDonlevy to be precise, U.S. Army—and, if I may say so myself, the world's greatest adjutant until some bureaucratic mixup in Washington forced my retirement. Not that it matters any more, but I do like to have these things straight."

"Yes, of course," Porterfield said. He seemed slightly taken aback, but the Major went on imperviously.

"I was just telling Tom here," he said, sitting down and crossing his short legs, "how much I admired your office. Makes me almost wish I wasn't such a rolling stone. Still," he added almost regretfully, "I suppose there are advantages."

"There are advantages to everything, Major," Porterfield said, back in charge of himself and again exuding heartiness. "It's just a matter of availing yourself of them."

The Major looked at him curiously. "You know," he said, "that was just the point I was going to make to Tom."

"Good," Porterfield said. "That means we see eye to eye. I take it that it also means you've decided to come in with us."

The Major cleared his throat. "I wouldn't say 'decided,'" he said. "I try to guide my life by the Good Book and where money is concerned I find it pays to be 'slow of speech, and of a slow tongue' until all the facts are in. Besides, I'd like Tom here to hear the proposition as well."

"Of course," Porterfield said. He paused, then rose as a light rap sounded on the outer door. "That must be Barnes now," he said. "I took the liberty of calling him when the girl told me you were here. He's the one you want to talk to anyway, because it's really more his project than anybody else's." He opened the door to admit a tall sallow-complexioned man. "Ah, Carl," Porterfield said, "you're just in time. This is Major McDonlevy—the man I told you about—and his associate, Mr.—ah?"

"James," I said. "Tom James."

Barnes gave me a limp hand, nodded distantly, then sat down across from the Major. "Arthur tells me you're interested in our little project."

"Shall we say I'm interested in considering it," the Major said. "I won't know whether I'm really interested until I know more about it."

"Fair enough," Barnes said. He was older than Porterfield and angular where the younger man was inclined to paunch. "What's Arthur told you so far, Major?"

"Only that you have what promises to be a highly profitable land speculation."

"Hardly a speculation, Major," Barnes said. "Or a promise. A fact. I travel a lot in my work, checking out potential factory sites primarily for eventual purchase or lease. It takes me to a lot of interesting places and into a lot of interesting records. That's only by way of background. The important thing is that in tracing down a title recently I came upon a situation of, shall we say, more than passing interest.

"It seems that about fifteen years ago a New York businessman named Elton Peters bought a tract of marshland in northern Indiana. The land was considered worthless and maybe it was. Peters' idea, however, was to turn it into a private sporting club and duck blind which he and his friends could use any time they wanted. Before he could bring it off, though, he was killed in one of those freak accidents the National Rifle Association says can't happen to experienced hunters but somehow seem to anyway.

"Be that as it may, his idea died with him. I imagine the attorney for his estate made some effort to sell the land, but found no takers for what was little better than a swamp and ended up writing the whole thing off as a dead loss. Loss or no, though, title passed to Peters' sole heir, a nephew, who still owns it.

"He wasn't hard to track down. He'd moved several times, but there's always a neighbor who remembers or a cousin who's kept in touch and one thing just leads to another. In any case, he lives in New Jersey and he thinks the possibility of finally getting some money out of 'Uncle's swamp' is the greatest joke in the world. What he doesn't know is that three years ago the river that fed the marsh shifted its course and as a result his 'swamp' is dry as a bone and worth at least four or five times what he thinks it is."

The Major shifted in his chair. "By George," he said, "I see what you mean about its not being speculation. Even if the deal falls through, all you stand to lose is your time."

"That's right," Barnes said. "At the worst we get our money back less maybe a few hundred for expenses. At the best, we make a four- or five-hundred percent profit—again less maybe a few hundred for expenses."

The Major smiled broadly. "Well," he said, "under the circumstances I don't see how I could possibly refuse. How much do you need?"

"$30,000," Barnes said.

"Thirty—"

"That's the total amount, Major," Porterfield put in smoothly. "Obviously no one of us has that kind of capital—otherwise why would we need partners?"

"Of course," the Major said. He seemed relieved.

"How much *can* you put up, Major?" Barnes said.

The Major shifted under his gaze. "Well," he said. He looked over at me. "Well, I think we could manage $5000. Yes, definitely, $5000."

"And that's all?" Barnes said. "Porterfield and I are putting up $10,000 each. We expected you'd be able at least to match that."

"Well, obviously I would if I could," the Major said. "Maximize the profits and all that. But I'm afraid $5000 is the most we could go."

Barnes shook his head. "I'm sorry, Major," he said.

"Oh, come now," the Major said. "What difference does it make how much each of us invests, since naturally we take our profits only in the same proportion."

Barnes continued to shake his head. "It's not that simple," he said. "I have another man on the string who will have the full $10,030 by the middle of next week. He won't settle for half. And there's no reason I should have to, because the only reason we considered you is that we thought you'd have the money now, and obviously the sooner we act the better." He shrugged. "A bird in the hand's always worth two in the bush, but all you can offer really is half a bird."

"Maybe the Major knows someone who'd be willing to take the second half," Porterfield said.

Now it was the Major's turn to shake his head. "I'm afraid my only other contact in town is the desk clerk at my hotel and really doubt he'd have that much money even if he were the type to put it up."

"I doubt it too," Barnes said. "I'm sorry, Major, but you can see my position."

"I feel bad about this," Porterfield said. "I really should have—" He broke off as the phone behind him rang. With a muttered "excuse me" he swung around to pick it up. "I thought I said I didn't want to be disturbed," he said into the receiver.... "I see ... No, I'd better talk to him." He looked over at the three of us and made an apologetic face, then spoke back into the receiver: "Yes, O'Connor?... It's here *now?*... No, no problem ... Yes, of course. This afternoon ... Yes, I understand."

He put the phone back down and sat silently for a moment, biting his lip. Barnes looked at him curiously. "Something wrong, Arthur?" he said.

Porterfield pulled himself back together with a start. "No," he said. He managed a smile. "Nothing I can't work out anyway."

"Good," Barnes said. He rose and turned to the Major. "I don't think there's really anything more to discuss," he said. "It's just one of those things. Too bad."

The Major nodded slowly. "I suppose," he said. "You will keep us in mind, though, in case this other man can't come up with the money either?"

Barnes smiled wryly. "It's hardly likely," he said. "But if it makes you feel better, sure." He nodded to Porterfield. "I'll be talking to you later, Arthur," he said and went out the same door he had come in by.

There was a short strained silence. Then the Major started rise. Porterfield waved him back. "Don't be in such a hurry, Major," he said. "Maybe we can work something out yet."

"How so?" the Major said. "You heard the man. He won't give."

"No," Porterfield said. "But maybe I will. How would you like to buy half of my share? Even-steven. For $5000, cash on the line."

The Major looked at him thoughtfully. "I wouldn't mind that at all," he said. "The question is, though, why would you want to sell?"

"And the answer is I wouldn't if I had any choice. The fact is, though, that not too long ago I took a big plunge. Without going into details, what I've done essentially is extend the franchising concept to the small manufacturing area. It's a wide-open field, and in the long run it will pay off handsomely. For the short run—well, all new businesses need lots of capital and frankly I was stretched pretty thin even before Barnes came up with his proposition. But—well, four-hundred percent profit. There was just no way I could turn that down."

"No," the Major said, "of course not."

"Anyway," Porterfield said, "to come up with the money I did what I had to. Nothing desperate, of course. I didn't embezzle or steal. But I did cut a few corners here and there."

"Like what?" I said.

"Well, for one thing I found I could buy industrial diamonds—which the franchises use in their cutting tools—for a quarter the price I'd pay here if I bought in Holland. So I arranged through a mutual friend for an airlines crewman to pick them up for me whenever he made a run to Amsterdam. The problem is he's here now—a good two weeks before I expected him. And since the deal is strictly cash and carry, I either pay up and take delivery this afternoon before his return flight or I lose the shipment, which I can't afford because it would mean reneging on the contract and forfeiting at least some of the franchises."

"I see," the Major said. He looked even more thoughtful. "I hate to profit by another man's misfortune," he said, "but on the other hand—"

"On the other hand," Porterfield finished for him, "you're a fool if you pass up the opportunity. Don't worry about it. In your place I'd do the same thing. The important thing is, are you willing to do it? And how fast can you put your hands on your money? Because there isn't much time to spare."

"Well," the Major said slowly, "I'd have to go to the bank—half an hour, say. Forty-five minutes at the most."

Porterfield bit his lip again. "That's cutting it pretty close," he said. "To be on the safe side, rather than come back here, you'd better take the money directly out to the airport. I'd go with you but I have to stay here in case O'Connor calls back."

"Of course," the Major said. "May I ask how we will recognize him?"

"No problem," Porterfield said. He rose and went to his coat closet to get out a brown-leather attaché case. "You carry the money in this," he said. "Then when you get to the airport, go to the newsstand in the international terminal, pick up a newspaper, and stand in front pretending to read it with the case on the floor beside you. O'Connor will contact you there. He'll have an identical case which he'll set down beside yours while he asks the dealer for an out-of-town paper—the *Louisville Courier Journal.* That's your cue to pick up his case and casually stroll off, leaving him yours with the money."

He paused as I frowned. "Something the matter, Mr. James?" he said.

"Yeah," I said. "Why all the rigamarole?"

Porterfield smiled self-consciously. "I suppose it does sound a little cloak-and-daggerish," he said, "but better that than risking some alert customs agent spotting an out-and-out exchange."

"Customs agent! You mean these diamonds are being smuggled in?"

"Of course," Porterfield said. "I thought you realized that."

"No," I said, "I didn't ."

The Major cleared his throat. "Ah," he said, "I think perhaps I did. Not that it makes any difference, though. In for a penny, in for a pound, eh?"

"That's the spirit, Major," Porterfield said. He held out the briefcase. The Major took it.

Later as we were riding down in the elevator, I said, "I hope you know what you're doing."

The Major smiled. "I haven't let you down yet, my boy, have I?"

"No," I admitted. "But isn't there something in that Good Book that you're so fond of quoting about there always being a first time?"

He looked at me blankly. "Not that I'm aware of," he said.

It was fairly crowded at the airport, but even so I had little difficulty staking out a spot near the newsstand to wait—or recognizing O'Connor when he appeared. He was a small sharp-faced man wearing a dark double-breasted jacket and matching trousers that suggested a uniform without quite being one. True to Porter-field's word he was carrying a brown attaché case that was at least a close match for mine if not exactly identical. He set it down about two feet from my own case while he browsed at the counter.

I hesitated even after I heard him ask for the Louisville paper, then, remembering the Major's "in for a penny, in for a pound," picked his case up and walked off. I didn't look back even when the commotion broke out behind me.

Porterfield's secretary wasn't at her desk when I got back to his office, but after a moment Porterfield himself came out to greet me. He looked at me curiously. "Didn't the Major come with you?" he said.

I shook my head. "No, he decided this was one of those times when two is a crowd."

"I see," Porterfield said. "I don't suppose it really matters. Everything went all right at the airport, didn't it?"

I shrugged. "I got this," I said and handed him the attaché case.

Porterfield looked at it lovingly. "Well, now," he said, taking a key from his pocket, "let's just check this out."

I'd discovered it was locked on the way back from the airport. Not that it mattered. What was or wasn't in it was his problem, not mine. Before he could open it, though, the door burst open and his secretary rushed in, flushed and out of breath.

"Thank goodness I got here in time," she said. "I was down in the lobby just now on my coffee break and I saw two men follow Mr. James in. I think they're police. At least I heard them talking and one said he'd call back to headquarters for instructions. I took a chance and followed him. Their car's got government plates."

"Oh, God!" Porterfield said. "They must have spotted O'Connor coming through customs and followed him to you and now from you to me." He turned away and shook his head as if lost. "I don't know what to say," he said. "It's all over."

"There has to be *something* we can do," the girl insisted. "All they know is Mr. James came in the building. They don't know he came *here.* Maybe if he got away—"

Porterfield shook his head again. "It wouldn't make any difference," he said. "O'Connor will give them my name to save himself. But," he added suddenly, turning back to me, "she's right about one thing. You can get away. O'Connor doesn't know you or your name. They're looking for me. And these." He rattled the briefcase. "You can slip out the back while they come in the front and be home free."

"What about the money? Our $5000?"

"Cry over it later," Porterfield said. "It's gone. The important thing, though, is for you to get out of this now while you have the chance and put as much distance between yourself and this town as you can."

"Sure," I said. "You tell me how." I sat down and shrugged despondently. "I knew this was bound to happen. Sooner or later. But he always knew better. Not this time, though."

"James," Porterfield said, "you don't seem to understand—"

"No," I said, "*you* don't understand. That $5000 wasn't just investment money. It was every cent we had in the world." I smiled bitterly. "The Major figured we could live on bluff and prospects until Barnes's scheme paid off. But now"—I shrugged again—"we owe the hotel. Restaurant charges. Bar tabs. You name it. If we try to duck out, there'll be five kinds of warrants out for us before you can say boo. So I might as well take my chances here. Federal prisons are supposed to be better than State anyway."

Porterfield glanced at his secretary. "You know what to do," he said. "Stall them." He turned back to me. "I got you into this," he said, "I'll get you out of it. Come with me. For God's sake, man, don't just sit there. Come with me!"

I got up then and followed him into his office while the girl stayed behind. Porterfield kicked the door shut, then rummaged in a cabinet for his cash box, unlocked it, and counted out some bills.

"Here," he said.

It looked to be about $100. I shook my head. "What do you think I am?" I said. "Besides, that won't cover two days at the hotel. We owe for two weeks."

"I'm not paying your debts," Porterfield said. "I'm giving you head-start money. Now take it."

I still shook my head. Outside a loud pounding broke out on the door to the reception area. Porterfield hesitated, then scooped the rest of the bills from the box and thrust them into my pocket. "There," he said. "That's all the cash I have in the office. Over $700. Now get out of here and get moving!" He shoved me out the rear door and slammed it behind me.

I looked up and down the corridor. Seeing it empty in both directions, I cut across to the door marked STAIRS, walked down two flights, then rode the elevator the rest of the way. Nobody paid the slightest attention to me...

The Major was waiting in the car half a block away. "Ah, my boy," he said as I got in, "how did it go?"

"Just the way you expected," I said. "The police showed up right on my heels. When I didn't panic, Porterfield did."

"I knew he would," the Major said. "He had no choice. But never mind that now. How much did you get?"

I took the bills from my pocket and counted them. "The son of a gun," I said. "There's only $500 here. He said there was seven."

The Major smiled. "I knew the man wasn't to be trusted," he said. "And hardly a major score in either event. But on the other hand, as the Good Book would have it, 'Sufficient unto the day.' Agreed?"

I nodded. "I don't suppose," I added after a moment, "there's any possibility there really were diamonds in that case."

"No more than there was real money in the one you carried out," the Major said. "I'm afraid, my boy, our friend Mr. Porterfield and his associates are working a modernized version of the old Country Send. And actually it's not a bad little scheme as schemes go. Only a saint could resist snapping at that bait. The only problem is what to do with your mark after he's hit.

"The ideal solution, of course, is not to be there when the sucker returns with his supposedly valuable purchase. Unfortunately, that option is open only to us rolling stones. If you have an expensive office to protect, the only feasible alternative, short of murder, is the old cops-at-the-door routine to panic the mark into running. And that, as I think even Porterfield will agree, has certain disadvantages—although for the moment at least I'm sure he feels $500 a small price to pay for the $5000 he expects to receive."

"Sure," I said. "The only thing I don't understand, though, is why O'Connor didn't call him from the airport to warn him our briefcase was only full of cut paper."

The Major cleared his throat. "That, my boy, is why I wasn't able to accompany you. After you left the newsstand I—shall we say inadvertently?—collided with O'Connor. It created quite a disturbance then and an even larger one a few moments later when I discovered my wallet was missing." His blue eyes twinkled ingenuously. "I'm afraid O'Connor has been tied up ever since explaining to the police how it happened to get into his pocket. And now if you don't mind, to avoid further complications I suggest we do what Porterfield couldn't—take the money and run."

Never Play Another Man's Game

French Lick Springs is a quiet little town set in the rolling Indiana countryside some 35 miles west of Louisville. Back in the early years of the century it had quite a reputation as a health spa. But then tastes changed or the mineral springs which had given it its name dried up, and French Lick settled back to its present sleepy existence—but not before somebody, with the prescience of Ford introducing the Edsel, built a sprawling brick hotel to house the hordes the railroad was sure to bring.

For years the hotel was an enormous white elephant. But then finally the Sheraton people took it over, turned it into a resort on the order of the Greenbrier and Homestead in the east, complete with golf course, riding stables, and the rest, and as far as I know made a very good thing out of it. At least, they were doing all right when I was there a few years back, and it was there, of course, that I first ran into Donner—in the literal sense of the word.

I was going up the broad central staircase while he was coming down, head cocked to one side so he could devote full attention to the much shorter, barrel-chested man accompanying him.

"$10,000," he was saying as I approached. "That's top price, Major, and you sure as hell won't do better elsewhere."

"Perhaps not," the Major said, "but the more I think about it, the less sure I am I want to part with it at all."

"Better stop thinking then," Donner said, "because—"

He never finished the sentence, because he became aware of me and ducked back instinctively to avoid a collision that otherwise would have been inevitable. "Watch where you're going," he said. He was a tall, almost lanky man with close-cropped graying hair and a long sleepy-eyed face. There was nothing droopy or sleepy about his voice, though; it was sharp and waspish.

"One of us should," I said mildly.

Donner's eyes narrowed, but then he nodded curtly. "You have a point," he said, and taking his companion by the arm guided him down past me. "Now, Major," he said, "as I was saying about that car—"

A bellman coming down behind them smiled at me ruefully. "You're lucky you caught him in a good mood," he said. "Mr. Donner's nobody to get on the wrong side of."

"Big man around here, is he?"

"Big enough," the bellman said. He looked down at the departing pair. "And I'll tell you another thing," he said. "If that fella with him has something Mr. Donner really wants, he might as well kiss it goodbye now. It won't be long before Donner gets it."

"I'll have to remember that," I said.

The next time was several days later and again it was a case of arriving at the same place at practically the same time—in this instance, the starter's desk at the golf course adjoining the hotel grounds. A balding, pudgy-faced man was with Donner and the Major this time, and since there were three of them and one of me, the starter—following his usual practice—asked if we'd like to play together and make up a foursome.

Donner looked at me quizzically. "I know you from someplace, don't I?"

"The stairway at the hotel," I said. "We nearly knocked each other over."

"So we did," Donner said. "I hope you plan to keep a better lookout today than you did then."

I shrugged. Impudence had paid off before. I gambled it would again. "Frankly," I said, "I was hoping the same about you."

It took him a couple of seconds to make up his mind. Then he laughed. "You've got spunk. I'll say that for you. And who knows? Maybe, for safety's sake, we should play together. My name's Donner. This is Mr. White." He nodded to indicate the pudgy-faced man "And—"

"McDonlevy," the Major said. "Henry T. McDonlevy, late Major United States Army, and if I may say so myself, still the world's greatest living adjutant."

"Frank Harris," I said.

"You have a handicap, Mr. Harris?" Donner said.

"Nothing official," I said, "and this is my first time on this course anyway. But I usually manage to get around most places somewhere between 90 and 100."

"In that case, you don't have to worry about anybody in this group overwhelming you—or vice versa," Donner said. "Now, shall we draw for partners? The two short straws against the two long? Or does somebody have a better idea?"

Nobody did, and the luck of the draw pitted Donner and the Major against White and me. It didn't seem to matter at the time, because

Donner apparently hadn't lied when he said none of us would overwhelm the others, and the first three holes went by uneventfully. On the fourth, though, a long dogleg backed up against a stand of trees and rough ground. White pulled out a long old-fashioned wood and stepped up to address the ball on the tee.

The Major, standing off to one side, folded his arms and frowned. "You surely aren't going to use that heavy a club on this hole, are you?" he said.

White looked at him curiously. "Why not?"

"Because you'll overshoot much too easily—even if you just tap the ball."

White glanced back down the fairway, then shook his head. "Not this boy," he said.

The Major shrugged. "Well, it's your business, of course," he said. "However—" He turned to me. "What do you say, Harris? After all, he's your partner."

"It's his shot," I said, "and his club. He should know what it can do."

"Wouldn't care to bet on that, would you?" the Major said. "Say, $50 to make it interesting."

I hesitated, then stepped over to where White was standing by the tee. "Let me see that club," I said. I hefted it, took a few practise swings, then handed it back. "You have a bet, Major," I said and started back across. As I did so, though, my foot knocked against White's ball, sending it skittering off and down a small incline into a patch of tall grass.

"Damn," I said. "No, wait. I'll get it."

I didn't, though. Nor did five or ten minutes of patient searching by the others turn it up either. Finally I said, "Sorry. I guess I owe you a ball."

White shook his head. "Don't worry about it."

"No, I insist." I dug down into my bag and came up with a ball which I set down on his tee, then stepped back again, careful this time to keep my feet well clear. "Let's see what you can do with that one," I said.

White hesitated, then glanced over at the Major, and after receiving only a slight shrug in response re-addressed the ball and swung. It was as clean a stroke as I've seen in a long time, but the ball rose only in a low arc and even after it hit and rolled barely made it halfway down the green.

I smiled. "Maybe next time," I said, "you'll know better than to judge a club by the size of its head, Major," I said.

"Maybe I will," the Major said. "And since it was my idea to start with, I doubt I should complain at the cost of the lesson. Still, I don't suppose it would be too remiss for me to suggest you give me some chance to get my money back."

"That would depend on what you had in mind," I said.

He shrugged. "A small standing bet," he said. "Say $10 a hole on low team score for the rest of the game."

"Just you and me," I said, "or everybody?"

"Make it everybody," White said. "If we're going to play partners, I'll feel bad if you lose and I don't. I'll feel even worse if you win. How about you, Donner?"

Donner shrugged. "I only feel bad when I lose," he said, "but I'll go along with the group."

Later, though, when we had all played and were trudging down the green to where our balls lay, Donner fell in step beside me. White and the Major were some yards back and out of earshot.

"Maybe I shouldn't have been so quick to get in on this bet," he said.

"Why do you say that?"

"Call it a feeling," he said. "But I wouldn't be at all surprised to find you kicked that ball away on purpose back there so you could ring in one with a dead center."

"And you wouldn't be wrong either," I said. "White couldn't have overshot with my ball if he'd used a rifle. If that bothers you, then I'm sorry, but I learned a long time ago never to let a setup stand or bet another man's game—unless I can change at least one of the givens. As for the rest of the game—well, if it's straight, I'll play it straight. But I'll fight fire with fire every time before I let anybody con me."

"You're sure then that's what they were trying to do?"

I grinned. "Well, maybe not," I said. "But on the other hand I couldn't be sure they weren't either. And there's no harm in playing it safe, now, is there?"

Donner smiled bleakly and continued to walk beside me. He didn't say anything, but I didn't think he disagreed.

Straight game or not, between us White and I managed to win nine of the last fourteen holes so that, far from getting his money back, the

Major ended up more out of pocket than ever. He seemed to accept it gracefully, though.

"As the Good Book, which I find a more than reasonably reliable guide, points out," he said, smiling, "'To everything there is a season.' And while winning and losing aren't specifically mentioned by name, I'm sure they're covered at least by implication."

"Well, implication or not," White said, "today sure wasn't your season to win."

"No," the Major said. "But tomorrow might be. Shall we try it again then for the same stakes? Or higher if you wish."

I shook my head slowly. "I'm sorry," I said. "I wish I could oblige you, but I'm really down here more or less on business."

"Oh?"

"I'm an architect," I explained, "and my company's thinking of submitting a design for a shopping center that some developers are thinking of putting up this side of Louisville. Before they commit themselves, though, they want somebody to go over the specs on the ground, and that's going to keep me tied up for the rest of the week."

"Well, there's always the weekend," the Major said. "Or perhaps it would be simpler just to change the game. Would you have any objection to continuing, say, over a card table in my room after dinner tonight?"

"What kind of cards?" White said.

"Poker?" the Major said. "Unless, of course, there's something else you prefer."

"No, poker's fine with me. Donner? Harris?"

Donner shrugged. "I wouldn't mind getting my money back."

That left it up to me, of course, and after scotching the golf rematch with $90 of somebody else's money in my pocket, how could I say no now?

I ate early that evening, but there were other things I had to do; so it was after nine when I arrived at the Major's room. The others were already there.

"Sorry I'm late," I said.

"No matter," the Major said. "We were just chatting anyway."

"You don't have to worry, partner," White said. "I was here. So they couldn't gang up on us." He grinned. "But that's the last of it. From now on in, it's every man for himself."

"Glad to hear you say it," I said. "It'll make me feel better when I take your money."

"If," White said.

The Major picked up the cards. "Seven-card stud all right?" he said. "$10 bet limit, no more than two raises each bet?"

"It's your funeral," White said. "Make it easy on yourself."

Now, a $10 bet may not sound like much of a funeral, particularly for the group we had there. But seven-card stud, despite its apparent simplicity, is not a game for beginners. Essentially, each player receives two cards face down, followed in turn around the table by four more face up, then a seventh card face down again, from all of which he selects his best five-card poker hand to match against the others in the game. As you might guess, it's a fast game with none of the delays inherent in other forms—dray, for example, where there is a discard and redeal.

The catch is that, in addition to the standard ante before the first card is dealt, you bet on the first face-up card and every card thereafter. So given four players, a $10 bet limit with two raises per bet meant that each individual pot could easily run over $600—and $600 even in these inflationary times will do a lot more than just feed chickens. Couple that with the game's speed and you can see why you can lose an awful lot of money very fast playing stud poker.

Most good players don't, though, and the reason is they learn very quickly to assess the odds and drop out fast if the early cards don't put those odds almost overwhelmingly in their favor. They also learn to assess their fellow players. And in this particular group, Donner soon proved himself to be a formidable opponent, punctuating an otherwise staid game with unpredictable bursts of seemingly reckless abandon. It was a deliberate tactic, of course, but all the more dangerous because it was impossible to guess when his play was backed up by cards and when it was not.

White, on the other hand, was as predictable as pie, while the Major's attention seemed to be everywhere and on everything except his cards. It didn't seem to hurt him, though, because after an initial loss he began to win and by midnight was close to $500 ahead.

That's when I called for a new deck.

White pushed his cards out into the center of the table. "I'll go along with that," he said. Most of the Major's $500 had come from him.

The Major looked helplessly at the two of us. "This is embarrassing," he said, "but, unfortunately, I just have this one deck. I suppose I should have arranged for more. Frankly, though, it never occurred to me we might need them."

White shook his head disgustedly. "Wouldn't you know it?" he said. "Even when I want to change my luck it stays bad."

It was the Major's deal and he reached out to pull White's cards over to stack them with the rest of the deck.

"They'll have cards at the front desk," I said. "Or the bell captain will."

"Well, yes," the Major said, "but it seems a little late—"

"If you don't want to call," I said, "I will."

He drew himself up. "Of course," he said stiffly, "if you feel that strongly about it."

Donner sighed. "What the hell," he said. "Why argue? If Harris has to work tomorrow, he doesn't want to make that late a night of it anyway. So why don't we just call it quits for a while. There'll be another time."

"So there will," the Major said, beaming again. "Shall we say tomorrow night the same time?"

"We'll see," I said and left it at that.

The next morning Donner was already in the dining room when I came down to breakfast. He was seated at a small table near the window. When he saw me just about the same time I saw him he beckoned me over to join him.

"You're an early riser," I said as I sat down.

"When it serves my purpose," Donner said. "In this case, to find out just what all that fuss about the deck last night was about."

I hesitated. Finally I said, "How well do you know Major McDonlevy?"

Donner shrugged. "I met him about six weeks ago," he said, "at an antique auto rally. He had a '55 Thunderbird on display which he indicated he might be interested in selling. Naturally I wanted to pursue the matter further."

"Why naturally?" I said. "Do you collect antique cars?"

"When it serves my purpose," Donner said again. "The problem with being rich today, Mr. Harris, is that there are so few ways to show it. Maybe that's why I like unique things and maybe that's why I want that car, because not everybody and his brother can go out and buy one. But what's that got to do with the Major and the cards last night?"

"Maybe nothing," I said. "But on the other hand, somebody was crimping the aces and kings so he'd spot them the next time around. I can't prove it, because I couldn't catch him at it, but I think it was the Major."

"I see," Donner said. He looked thoughtful. Then his eyebrows lifted and a slight smile played around the corners of his mouth. "Speak of the devil," he said, looking past me.

"The Major?"

"No. White."

I looked around then. White had spotted us and was making his way across the floor toward our table. "Well," he said, coming up, "I caught you, didn't I? Plotting strategy, eh?"

"You think that's necessary?" Donner said.

"Some people might," White said. He sat down without waiting for an invitation. "After the game last night I got to thinking," he said to me. "Your luck wasn't all that bad, so why would you want to change it by changing the deck?"

I glanced over at Donner, who gazed impassively back. "We were just talking about that," I said. "I think the Major was trying to mark the deck."

White laughed harshly. "I figured it had to be something like that," he said. "The Major, huh? I wonder just where that's covered in the Good Book he's so fond of quoting."

"I don't think it is," I said.

"No, I wouldn't be surprised if you weren't right. But I'll tell you what is," White said. "Do unto others. And an eye for an eye and a tooth for a tooth. I say we get some of our own back tonight."

"How? By crimping our own cards?"

White shook his head. "That's for suckers," he said. "What I had in mind was more like stacking the deck. Let me show you what I mean." Without waiting for a response he rose and made his way back out of the room.

Donner looked down at the back of his hands. "Curiouser and curiouser," he said.

"That's one way of putting it," I said.

A few minutes later White was back, carrying two identical packs of playing cards, one of which he passed over to Donner. "The way to do this," he said, "is call McDonlevy and tell him we'll play in your room tonight. That way—if you're game—we can start out with your deck and then later when the time's ripe switch to mine—without, of course, letting the Major know that's what we're doing."

"That might not be as easy as it sounds," I said. "The Major's no fool."

"You leave that to me," White said. "All you have to do is make sure you two sit down across from each other. It doesn't matter which of you gets the winning hand as long as we're all in it together, but the only way to make sure the Major gets the hand he's supposed to is to put him in the middle across from me. Okay?"

White opened the pack and took out the cards. "Now, let's see what kind of hand we ought to give him." He thought for a minute, then went through the deck quickly, pulling out three of the four aces and setting them down in a neat row followed by the king of hearts and the king of spades. "How about that?" he said. "A nice full house."

"A good hand," Donner said.

"Sure," White said. He turned over the top card remaining in the deck. It was a seven. He set it on the table, then pulled out the other three sevens to place beside it. "But not as good as four of a kind."

Donner looked thoughtful again, the way he had when I had first accused the Major of crimping cards. White grinned and took a card from the top of the deck again, then picked up the ace of spaces from the Major's hand and the seven of clubs from Donner's and put them under it followed by another two cards from the deck, then another ace and seven—and so on until he had the whole sequence arranged the way he wanted it. "That's it," he said. "Four hands, seven cards each, and whoever's to my right is guaranteed to be the winner. How about it?"

Donner continued to look thoughtful for another long moment. Finally he said, "Do you know where my room is?"

"I can find it," White said.

"Good," Donner said. "Be there tonight. Bring your cards."

White grinned. "I knew you'd see it my way," he said. He placed the stacked deck back in its box and put it in his pocket, then rose. "I'd better be going," he said. "It wouldn't do for the Major to walk in and see the three of us together. It might give him the wrong idea."

"So it might," Donner said.

I didn't say anything, but after White had left I sat for a long minute frowning out the window. "I don't like this," I said at last.

"Why not?" Donner said.

"It's too pat. Maybe White wasn't working with the Major to set me up the other day. And then again maybe he was. And maybe he still is. Because all it would take to make those four sevens of yours look mighty small is for the Major to draw a fourth ace. And if White slipped it to him on the seventh card—as he would—face down, we wouldn't realize what was happening until all the bets were made. And what would we do then—admit we had been part of a conspiracy to cheat at cards? That would look really great when it got out, wouldn't it? I don't know about you, but I care about my reputation."

"So do I," Donner said. "Perhaps even more than you."

"And you're still willing to risk it?"

"Why risk anything?" Donner said. "What was it you said the other day? Never play another man's game—unless you can change one of the givens?"

"And which of the givens are you going to change now?"

He leaned forward and told me.

That evening I made it a point to get to Donner's room early but deliberately held back from taking a seat while Donner puttered around playing host. White gave us a couple of curious looks, but the Major solved the problem neatly by sitting down almost as soon as he came into the room. I promptly sat down to his right so that when White took his place opposite him Donner would be placed seemingly by chance in the winner's seat.

Actually it had been his suggestion. "It'll look more natural," he said, "when the heavy betting starts if I'm the one to initiate it." There'd been no reason to disagree, of course, and in any case, the three of us—White, Donner, and myself—had already agreed that even though we had the deck we wouldn't use it unless it was clear the Major was trying to cheat us as well.

Even as we said it, though, at least two and probably all three of us knew we were lying. But as it turned out, of course, it was a moot point, because the Major was his usual expansive, larcenous self and those telltale minute nicks and creases marking the high cards began to show up shortly after we started playing.

I caught Donner's eye and was rewarded with a short, almost imperceptible nod. He'd spotted it too. White's face gave nothing away, but after a couple of more hands he asked Donner if he could have something to drink.

"Sure," Donner said. "There's no gin, but I've got just about everything else. Scotch? Bourbon?"

"Just water," White said. "Or plain soda."

The Major nodded approvingly. "Very wise," he said. "Liquor and cards mix even less well than oil and water—although I suppose in a friendly game it wouldn't hurt to stretch the rule to the extent of a weak bourbon and water."

"Sure," Donner said again and rose to get the drinks, including a Scotch for himself and a bourbon for me. I sipped from mine and if the Major's was any match for it, it was far from weak. But the Major didn't say anything and neither did I. White placed his glass on the edge of the table between him and Donner, where it remained ignored and forgotten until the deal came around to him again. He shuffled carefully, then as he reached out to offer the deck to Donner for the cut, he brushed against the glass, knocking it over.

The liquid inside spilled out and away from the table, but Donner jerked back instinctively anyway, jarring the table and setting his and mine and the Major's glasses rocking precariously—and making it easy in the confusion that followed for White to drop the clean deck smoothly into one pocket while pulling the other out from the other. When everything had settled down, he re-offered the cards to Donner.

"Want to try again?" he said.

Donner hesitated, then rapped the cards lightly with his knuckles. "Why cut your luck," he said.

White nodded and dealt out the first two cards face down impassively: a queen and a ten to me and by the plan a pair of aces to the Major and two sevens to Donner and God knew what to himself. "Anybody care to go out on a limb and open?" he said.

Donner stroked his fingertips across the backs of his cards for a long moment, then tossed some bills out into the center of the table. "Let's cut out the fooling around," he said. "$50 to start."

The Major looked up quickly. "I thought we had agreed to a $10 limit," he said.

Donner grinned. "That was last night, Major," he said. "This is a different ball game and I don't remember anybody saying anything about any limit at all. Of course," he added, "if it's too rich for your blood—"

The Major smiled faintly. "No," he said, "I think I can keep up." He added $50 of his own to the pot. White and I followed suit, and then White dealt out the first of the face-up cards: the queen of clubs to me, the king of spades to the Major, a ten to Donner, and a jack to himself.

It was the Major's bet since he had the high card showing. "Since the limits are off," he said, "shall we go all the way and say $100."

Donner grinned. "You're a man after my own heart, Major," he said. "Your $100 and another $100 on top of it."

It was awfully early in the game for that kind of betting and raising but no one objected, and White waited until all the money was down, then dealt again. This time I drew a second ten, giving me two pair and a reasonable excuse, should the question arise, for staying in—but only an excuse since the ace and seven he dealt in turn to the Major and Donner raised them to three of a kind each while White contented himself with a lowly four.

The next round was a seeming throwaway: eight of hearts to me, jack of spades to the Major, a meaningless king to Donner, and a queen to White. The sixth round was something else again, because this was the round that should put Donner squarely in the driver's seat, and White called out the cards as he dealt them around: "Five of diamonds. Ten of spades. Pair of sevens. Two of clubs. Pair of sevens bets."

Donner pursed his lips. $50 and $100 bets had become the rule rather than the exception and there was a large amount of money in the pot. But apparently not enough. Very deliberately Donner took an envelope from his inside pocket and laid it on the table. "All right, Major," he said. "Let's really separate the men from the boys. There's $5000 in that envelope and it says I've got the best hand. What do you say?"

"You know I can't match that kind of bet," the Major said.

"Sure you can," Donner said. "You've got the Thunderbird, haven't you? Put up the key and we'll call it all even."

The Major shook his head. "Not for $5000," he said. "I won't let you force me out, but I won't be stampeded either. Make it $10,000 and you've got a bet."

Donner grinned. "I thought you might say that," he said. He took a second envelope from his pocket and laid it on top of the first. "$5000 more," he said. "Back to you."

Without hesitating, the Major placed his car key beside the two envelopes. I folded up my cards and pushed them off to one side. "Too rich for my blood," I said. "I'm out."

White looked up sharply. "Now wait—" he began.

Donner rounded on him savagely. "Now wait nothing. I said this was a new ball game and it is—just the Major and me. All you do is deal."

White regarded the two of them silently for a moment, then dealt out the last two cards face down. Donner smiled with satisfaction, because by dropping out, of course, I had upset the sequence that White had planned so that the Major now drew the card that in the normal course would have gone to me, and Donner the one that would have gone to the Major. Donner leaned back now without bothering to look at it. "I'll stand," he said. "How about you, Major?"

The Major nodded. Any additional betting would have been anticlimactic anyway.

Donner turned over the first two cards White had dealt him. "Four sevens," he said. "Not much maybe but enough to beat three aces."

The Major nodded again. "But not enough to beat a royal flush." He turned over the seventh and last card he had drawn. It was the queen of spades and around it he grouped the ten, jack, king, and ace of spades. "Ironic, isn't it," he said, "but three aces is the hand I was betting on. I thought you had two pair." He shrugged. "If you hadn't gone for the really big bet and forced the others out, I wouldn't have drawn the queen of spades and you would have won. Still, I suppose it's as fruitless to speculate on might-have-beens in poker as anything else."

Donner didn't respond and after a moment the Major picked up the two envelopes and his car key, then rose, and almost as an afterthought scooped up the rest of the pot. "I realize it's bad form to quit while you're ahead," he said, "but somehow I don't think the game could ever be quite the same."

Donner still didn't say anything as the Major went out. In fact, there wasn't much left for anybody to say. Or do. And shortly afterward I left myself. Instead of slinking back to my room, though, I rode the elevator down to the main floor and left the building through a side entrance. Moments later a sleek low-slung car pulled up to the curb beside me and I got in.

"Well, my boy," the Major said, "I must say that went well."

"I won't argue," I said, "but one of these days you're going to go too far. What would have happened if Donner hadn't suggested I drop out so we could get you that queen?"

"But that was the whole point of planting the idea," the Major said, "and setting it up so he'd get his fourth seven on the sixth card. So he would suggest it. If he hadn't, then I'm afraid all our hard work and preparation would have been in vain. But," he added expansively, "it wasn't, and as the Good Book so aptly points out it's what happens that counts, not all the what-ifs and might-have-beens."

I looked at him curiously. "Is that really in the Bible?" I said.

"Oh, I'm sure it is someplace," he said, "and if it isn't it should be. You can look it up sometime. But for now I'd suggest we'd do better to arrange to forward White his share and then shake the dust of this place from our feet before Donner recovers enough from his shock to discover that not only is there no shopping-center project planned for this area but that the young architect he knew as Frank Harris is none other than my valued associate and friend Tom James."

Bibliography

Short Stories by Robert Edward Eckels

Those stories marked with an asterisk (*) are included in *Never Trust a Partner*.

"The Man in the Revolving Door." *Ellery Queen's Mystery Magazine*, June 1969.
* "The Blue Lady." *Ellery Queen's Mystery Magazine*, October 1969.
"Double Jeopardy." *Ellery Queen's Mystery Magazine*, January,1970.
"After the Fact." *Ellery Queen's Mystery Magazine*, April 1970.
* "A Question of Honor." *Ellery Queen's Mystery Magazine*, June 1970.
"Milk Run." *Ellery Queen's Mystery Magazine*, August 1970.
"Payment on Demand." *Ellery Queen's Mystery Magazine*, October 1970.
* "Only Bet on a Sure Thing." *Ellery Queen's Mystery Magazine*, January 1971.
"Game with One Rule." *Ellery Queen's Mystery Magazine*, April 1971.
"Vicious Circle." *Ellery Queen's Mystery Magazine*, June 1971.
* "The Waldemeer Triptych." *Ellery Queen's Mystery Magazine*, July 1971.
"To Catch a Spy." *Ellery Queen's Mystery Magazine*, September 1971.
"The Munich Courier." *Ellery Queen's Mystery Magazine*, January 1972.
* "Never Trust a Partner." *Ellery Queen's Mystery Magazine*, March 1972.
* "The Kidnaped Painting." *Ellery Queen's Mystery Magazine*, June 1972.
"One Man's Ignorance." *Ellery Queen's Mystery Magazine*, December 1972.
"Bread Upon the Waters." *Ellery Queen's Mystery Magazine*, March 1973.
"One Born Every Minute." *Ellery Queen's Mystery Magazine*, June 1973.
"The Chance of a Lifetime." *Ellery Queen's Mystery Magazine*, October 1973.
"The Hard Part." *Mike Shayne Mystery Magazine*, November, 1973.
"Nobody Can Win 'Em All." *Ellery Queen's Mystery Magazine*, February 1974.
"The Last One to Know." *Ellery Queen's Mystery Magazine*, April 1974
* "Hobson's Choice." *Ellery Queen's Mystery Magazine*, June 1974.
* "The Switcheroo." *Ellery Queen's Mystery Magazine*, September 1974.

"The K'ang Sheng Memorandum." *Ellery Queen's Mystery Magazine*, October 1974

"The Great Bread Swindle, *Ellery Queen's Mystery Magazine* July 1975.

"Site Unseen." *Ellery Queen's Mystery Magazine*, December 1975.

"Attention to Detail." *Ellery Queen's Mystery Magazine*, September 1976.

"Judgment Postponed." *Alfred Hitchcock's Mystery Magazine*, December 1976.

"The Last of the Breed." *Ellery Queen's Mystery Magazine*, December 1976.

"Buchanan's Squeal." *Alfred Hitchcock's Mystery Magazine*, February 1977.

"Account Settled." *Ellery Queen's Mystery Magazine*, May 1977.

"The Long Arm of the Law." *Ellery Queen's Mystery Magazine*, July 1977.

"Snow from the South." *Alfred Hitchcock's Mystery Magazine*, July 1977.

* "Lang and Lovell Go Legit, *Ellery Queen's Mystery Magazine* November 1977.

"Manhunt—Indiana Style." *Alfred Hitchcock's Mystery Magazine*, July 1978.

"Only One Way to Go." *Ellery Queen's Mystery Magazine*, August 1978.

* "Quit When You're Ahead." *Ellery Queen's Mystery Magazine*, December 1978.

"Sufficient Unto the Day." *Ellery Queen's Mystery Magazine*, March 1978.

"The Right Circumstances." *Alfred Hitchcock's Mystery Magazine*, March 1979.

"Night to Remember." *Alfred Hitchcock's Mystery Magazine*, November 1979.

*"Never Play Another Man's Game." *Ellery Queen's Mystery Magazine*, November 3 1980.

"Maybe It Didn't Happen." *Ellery Queen's Mystery Magazine*, January 28 1981.

"The Swindle." *Alfred Hitchcock's Mystery Magazine*, May 27 1981.

* "The Canadian Caper." *Ellery Queen's Mystery Magazine*, October 1982.

"The Kapalov Proposal." *Ellery Queen's Mystery Magazine*, May 1983.

"The Pearson Affair." *Alfred Hitchcock's Mystery Magazine*, August 1983.

"The Export Specialist." *Ellery Queen's Mystery Magazine*, November 1984.

"A Nice Thing Going." *Ellery Queen's Mystery Magazine*, June 1984.

"The Benefit of the Doubt." *Prime Crimes 3*, Davis Publications, 1985.
* "The Bellman Portrait." *Ellery Queen's Mystery Magazine*, September 1986.
* "Major McDonlevy Does the Math." Included as a separate pamphlet with the limited edition of this collection.

Published as by E.E. Roberts**:

"Mug's Game." *Ellery Queen's Mystery Magazine*, February 1971.
"Where There's Smoke." *Ellery Queen's Mystery Magazine*, May 1971.
"A Little Ride in the Car." *Ellery Queen's Mystery Magazine*, February 1972.
"The Enumerators." *Isaac Asimov's Science Fiction Magazine*, November/December 1978.

**Note that some sources credit Eckels with two other stories written by E.E. Roberts for *Esquire* magazine, but that was an entirely different E.E. Roberts.

Never Trust a Partner

Never Trust a Partner: The Con Games of Robert Edward Eckels is printed on 60-pound paper, and is designed by G.E. Satheesh, Pondicherry, India. The type is Adobe Caslon Pro. The cover is by Joshua Luboski. The first edition was published in two forms: trade softcover, perfect bound; and one hundred fifty copies sewn in cloth, numbered and signed by Robert Edward Eckels. Each of the clothbound copies includes a separate pamphlet, "Major McDonlevy Does the Math", a short story by Robert Edward Eckels. *Never Trust a Partner* was printed by Southern Ohio Printers and bound by Cincinnati Bindery. The book was published in June 2021 by Crippen & Landru Publishers, Inc., Cincinnati, OH.